D1232184

RAZOR STRIKE

RAZOR STRIKE

LEE SARPEL

Copyright © 2022 Lee Sarpel
Published by Nova Civitas Press

Content edits by Red Circle Ink
Copy edits by Johanie Martinez-Cools for Tessera Editorial

Cover art by Kanaxa
Interior design by John Leen with LaTeX and Octavo
Set in Charter with titles in Bebas Neue

All rights reserved.

ISBN-13: 979-8-9861585-0-1

To John

ONE

Blood rushed through Trez's head as she ran. The Michaud goons were less than a minute behind her, and she had a plane to catch. When she got to the landing zone, she had to lock her knees to stay standing.

The copter that came to extract her announced its arrival by slamming into the pavement. She'd thought Shlomi would pick her up, since it was his shift, but when the hatch opened, she saw her handler was Jenna Garcia. Trez stumbled toward her and Jenna caught her, lifting her by the armpits as her knees gave out.

"Jesus, Trez, what the hell happened to you?" Jenna hauled her into the copter's passenger space.

She could crash now. Once Jenna got her to a pallet, she collapsed. "'M fine," she mumbled into the bedsponge.

Jenna tussled to get Trez's helmet off. "And I'm the king of Siam. You're high as a fighter jet."

Coming down fast, she thought. "Since when're you a medic?"

"Don't need to be, I have eyes. Also first aid training. Your eyes are all pupil, your breathing is shallow, and you're shaking like a tweaker," Jenna said. She looked fuzzy and her voice sounded metallic.

"Charcoal," Trez said.

Jenna shook her head. "We need to get the hell out of here before Michaud security catches up. Last time you got captured, they fucked you up wicked hard."

Trez shuddered with the memory. Her legs throbbed with remembered pain.

Jenna dragged the bedsponge up closer to the open cockpit and secured Trez to the side of the copter with some flex cord. She returned to the pilot's seat and initiated takeoff at the console. The shuttlecopter lurched to the side. Trez was glad she hadn't eaten anything.

"Need Charcoal." Her heart sped up as the pharma wore off.

Once the copter had ascended, Jenna partially undid Trez's bodysuit, hooked the comm in there up to the vitals machine, and opened the aid kit. Trez managed to roll over and open her mouth. Jenna lifted her tongue with her other hand and deposited a tab sublingually. Trez let her head drop back. Her teeth chattered.

They must be safely away from Michaud territory by now. Trez opened her eyes to check. Harbor Securities and Fairchild Heavy Industries had repurposed the old bank skyscrapers for their own business. The lights were still on at 10 p.m.

Jenna took the opportunity to be chatty. "Haven't seen you in a while. You've been avoiding me."

"Have not," Trez slurred.

Jenna dismissed the denial with a shrug. "I used to see you every day at lunch, and three weeks ago, poof! You stop showing up. Then I realized I didn't see you after the weekly meeting anymore. You didn't respond to any of my comms. So I asked Velrain and he said he'd noticed the same thing."

"Been busy," she said.

Jenna harrumphed. "You've been signing up for strikes

when I'm not on duty. A fuckton of them. You're not resting in between them."

"More strikes means more money." She closed her eyes again. She got about two minutes of silence while the pounding in her head spread to the rest of her body. Her shoulders shook as the Charcoal did its job, helping her sweat the poison out. Trez knew it didn't really work that way, but she swore she felt her pores weeping. All of them.

"You're still twitching like you took enough stims for a horse. This was a routine strike." Jenna wasn't content to leave this alone, it seemed.

"Huh? What?" It was hard to do the brainwork to figure out what Jenna wanted to know.

"This wasn't a risky strike. You tussled with two guards who didn't give you much trouble before you dispatched them and downed the target. *Kirisute-gomen*, done and dusted."

"Mmmfh." Could Jenna just shut up?

"I've picked you up from strikes dozens of times. Analyzed plenty of data from your encounter suit. That many drugs, your heart rate through the roof, that isn't normal."

Trez had stopped tallying her strikes. That was her comm's job. She couldn't even remember how many missions she'd been on since she last saw her personal pharmadoc. She made a note to schedule an appointment. The side effects of the mix of pharma she used on strikes were getting much worse. The shuttle lurched into semi-freefall, and what little water she'd had, came up.

The landing jarred her since she couldn't brace herself well, but at this point, that pain was superfluous. She could only manage a weak protest as Jenna unbuckled the makeshift harness, opened the hatch, and called for a stretcher. "I don't need—"

"You can't walk, and I sure as hell can't carry you all the way."

Outside the copter, advertisements for tooth whitener and a new stimsense movie about giant robots lit up the sides of buildings. Several indigents in their municipal-issued sweatsuits were shooed away from the Harbor areas by security forces.

Trez listened to the noise. Loud music from those with hearing damage or clubs who didn't care about noise ordinances. Someone screaming at someone else, probably a domestic fight. Rumbles of vehicles without mufflers.

"Beatrez Kufo Harris?" asked the medic. Shit. When had he arrived?

"I ... yeah," she said.

The medic took her wrist and squeezed it with one hand, scanned her head with the other. "Temperature's normal, BP is fine, but your heart's going one twenty. Are you in any pain?"

"Nah." A thorough explanation would take energy she didn't have.

"Were you injured? Hit? Did you take any falls?" He undid the top of her encounter suit.

"Don't remember."

The medic's eyebrows went up a fraction. "I think we'd better wheel her to Menendez. He's her designated medic. You can come with us if you like, Garcia."

"Good." Jenna's voice sounded tight.

The medic rolled Trez in. Infirmary was attached to R&D 2. Several floors down. When the gurney stopped, Trez heard heavy footsteps. Menendez couldn't do anything but stomp around, even though he was at most seventy kilos. "Harris," he said. He peered over the stretcher, his lips compressed. "I hear you ODed? You look like a mess."

"Tell me something I don't know," she said.

"Found her after the mission tweaking wicked hard." Jenna was trying to be helpful, but Trez wished she'd keep her mouth shut.

"Is any of the blood yours?" Menendez probed at Trez's ribs.

"Don't think so." She thought most of it was from the goon squad she'd dispatched, but she couldn't remember what minor injuries she'd sustained. Trez flinched as the medic took her shoulder and checked its mobility. She must have hit the floor at some point during the mission. Fucking sadist doctors.

"There's a strain here, but nothing dislocated or broken," he noted. "Vitals within normal bounds. No visible signs of infection." He stung Trez's left arm with a needle and hooked her up to a diagnostic machine. She grunted.

"She's been semi-lucid since I picked her up," Jenna said. "She couldn't walk unassisted though. I had to secure her to the shuttle seat because she kept jerking around, even after I dosed her with detox."

"Sample shows … Hoo, you've been behaving badly, Harris."

At this point, commenting would use energy she didn't have. Trez couldn't fake unconsciousness with a medic and equipment around, but she stayed silent.

"Two of these stims are normal for field ops. The Redeye not so much," he continued. "Ahhh. Probably to keep her going with the Poppy downers. Mild painkillers to complement the stims, cannabinoid, dissociatives, and several sedatives I'll need to analyze further."

"You're the medic," Jenna said. "How much should I worry?" She began to pace.

"I'll have the lab run some tests." Menendez looked up from his arm console. His voice was clipped. "Garcia, I appreciate the data you were able to give me. We'll talk to her emergency contact and keep her here until she recovers." Menendez softened his voice. "I understand that this is a stressful situation, and your concern for Harris is understandable. As soon as she's released, we will let you know."

Jenna had stopped in her tracks. "Eight years of strikes, and she's never overdosed before. This isn't the first time she's done a strike at Michaud's building 17. I have no idea what went wrong."

"It's Corpfare. Strikers lead high-risk adrenaline-fueled lives." Menendez shrugged, bemused. "Garcia, I'm going to kick you out while I monitor Harris further. You need to report this to your boss and hers." He flicked his fingers at Jenna. "Shoo, shoo. The patient needs rest."

Jenna left without any resistance, muttering to herself about how this week felt too long. Menendez waited until the door slid shut behind her.

"From this preliminary data," he said to Trez, "I don't know what you think you're doing. Most strikers I treat take a shit ton of pharma on a regular basis, but your lot always teach me new ways you can fuck yourself up. Propofolite-class drugs usually cause sedation, so you're trying to compensate with enough stims to give a bear a heart attack."

Trez blinked. "You're exaggerating."

"Never mind. I'll get the analysis from the lab shortly. But based on your vitals and current organ function data, you need to rest. I'm giving you a few days of downtime after this. Don't do anything strenuous."

She was so tired, but nodding was easy enough. She would

need a dark, quiet room, and a steady, low stream of caff. "Right. Sure." She took a deep breath.

"Before you go to what I'm sure will be a disturbed toss-and-turn sleep, I have some intake questions." Menendez's face lost its tension, his mouth relaxing. "I have to ask these questions. Did anything unusual happen out there, Harris?"

"Got it on bodycam. Better than eyewitness junk."

"I would like your subjective experience, even though you were in an altered state at the time."

"It's all ... When it's getting kinetic it all goes by so fast. Target downed, mooks downed. Success. Yeah."

He shook his head. "I'll look at your suit readout. I'm going to have to tell you what I have to tell too many people: Performance enhancers have tradeoffs. With the doses you're taking, you gain very little edge at significant risk to your short-term condition, not to mention the long-term."

"Gotta ... I need ..." So many things now, but her mouth had trouble shaping words.

"Good grief. Aces, always trying to one-up each other with no regard for their own safety. Pity I can't do a stupidectomy." Trez made a weak groaning sound, and he paused. "I'll leave you to your rest. Remember doctor's orders and you will feel better."

She heard his footsteps tromping away as she crashed into familiar fever dreams.

———————

Trez's bed shook while her custom alarm yelled at her.

"Wake up and chew the caff, persons and unpersons! Dinochildren and flat earthers alike! We got plenty of flat earth listeners, and I gotta say it's not just them, you're all loobies for listening to me! That's what I'm here for, bringing people together. Maybe today's the day two of you listeners will meet each other, and start a beautiful friend—"

Trez had to stand up and walk across the room to deactivate her alarm. Otherwise she was prone to mute it and go back to sleep. She doubted she'd meet other Dinochildren today; the audiocast had stopped publishing over twenty years ago. The only reason she'd known about it was an old family friend who'd played it for her when she was a child.

She had just deactivated her alarm when the comm blared again. It was Linus calling. She shook the remnants of her nightmare off, stumbled over to the nearest chair, and chose the voice-only option.

"Baby girl," her father said. "What's doing?"

"Nothing special. Day off."

"You sound like you been out late partying."

She tried to remember the last time she'd gone to a club or party. Months? She'd enjoyed dancing, once upon a time. "Sure, that's me. All play and no work."

He laughed. "That's my girl. You deserve it on your off time." Linus Harris had never understood why Trez had become a striker for Harbor, despite them both being adrenaline junkies. "Gonna retire soon? This Corpfare business seems hard on you. It's not a life choice I'd make."

Of course it isn't, she thought. That's why they were in this clusterfuck, why she needed to cover for him. She kept her tone level. "We all have to get our thrills somehow."

He laughed. "Bee, I'm just gambling with creds. You've got a little more skin on the line, and Harbor's the one anteing you up."

Don't I know it. "Harbor protects its investments." Her

finger blades, arm blades, optics, muscle actuators, and internal body armor weren't cheap. Not to mention the hours of training needed to use them properly. Security's Corpfare division upgraded a body with the expectation that it would pay off for them. The sunk cost fallacy worked in her favor.

"Well, if you want to believe that ... maybe it lets you sleep better at night." Like most civilians, he didn't know or bother to learn the details of how Corps operated. In his mind, Corps were a vehicle for psychopath executives. They preyed on the public to line their own pockets and spend the creds on the newest designer drugs. They probably also hired high-end sex workers to do it with them. She couldn't tell him the details anyway thanks to the nondisclosure agreement clause in her employment contract.

"Doesn't do the trick." She grimaced. When had she last slept straight through the night?

"Well, ah, speaking of sleeping ... I found a new place to crash, in Cape Elizabethtown."

"New buddy? Old one?" Tracking his "friends" was difficult sometimes. Mostly indigents with rental comms and without addresses.

"Ah, a new one. Should be okay for a while."

"Wait, a friend friend, or a friend you sleep with?"

"Nothing you need to wonder about, Bee. You know, most people don't ask their parents that kind of question."

"You always say I'm not most people. A little different. Like Ma." She regretted saying that immediately.

There was a pause. "Not like that."

Shit. She hadn't meant to derail the conversation. "Things, ah ... okay for you?"

"What? You mean with Withers?"

"Yeah. She and her goons not giving you any trouble?"

"Nah. They're not bothering me. They got better things to do."

"Let's keep it that way." Trez needed to keep them happy for just a few more months.

Linus attempted a chuckle, but it came out like a coughing fit. "You've got this part under control, seems like."

Her head was beginning to throb. "I should go. Anything else?"

"Nah, that's it. Take care of yourself. Don't work yourself to death." He always worried for her. Never about himself.

Trez arched a brow. "Ha ha." Her face muscles were too tired to smile. "You too. Just let me know if you need anything."

"I'm doin' just fine." That's what he always said. She was not sure whether he walked through life with low standards or simple obliviousness.

"Stay that way."

"You too, baby girl, you too."

She closed the connection with a flick of her right hand and plunked back down on her bed, slouching. A spike jabbed right above her brow from inside her skull. Tea would help. She'd prefer sleep, but she was good and awake, now mulling over her father and his call.

Linus was such a goddamn idiot. Hopefully the place in Cape Elizabethtown was actually safe and he wasn't being led around by his dick. "Motherfucker," she muttered, then giggled for a moment before coughing a few times. They'd just been discussing that, hadn't they? She must have brought it up because of the nightmares.

Trez pushed herself up off the bed using her forearms, unsteady for a moment. She could hear her heart pounding almost as loud as she'd heard her father's voice. Fuck, these mornings after strikes kept getting harder. Old injuries tried to reassert themselves every chance they got. She braced herself with a hand on the wall while she walked to the kitchen area. This was one of the times she cursed shelling out for a separate bedroom.

Trez made her way to the food storage, picked up a cup, and fished around for a tea capsule. The gold powder looked the least offensive today. Supposedly had relaxing properties. Quackery, she was sure. It had caffeine, so how was it supposed to relax anything? Trez sat to sip her tea slowly, less to savor and more to accustom her stomach to having anything in it again.

She should touch base with her boss. She hoped Sloane wasn't concerned about her performance. Trez could probably argue that the strike itself had gone fine and she hadn't cost Harbor anything extra; her stint in medbay was priced in by the quants who regulated Corpfare's resources. Sloane would understand that sometimes you needed some extra pharma to get through a mission. They might be the Vice President of Security, Competitor Relations, but they were also a retired striker themself.

Linus had mentioned retirement again. Her employment contract was technically at-will, but leaving her job wouldn't be simple. All of her cybernetics required maintenance, Linus required bailouts sometimes, and she liked having a separate bedroom. She wouldn't be able to get at her pension for decades. Her remaining savings were earmarked for the Makos. Her stomach churned. She needed to continue striking for a few more years before she could think of hanging her encounter suit up.

Trez smoothed the lines on her brow, massaging the skin on her forehead until she hit her temples. Maybe some ice would help her headache. She didn't see her cold pack immediately, so she started sorting through the assorted objects piled up next to her bed. Buried under yesterday's pants. She'd have to clean it first. She tossed both into the sterilization unit.

The wall console chose to sing at that point. Jenna was comming. Fuck. She wasn't going to answer that. She waited to find out whether Jenna would leave a message.

"Hey-oh, Trez. Wanted to see how you were doing now that they let you out of medical. Sorry for freaking out on you. Let's get lunch or a drink. Any place you recommend?"

Jenna was right. Trez had been avoiding her. That episode in medical would no doubt lead to an inquisition, even if Jenna had seen plenty of fucked-up coworkers. Maybe she could spin this as no big deal. Almost every striker took a little extra pharma to stay short-term sharp. She didn't know how to explain the propofolites though. Trez scrunched her eyes shut. Jenna was right to be worried. But there wasn't anything Jenna could do to help. Her pay grade was lower than Trez's, and she had dependents.

There were probably other comms for her to sift through, although she'd probably ignore most of them. "New Comms," she muttered. Translucent colored panes popped up on all sides of her. She had to push most of them aside to sort through the morass of information.

First she discarded the usual ads promoting hair products, this season's fashions, sexual enhancements, and attractive local singles just waiting to hotsync. All things she never bothered with. There must be enough people who responded to non-targeted ads to make it worth the time to draft them.

Semiannual sale at a jewelry shop. Her friend Imei

Vanchen talking about a new club on the waterfront that had some "sweet sweet eye candy," whatever that meant. With Vanchen it could be attractive men, an art installation, or drugs you injected in your optics. Possibly more than one of those. Lafarge from Central Security asking her if she were interested in going to a skidder race. Eric's most recent comm, which she'd saved. Trez couldn't stop herself from replaying it.

Trez. I just wanted to check that everything's okay. I miss playing Ninja with you. I don't know what's going on, but if you need your space I'm going to respect that. If there's anything I can do . . . well, please comm me, okay?

Trez grimaced. *Eric . . .* Why was he being all smooth voiced and understanding? She'd treated him the worst of all her friends. Hotsyncing, cuddling, then ghosting him.

She'd told herself he deserved better than to deal with her personal shitshow: her dad, her capture several months ago, her flashbacks to the disastrous mission where she'd killed a civilian. She couldn't let him see her like this, fatalistic and stove-up by pharma. But that didn't excuse her behavior. She'd apologize, explain later. After. If he still wanted to talk to her.

She had to see this through first. Hold it together for a few more months. But the last message in her comm queue was from a name she hadn't said in years.

Hello. I've returned to the city with some friends and associates. If possible, I would like to see you. I regret not being able to meet you previously. It wasn't safe for me to come back to Portland yet. —Felicity Santorini

Trez sat still for a minute, counting her breaths. When she finished with that, she let herself think again.

She hadn't heard a peep from Santorini for more than

half her life. This comm had to be a nasty prank. Somebody pulling her leg. She didn't know why anyone would pull a prank like that though.

But what if it wasn't? What if it really was Santorini? Trez slumped in her chair. Had the woman been keeping tabs on her? She hadn't wanted to hope for that.

Santorini had to want something. Maybe she just wanted to see Trez. Maybe try to make amends. Trez wasn't sure she had that forgiveness in her. She'd trusted Santorini with her heart, and that hadn't ended well for her.

Linus had told Trez that Santorini only wanted what was best for Trez, and that nobody was a bad person here. He believed it too. Trez had a harder time swallowing that one.

Vanchen was a Runner. Trez could ask her about whether the one-time pad was legitimate. If it was ... maybe she could give Santorini a piece of her mind. A little shiver, some glee mixed in with her anxiety, went through her at the prospect. Or maybe it was from the pharma wearing off. Either way, she couldn't pass up the chance to see Felicity Santorini again. Show her that she'd been successful without her. If she could do that.

But how? What would impress her? What would prove that Trez didn't need her and never had? Write a resume? Do some kind of combat demonstration? No. Santorini wouldn't take those seriously. Maybe talk about the places she'd infiltrated? That seemed more like something Santorini would value.

She had to stop thinking about Santorini. No way she could nap and rest up with her mind swimming laps. Time to see if Doc Ten was available. She was practically vibrating in her seat.

TWO

A blast of cold air greeted Eric when he opened the door of R&D 4 room 203. The server laboratory's heat exchangers kept the computer parts cool and vented most of the heat out the side of the building. They weren't perfect though. Parts of the room were sweltering.

Eric wasn't on duty, but he'd left his red-and-green paisley earmuffs in 203 last shift and forgotten to take them home. Sam had gifted them as a joke, but he'd ended up using them. People already looked ridiculous enough with earmuffs on that he might as well wear garish ones. Today was back to freezing, despite yesterday's warmth. March in New England meant he needed to have both his winter and summer wardrobe on hand.

A few steps in, he heard a scraping noise above the hum of the electronics. He peeked his head around the first rack of servers.

Someone he didn't recognize was fiddling with one of the servers, pushing something into a drive. Their breaths fogged in the cold. They were wearing a teal padded coat. Sections of their hair were shaved off, the rest of it left long. For a moment he wondered if they were one of Seymour's new helpers. Doubtful.

He summoned his heads-up display with a turn of his

wrist. Employees upstairs and downstairs registered. Teal Coat didn't have a Harbor ID, which put the odds at 100:1 that they were not supposed to be there.

The intruder likely wasn't a striker—no encounter suit. Eric signaled for backup anyway, then walked toward the stranger. He noticed that one glove was not like the other. He'd first thought it a punk fashion statement, but when he switched his HUD to detect electronics, it indicated that they were wearing a Gauntlet on their left hand.

His footsteps weren't quiet. The punk turned their head and saw him. Then they jumped to a standing position and threw a circuit board at him. He managed to dodge the makeshift missile, but it gave them a second to dash around the corner.

Eric chased them around the lab, the two of them trying not to trip on cables trailing on the floor. He couldn't tackle them without potentially damaging server equipment, and he'd rather not have to justify that to Seymour.

They were wicked fast. Agile too. They escaped Eric's first attempt to grab them. A hologram burst from the Gauntlet, displaying text Eric couldn't read. He chased them to a corner, trying to box them in. When they turned, he got a better glimpse of their face, unlined and glassy-eyed.

His comm beeped. Dispatch informed him that backup was headed his way. Teal Coat drew a knife from inside their coat. Eric might have enhanced muscles and years of hand-to-hand combat training, but that wasn't proof against stab wounds. He braced his shoulders, took a quick breath in, and expelled it as he jumped to tackle them.

Teal Coat didn't go down when Eric landed on them though. They shook him free and he had to regain his footing.

He felt a sting at his shoulder, but they left themself open while swinging the knife. Eric finally succeeded in getting ahold of the punk, but they were freaky strong as well as fast. Elbowing them in the chin got some swearing, but didn't knock the intruder down. The two of them tussled some more until Eric finally got enough leverage to throw the guy onto the stone flooring.

He attempted to secure their limbs, but they kept Eric off-balance with their bucking. They must be high as a helicopter on some pharma. Drive, most likely. They swung the knife at him again, but he got out of the way in time.

Uneven footsteps thudded from the direction of the door as backup arrived. "Just one guard?" he asked them. Odd. He continued to tussle with Teal Coat until another pair of arms grabbed the intruder's legs from the other side.

Vail Makarov, Eric's teammate and patrol partner, snorted. "Afraid so."

With Vail's help, the two of them got Teal Coat by the limbs. Eric didn't have restraints handy, so he punched the punk in the temple. They relaxed in his grip.

Vail raised their brows. "I don't think that was necessary." They fished around in the bag they'd brought for some cable ties.

"Where's everyone else then?"

"Let me check." Vail rotated their wrist and brought up their HUD. "Attending to something else, it seems. I just sent a second request for a team, but who knows when they'll get here."

"Criss."

"Am I going to get treated to more of your Quebecois sacres?"

"Maybe," Eric said. "But I guess we didn't need more than two people for this kid anyway."

"Doesn't look like a striker," Vail said.

Eric rifled through Teal Coat's clothes. "No identifying effects." That ruled out the person being a striker then; strikers always kept their CorpIDs on them in case of capture so that they would be ransomed properly.

"You're bleeding," Vail said.

"Oh. Right." His shoulder throbbed. "I don't think it's deep."

"Save me the fuss and let's see the wound."

"Fine." Eric removed his jacket.

"I don't know if that's technically gaping or not. But I can try to seal it for you," Vail said. "I have a cleaning swab and some glue on me. Hold still."

"I wasn't even supposed to be here." Hopefully that didn't sound too whiny to Vail.

The corner of their mouth lifted in bemusement. "So why were you?"

"Forgot my earmuffs," Eric said. He inhaled sharply when Vail swabbed him.

"Where?"

Eric gestured with his uninjured arm. "Two racks over, at one of the electronics carts."

"Talk about bad timing," Vail said. They opened a glue packet and spread it over the cut. Hopefully it would hold and he wouldn't need a medic to see it. "The guards nearby are disposing of a suspicious package that they found in one of the first-floor offices."

Now that the fight was over, his sweat chilled. He shivered. "Check out their fancy glove," he said.

"I was wondering about that," Vail said. "Not everyone with a Gauntlet is a Corp striker, but ... those babies aren't easy to get your hands on." Corps owned the vast majority of Gauntlets, loaning them out to strikers and elite operatives for the duration of their missions.

Eric supposed there were a few Gauntlets on the black market. Probably several million a pop, enough to buy a mansion. A Gauntlet hosted a full kit of lockpick programs, biometric and otherwise. The proprietary technology in them, additionally, could crack almost any server the wielder could get physical access to.

"Any idea how they got in?"

"Nah."

"Marde. I'll have to file this with Seymour."

Vail shook their head. "Good luck with that one."

"What, you don't want to take the credit?"

"More like taking the blame, if you ask me."

"You're not on duty."

"Neither are you."

"But she's going to get the report from our backup anyway. Speaking of which ..."

A team of four guards arrived, faces haggard and morose. "The fuck's going on here?" one of them asked.

"An intruder. Light-skinned person, 1.8 meters, 75 kg, brown hair roots, single IR optic, Gauntlet proficient. Beyond that, we don't know anything." Eric gestured to Teal Coat. "I'm going to file the report."

"We'll search for their ident," Vail said to Eric. "You file your report and wait for Seymour's response. Five hundred americreds it comes in less than five minutes."

"Thanks. I won't take that bet though." He sidled away

and filled out an incident report for Seymour. Eric smoothed his brow with his fingers.

———————

Thirty seconds later, Eric's comm buzzed. He gestured with his head to Vail before going into the hallway for a smidgen of privacy.

"Greis."

Seymour's holo showed her standing in her office. Her chair lay on its side. Eric would bet it was a casualty of one of her tantrums.

"Director Seymour." Omitting the title director would not be a good conversation starter. Sarah Seymour oversaw several of the labs in R&D 4, several more in two other buildings, and she made sure nobody forgot it.

Her mouth was a flat line. "I just got your preliminary report. What's this I'm hearing about a break-in at R&D 4?"

He wasn't sure what kind of answer she was fishing for. "Is there any information missing in the report?"

"You're in R&D 4 right now. With Makarov. And an unconscious person, identity unknown. Is anybody else there?"

"Four building security officers. Matthews, Molyneaux—"

"And you've done a DNA test to identify the intruder?"

"Working on that." They'd have those results in half an hour.

"Let me know as soon as you get the results." She tilted her head and smoothed her hands on her dress pants. "You were alone when you found them?"

"Yes."

"Your report says you called for backup, but Makarov was the only guard available at the time."

"Yes," he said. That part still confused him. What had everyone else been busy with?

"And, of course, the security footage on that floor was jammed, so we don't know how they got in. How convenient." She sneered.

Well, if he were breaking in somewhere, he'd disable the security cameras if he could. But he was pretty sure she already knew that, and he wasn't about to defend himself with snark.

"You caught them in 203, and they have a Gauntlet," she continued. "Do you know its origin?"

"No serial number, so I'll turn it over to the Runners in InfoSec."

"Don't do that just yet. Did they steal anything?"

"Nothing physical that I could identify."

She pursed her lips. "Either they were going to remove something to do damage, or copy it to steal it. Do you know what they touched in the room?"

"I'll go check." Eric walked back into the lab, to the server rack where he'd originally found the intruder. Vail and the other guards were busy talking. "Not sure. It's rack G-23. My HUD shows some fiber traces on some of the drive casings. Nothing seems to have been disassembled or removed though."

She compressed her mouth then took and expelled a breath. "G-23. Well then. Of course."

"If they copied any data, it would be on either the Gauntlet or their personal comm. Unless they ate the data chips."

Her nostrils flared. "I need to know if any data on the

servers in that rack was copied anywhere, and if so, whether the intruder managed to upload it. Get the Forensics Division in InfoSec to pull the Gauntlet's logs for the past few hours. But if they don't find anything, close the issue with them. We don't want to make a fuss about this to InfoSec."

"All right." If she was going to be hush-hush about the break-in, chances were that she had some work she wanted to keep off the books. No doubt he wasn't supposed to know about the server. He filed that information away to think about later.

"But you need to look into it." She smiled, but deliberately kicked her overturned chair. It slid a few centimeters across the floor, making a scraping sound.

"Me?" He wasn't an InfoSec specialist. Sure, he'd been looking at the department, and kept checking if there were openings for a transfer, but he didn't have any formal Forensics training. Just because he guarded servers physically didn't mean he could crack complicated ciphers. He'd tried to learn more about the technical parts of their job, and he'd even bought some equipment, but he hadn't gotten beyond the basics.

"Yes, you. Find out what you can. Don't escalate the case any more than your initial filing. I'll put it down as something we need to watch."

Criss, she must really want to keep this project on the down-low. "I'll see what I can do without consulting InfoSec."

"See that you do." She stared off into space. "I expect results in two weeks."

He blinked. What kind of . . . Had she lost her mind? "I'll do what I can. Though I'm not exactly a forensics specialist."

"You have next week on standby. Use that time for your investigation. I'll talk to your supervisor. I'll tell them you're doing some Forensics training for me. You've shown interest in InfoSec before, so let's see what you can do."

"Yes, Director." Eric wasn't going to ask about the week after that. She didn't seem in the mood for answering questions.

Seymour let out another heavy breath. "I'm disappointed, Greis. This needs to never happen again. If you can't make headway on this, maybe you need to go back to guarding something less critical." She said the words lightly, but he heard the threat in them.

He swallowed. Not too noticeably, he hoped. "Understood."

"Keep me apprised of any developments."

"Yes, Director."

She disconnected, and he allowed himself to slouch a bit.

He poked his head back into 203. "Found anything on our guest?"

"Their DNA doesn't show up in any municipal records," said Vail.

So either Teal Coat was new to the area, had never seen a doctor or held a job that the municipal government recognized, or their records had been wiped. Too many possibilities to be a good lead.

The guards had trussed up Teal Coat fine, and two of them carried the unconscious body out the door.

"We done here?" Eric asked.

Vail nodded. "Seems like it. You talk to Seymour?"

"Ah-yeah. She gave me a lot of food for thought." He wasn't sure where to start if he wanted to keep his job. "I'll want to talk to you about it later."

"I'm on tenterhooks." Vail didn't smile at him, but their eyebrows arched. They held out Eric's jacket for him.

"Thanks." He put it back on, along with his gloves. They were old, and he enjoyed their smooth feel, but they were fraying at the fingertips. He should have bought new ones instead of coming back to the lab today.

Eric exited R&D 4 and shook his shoulders out before he headed to the train station several blocks from the lab. He liked taking the train and found the ride relaxing. He hadn't boarded a train until he was sixteen though. Dad thought them the devil's work. But Dad didn't know enough to disapprove—the two of them hadn't spoken in years. Eric wanted to make his life in Portland, and Dad wanted to stay off the grid and in the forest.

When he boarded the train, he stood and held a bar, despite some seats being open. The seats in the car all faced into the center, in case you wanted to converse across, he supposed. Or just cram more humans into it. Since Eric didn't work first shift, it wasn't crowded tonight.

Most of the other riders on the train were late commuters, holding corporate jobs like him. Some of them wore trendy suits. Others wore flannel and sweatpants that had seen better days, probably last decade. The most unkempt people were either indigents or well-compensated tech workers with nonpublic-facing careers.

Most of the suits the corporate drones wore fit poorly. Those folks were probably low or middle management. Execs like Seymour tended to have theirs tailored. She only wore one suit design, powder blue. Even though she'd gotten covered in her bodyguards' blood three of the past four strikes this year. She'd gotten popular, if he could call it that. When he'd first joined Research and Development's Security department, she'd been the target about once a year.

operate with eyes on them. Namely, make their dealings not the Big Three's problem. Make stamping them out more trouble than it was worth.

Eric didn't object to the Makos' activities. He didn't own a small business, and didn't know anyone who owned one. Unless you counted his sister, Sam's, boss, who was a sculptor with a studio. He wondered if the Makos squeezed artists. He'd asked once, and Sam had said not that she'd known of. The artists who made enough money to be worth squeezing lived in the areas where the Makos didn't operate anyway.

Sam said one of the Makos liked old-fashioned paintings, and even sponsored a few artists. She'd laughed and said it was like Renaissance Italy. He didn't get the joke. Probably because he'd never studied art history. She hadn't formally either, but she'd taught herself.

Eric still wondered why backup had taken so long to arrive. He wasn't about to mention it to Seymour though. Vail had mentioned that the other guards assigned to the building were elsewhere resolving a different incident. He'd have to look into that after he got home and rested a bit.

Eric rummaged through the pantry for protein powder. Maybe some carbs would help too. Make him less cranky. The kitchen comm rang and popped up an image of his sister.

"Yo."

"I got an invitation to the Founders' Day gala," she said. She stood amidst some drafting equipment.

"Uh, that's cool." He found the packet he was looking for and emptied it into a tumbler. "You went last year, right? With uh … Aron?" Eric couldn't keep track of his sister's flavors of the month.

"Yes. With Aron. He's not available this year though. He's going with Jancee Rees."

Who was Jancee Rees again? He added water and stirred. "Okay."

"So I need an escort this year."

"Ah-yeah." Right now he didn't feel like digging for information.

"I haven't been able to find anyone yet. Except Hien, and I'd rather go with a scorpion."

Eric sat on his sofabed, exhaling hard. *Ouch.* The numbing agent was wearing off. "What's wrong with him?"

"Hien's a girl, you yokel. Nasty gossip. She'll inflate everything she sees. I've talked about her before. So stupid of me to get involved."

"I can't keep track of all of your friends, conquests, whatever, Sam." Eric sighed. "Did you call me just to bitch, or do you want me to actually say something?" He was fine with the former, but he had no brains left today to deal with anything more.

"No, I already bitched to Yavis." Yavis, a hyped sculptor, was Sam's boss. "He told me to call you."

"Oh no. No no no no." Galas were a throwback in socialization. They required physical attendance. He'd attended two of those as Sam's escort, and a few more guarding Harbor execs.

Eric grumbled to himself, disgusted. He'd have to get his suit out and pressed, only to drink whatever sweet cocktails were a la mode this month and avoid people who were just there to gossip.

Eric sent Sam money and didn't get involved with her socialite arts scene, and he liked it that way. Too many people wearing what he guessed was supposed to be art, acting all fancy and glamified.

"Please. This is important. Jack den Liu is presenting, and I've got to meet him."

"You know I can't talk the talk." He owned two suits, which was at least one suit too many.

"Neither can most of the businesspeople there." She twisted a loop of hair around a finger. "I know you'll be bored to tears, but I don't want to be seen without an escort." His face must have told her what he thought of that. "S'il vous plaît?"

"Let me check my calendar," he said. He put down his drink then flipped through his scheduler. "Nothing that night. Fine. But I'm doing this under protest."

He spoiled her, but she knew how to make nice. "Thank you, Eric. If there's anything I can do in return ...?"

He shook his head. "I'll take an IOU."

"You must have at least five of those by now. What are you saving them up for?"

"Nothing in particular," he answered. "You never know." He doubted anyone in the art scene could help him with his problems at his job, and he wasn't about to involve Sam in his personal bullshit.

Sam gave him a long look. "You looked pretty stove-up."

The abrasions on his face would heal the fastest. "Just some scrapes at work today." He waved dismissively. "The usual. Don't worry about me. You go and find an outfit for the gala."

"If you say so." She always commented, but rarely pressed hard. "Well, anyway, I'll arrive at your place beforehand, then we can go together. I'll try not to let anyone talk your ear off too much."

"You do that." He signed off and chugged his drink. Ugh. He still felt amped up. Time for a walk to clear his head. He'd just gotten home, but he could postpone the shower. Not like he had further plans for the evening. Throw a shirt and coat over his work gear, and he'd call it cool. He didn't bother with a hat before he walked back into the drizzle.

Eric took his regular route through his drab neighborhood. No blinking light signs. All the buildings had been painted gray or beige, and some of them needed new siding. The roads had rubbish piles, but not enough to get in his way. The stench of rot wasn't overwhelming.

Mako territory, which made it moderately safe. The gangs and petty criminals around either knew Eric or were too small-time to give him much trouble.

Maybe it wasn't Eric's business, but he did wonder if the punk had successfully kifed whatever he was after. He doubted Seymour would tell him if he asked though.

Normally, Corps tried to steal information from each other as part of Corpfare. Large corporations had agents they'd send out to kife or damage each other's assets. So each corporation built up a large Corpfare division in Security. Eric thought it was baroque, but it kept him employed.

Corpfare was supposed to be conducted openly. All registered agents were easily traceable so that in the case of capture, the captors knew where to send the ransom demands. So if the kid was working for a Corp on the down-low or wasn't involved with a Corp at all, something was off.

Gauntlets were rare high-end equipment, unique to a corporation's Corpfare division due to their astronomical cost. Eric didn't know how to use one. Few agents were trained. They'd borrow a Gauntlet for their strike and use it to brute force break any cybersecurity they encountered. How had some kid not affiliated with any Corp known how to use one, let alone get his tattooed hands on it?

Eric was no forensics expert, but he'd thought R&D 4 a secure facility, and room 203 had extra locks on it. How had the punk gotten past all of them? If he could figure that out, maybe he could advance another rank at Harbor.

He thought about going over this puzzle with Trez, but she'd bugged off and out. A few months ago she'd been his favorite Ninja opponent. After all, it was her job to get past guards like him to the target.

Corpfare personnel often played Ninja with each other when they were on standby or bored. They talked out scenarios and fights, theoretical or actual, and tried to one-up each other. Eric thought himself pretty good at it, and Trez always gave him a challenge.

Something was very wrong in Trezland. He'd been interested in her for months, and he'd thought she'd been into him too. A sparring session a few weeks ago had ended in hotsyncing. Then she freaked out and became a shut-in.

He'd seen her once since then, and she'd quickly apologized for not staying in touch. Then she'd booked it before he could get in a word.

He would have thought he was getting the kiss-off because she'd regretted their hooking up, but some of her other friends had also said they were confused by her withdrawal from social interaction. Plus, she'd looked awful of late. Not that he'd asked them. No, he wasn't mooning over a woman like that. Just concerned about an old friend.

A sudden screeching noise made his danger sense flare. *What could be* . . . Eric's eyes widened. That was one pimped out dirtcycle headed his way. It careened hard into a nearby storefront with a loud crunch, throwing the rider a few meters down the road. Eric ran toward the cyclist even as the other pedestrians gave the bike some distance. Dirtcycles spruced up like that often had some crazy volatiles in their tanks. You never knew what could explode when.

"You all right?" He checked the crumpled figure for obvious injury. The rider was breathing and conscious. The half helmet, now dented in near the right ear, had taken some of the impact. He wore a suit with a sharktooth motif. Mako member then. Probably suffering massive road burn under there. Maybe even broken bones.

"Ugh," said the cyclist. He shook his head as if there were an object in there he needed to jar loose. "What the . . . Shit . . ." His face turned toward his bike, now embedded in the cement next to the front door of a building signed ANUPAM'S SYNTH SWEETS. "Well, fuck me." He grimaced, and braced his hands on the road to get back on his feet. He failed to push himself up then he collapsed.

A beat-up truck swerved onto their street, and two goons wearing flannel bandannas to cover the lower half of their faces came out. They didn't sport any Mako symbols, and red-and-green plaid was definitely not a Mako color combo. One of them had a baton attached to their belt. Eric's metal detector didn't pick up any other weapons.

He hadn't acquitted himself well in the earlier fight today. Here was a chance to impress the Makos. Never hurt to be in good graces with the mob.

Eric's heartbeat sped up. He had been tired, but he could feel a second wind coming on. This could be more fun than he'd expected. He turned to face the thugs, angling his body and putting one foot forward. His farther hand made a fist. "Looking for something?"

The two figures stopped short. One tilted their head at the other's. "This isn't your business."

The words came easy. "Sure it is." *Come and get it.* He smiled, not kindly.

"You're not one of them. He probably squeezes you for protection money. What do you care?"

"I don't like jerkass squirts hanging around outside my apartment and doing whatever they want. Lowers the property values."

The male thug wound up to strike Eric. Eric caught him by the wrist and pulled him in close, grabbing his other wrist. The baton smacked into Eric's side, and he gritted his teeth from the impact and electrical shock.

Eric bent both of the thug's trapped wrists back. Painful, but the idiot didn't deserve anything more permanent yet. The other thug's eyes darted around, but she made no move toward Eric to attack him or rescue her partner.

"You can leave, or I can have more fun testing your flexibility. Nod if you agree." The man grunted, but nodded. Eric dropped him and he scurried away. His companion made a slight move toward them, but Eric moved his head to stare at her. Wouldn't do for her to think he'd forgotten about her. She raised her hands a little then backed up and jumped into the driver's seat of the truck.

Eric watched the beater leave then turned to the prone crash victim. Still conscious. None of his limbs were obviously broken.

"I'm going to check your vitals first, okay?" Eric said. He checked the guy's pulse and reflexes. "I'm going to take off your helmet."

"You some kind of— Look, I don't need—" the cyclist said,

or something like that. His voice was a little muffled. Eric ignored his protests and took the man's jaw in his left hand and removed the helmet. Eric recognized him: a fixer Eric had dubbed Staplehead due to his mostly shaved head and the glint of staples from a chop shop. No obvious head injuries.

"Look, you big lug, I appreciate a Good Samaritan, but I'm all set."

"How many fingers am I holding up?" It was dark and his gloves were black, but the street was lit well enough for his reluctant patient to see.

"Three."

"Now how many?"

"I get it, your thumb's up, very funny—"

"I have first aid training, Staplehead. Now follow my finger with your eyes and shut it." Eric looked at how the guy tracked his movements. "I'm going to guess you have at least a first-grade concussion. Go see a medic. I'm going to call HES for you—"

"Don't bother. I'll go see a doc myself."

"Your bike isn't what I'd call drivable right now."

"I'll comm a friend for a pickup." Staplehead activated his comm. "Ayuh, it's me. Can you come get me?" He blinked several times before raising both eyebrows. "No, it's not an emergency per se, but I'm stranded and there's a big lug here saying I need to see a doc." Eric sat on his haunches and monitored the foot traffic. Could be more goons where the last two had come from.

"Crashed the bike. Minor injuries. I've fallen and I can't get up." The man had a thick Aroostook County accent. "All right, I'll wait here. Got my painkiller spray if I need it."

"And also, the big lug," Eric commented. Half his mouth couldn't stop smirking.

"Fine, fine." Staplehead disconnected and met Eric's eyes again. "Are you just going to wait around here until my friends come to get me?"

"Can't exactly leave you out here alone. Those thugs might have buddies."

Staplehead winced. "Well, I could say I'm not in a gaum but that's obviously not true."

The other half of Eric's mouth joined the smirk. "Pretty much, bucko. I'm guessing you're bleeding under your suit." Marde, that reminded him of his own injuries. He held in his breath and counted until the pain subsided. Shock baton contact hurt like a bitch, even with heavy muscle weave to dampen the impact.

A dark gray stove-up van pulled up to them. "You numb stump," said the person in the driver's seat. Out the passenger's side came a slick-haired goth. His jacket was open, and his shirt had "BITE ME" written across his nipples. He walked to Staplehead and picked him up by the underarms.

"They were trying to run me off the road," Staplehead said.

"Yeah, yeah, excuses. You and your persecution complex," Mr. Bitee opened the backseat door and tossed his charge into the vehicle. He closed the door and gave Eric a long look. "You helping?"

"I'm the lug," Eric said. "Your friend hit his head decent bad." He picked up the helmet. "Want this back?"

Mr. Bitee recoiled a little. "Sure." Eric tossed it over and the Mako made a good catch.

"What about the bike?"

"Fuck. Kalla can share the backseat with it."

Eric helped him try to wedge the bike into the footwells, partially squishing Staplehead, who protested.

"Enough of this," said the driver. "Get in the van, Dorgo."

Dorgo, a.k.a. Mr. Bitee, opened his own door. "I won't say thanks for this idiot here, but I guess you may've helped." He stepped in and the idling vehicle was off before he had the door shut.

Eric watched the van rumble off, worrying a strand of hair from the helmet in his fingers. Shit, he'd forgotten to get some DNA from the thugs. That might have been useful. It never hurt to know who you'd picked a fight with.

THREE

Trez disembarked from the train. Nobody else got out of her car at this stop. There wasn't much in this neighborhood besides hazardous waste disposal and incineration. It had gotten gray out: some ungodly mix of ash, pollution, and clouds. The buildings were mostly gray too, the paint had worn off the concrete ages ago. Nobody had seen fit to repaint anything except a few candy-pink triple-deckers.

When she arrived at Doc Ten's office, she checked that she hadn't forgotten her anonymous chip to pay him. She'd chosen Ten's office because of its reputation for discretion. Ten didn't know her full name or occupation. At least, he claimed not to.

Trez scuffed her boots on the pavement outside the doorway. Her knees weakened for a moment. She stumbled. She bit back a swear then commed Ten to tell him she'd arrived.

Ten eased the door open. Trez didn't know when the sliding mechanism had last worked. "Kufo, come on in."

She followed him down a hall. The office had always been dingy, featuring stucco walls somewhere between gray or blue, concrete floors with gray rugs, and bare light sources. A grimy kid lay on a makeshift pallet, mumbling in his sleep and shaking.

Doc Ten ushered Trez into an exam room. He swiped a wand across her forehead. Many medics had robots or assistants to do initial diagnostics for them, but he'd told Trez he'd rather blame his errors on himself.

"BP's up a bit. You need more water." No matter what her vitals were, he always told her she needed more water. He glanced at her file. "Aaaaand ... ears, nose, throat, ports." He retrieved his scope from the wall and began sticking it in the more inoffensive places the sun didn't usually shine. "Good thing I had space for you on short notice."

"Thanks for taking the time for me. It's urgent."

"All right. Let's start with the obvious intake questions. How much sleep do you get a night, on average?"

"My comm says four or five hours."

"With interruptions?"

"A few."

He scrolled through his patient notes. "So ... screaming nightmares, sweating, paralysis, and shaking?"

"Yes. No change in that."

"Would you say this is better or worse than four weeks ago?"

"Maybe a little worse? I'm not sure."

Ten stood up to go to his needle dispenser. "O-kay! Time for the bloodwork!" She wondered how many needles he used in a day. Some Security personnel, guards or ninjas, were still squeamish about doctor needles. Eric hated them, even though his job was essentially to shed blood at a moment's notice.

Ten grabbed Trez's arm and tapped it, massaging her forearm until he found a vein. There were less invasive ways to do it, but the doctor talked about being "cost conscious" when he could.

"That should do it." He flipped a plastic bit from the draw apparatus toward the compactor, but missed. He giggled. Trez was decent sure the bit was clean, but she didn't feel like asking right then. He'd no doubt say something to plant seeds of worry in her mind.

"Now it's pee-in-a-cup time. On with you!" He handed Trez the receptacle and waved her to the bathroom. When she returned, Ten was poring through a bunch of charts. He looked up at her approach and put his left hand out to grab the sample from her. He deposited it into a machine and frowned.

"Your body isn't handling the pharmaceutical load well. Your blood has mad chemtrails. Sieve, trace. Stims, gone. Dissociative, lurking. It's good that you're not building those up. Huh, Charcoal detox. You needed that? When did you use it?"

"Yesterday, after the job."

"Ah-yeah. Opiates, you'd better watch those. You're getting near the dependence stage. How much of the scrip did you take for god's sake?"

"Everything that I had left."

"Jesus. I can't imagine what your job must actually be. My newest guess is professional clown. You'd have to be elite though. Those boots may be dirty as Times Square on garbage day, but they can't be cheap."

"Clown?" Trez tried to imagine several of the other strikers as clowns and failed. Some of them were decent entertainers or showpeople. Some Corps in other regions sold strike footage.

"Yes! Requires agility, precision, coordination, so that's why you need all the stims. You're hiding it from me because of the shame and fear that accompanies clowning, as coulrophobia is one of the more common intense fears people share. The dissociatives and Sieve are for your internal terror."

"Uh, I'm not afraid of clowns." She had never considered it as a career though.

"Your hair would be perfect for it. Some people need a wig, you'd just apply dye and go! The old American style popularized in the twentieth century. Well, maybe grow it out." Ten tugged at his own wavy hair and gave it an accusatory glance. "Work what you've got."

Trez fought the smile creeping onto her face. The process made Ten's eyes widen. "Growing my hair that long would take years. That aside. You were saying something about my body being stove-up?"

"You even have a freaky clown smile! Ugh! Anyway, you have some kidney and liver damage. Nothing irreversible at this point, but I don't want to give you anything that'll stress them any more. So if you want to continue your peculiar brand of performance enhancement, you need to change it up."

"I'm listening."

"Long story short, I'm making you two new cocktails. The first one, which I will call Cocktail A, should give you the effects you desire, but will take a while to work. Two hours or so. Cocktail B, meanwhile, you should only use on short notice. Like last-minute clowning gigs."

"I really am not clowning."

"Aren't you? Metaphorically?"

"It's a stupid metaphor."

"Knowing as little as I do, I can't comment on its metonymy."

"Meto what?"

"Never mind." Doc Ten was no doubt doing a few too many stims himself. "Any questions so far?"

"Will there be any change in half life or side effects?"

Ten waggled his fingers. "For Cocktail A? Dehydration, fatigue, and muscle weakness several hours later. You will hate that you are still alive or ever were. You will curse my name and your own. For Cocktail B, expect a hangover the next morning. No dairy, real or synth, for two days after; it'll give you wicked gas. You'll be farting a symphony."

"That's not a lovely image."

"Well, it'll also do dastardly things to your blood sugar, but patients tend to take the farting more seriously somehow."

Trez didn't bother acknowledging that with words, but she tilted her head to the side and narrowed her eyes.

"I'm only prescribing one dose of each. Comm me after you use either of them so I can run some tests and adjust the scrip. You want to come see me?"

"Okay. Sure." She couldn't muster much enthusiasm for dragging herself out here again soon, but she didn't feel confident about the privacy of the local courier services.

"I'll give you your test results and the pharmacological details of the cocktails on a chip," he said.

"Anything else?"

"Just payment. You got cash?"

"Give me a moment." She ejected the wafer from underneath a fingernail.

"That always creeps me out." He took the chip and put it through the sanitizer with an expression of distaste. Trez couldn't help but find that funny. "When we get metal bits out of people, as opposed to installing them in, it reeks too much of those old war movies with fragmentation grenades."

"Have you ever had to treat someone for that?"

"For grenades?" The sanitizer ultrasound beeped. "Not frags. But other related injuries, sure." He withdrew the chip and put it into the terminal. "There. That's your test results, mixtures, dosages, contraindications, and some illustrative diagrams. Any info you could possibly need, loaded. Just covering my ass here."

"Thanks." He handed the chip back to her.

"Got some alcohol to swab it?" Trez asked. She smirked when he grumbled and gestured at the ultrasound.

She stood up a little too fast and had to wait until she didn't feel faint anymore. Ten made a move to assist her, but she waved him off. She cleaned her chip in the sanitizer then reinserted it. "Thanks, doc. I'll see you in a month, or sooner."

"I might hope sooner, you would hope later. Ta!" Ten waved goodbye.

"Take care," Trez said. She let herself out of the office and the building. As soon as she got to the rail station, her comm alerted her to a new strike she could sign up for. She skimmed over the assignment parameters. Good pay, site access secured, coordinates ... odd location. There would be civvies on location. She didn't like that. The target had a team of three personal guards, but one of them was out on medical leave. Lethal force authorized. Which was rare, she hadn't had a job with permission to murder in three years. She accepted even though the assignment seemed irregular. It wasn't as if she was in a position to be choosy.

The train pulled in. Time to rest at home and not think about Linus, debts, pharma, or Eric. How about purple elephants while she was at it? She stepped into the car, worrying the finger with the now-creditless chip in it.

FOUR

Breakroom coffee came from a low-quality dispenser. Somehow the drinks turned out both weak and sludgy. Eric had suggested taking up a collection to get a better model, but nobody else in the office had been interested.

Security guards went through rotations: a week guarding important personnel from Corpfare, a week patrolling buildings, and a week of standing by for deployment. That meant hanging out in the lounge, talking shop, doing administrative work, and trading barbs unless violent excitement called in. The emergencies were where they earned their salaries, Vail said.

Eric wasn't keen on filling out the mountain of reports he had pending, but he'd better learn to deal with it if he wanted to transfer to InfoSec. InfoSec used a lot of reports and classification in their workflow. But if he wanted to stay off Seymour's shit list, he needed to focus on his immediate problem. "About yesterday," he ventured.

"What about it?" Vail was sitting back on a small couch, fussing with their hair. They'd shellacked it back to a flat top, but they didn't seem pleased with the results.

"The dustup at R&D 4. Seymour wants me to look into it personally, and I'm drawing a blank as to what to do. How to investigate."

They took their hands out of their hair. "Huh. I shouldn't be surprised Seymour left it on you. Sounds like her."

"Going to ask to bounce some ideas off you. If that's okay"

They hesitated. "You want my help?"

"You are the other person with firsthand experience of the incident. I'm not afraid to ask for help. Especially since Teal Coat corrupted all the security feeds and footage."

"You're right. I'm just . . . wondering how useful I could be to you." A bit of bitterness slipped out.

"You know plenty."

Vail shook their head. "Not sure if management thinks so." Eric had been Vail's subordinate five years ago. Now he outranked them. Vail didn't seem to hold him responsible, but he tried to step lightly around the subject.

"The fast track's not all it's cracked up to be." Eric couldn't meet Vail's eyes. He hadn't told them about his transfer request explicitly, but Vail had somehow known anyway. They had never abused their authority around Eric, even when it was easy to use your grunts to make yourself look good.

Vail exhaled through their nose, a bit of a reverse snort. "Finally figured out you could cut someone on those skates."

"What?" Vail said shit that didn't make any sense sometimes.

"That or you wanted the extra heavy muscle weave Protection Detail gets to impress people you'd like to fuck." They scanned their comm for a moment.

"Sure, like I go around performing feats of strength in restaurants or people's apartments."

"You could move someone's furniture for them. Or save them from getting crushed by debris from a collapsing building. Hero-man. People dig the hero-man."

"Damsels aren't really my type."

"Nah, you like them dangerous. Femmes fatales."

Eric put up with this shit from Vail because even though they were nosy, there was no malice. They tended to meddle like a concerned older sibling. One who wasn't a psychopath anyway.

"Well, at least you don't need to worry about breaking her," Vail continued musing. "Woman like that, bet she could flip you if she wanted."

Eric pressed his lips together. Trez knew how to use her leverage for a bit of spice. No. He pulled his thoughts from that path.

"Hey. Greis." Vail's brow furrowed and they sat up straighter then winced. Their replacement leg and hip hadn't integrated well. Eric had given up asking them how often it hurt and how much. They never said anything except "tolerable."

"Yeah?" He rubbed his temple with his fingers.

"She kick you to the pavement?" Oh, great. Now Vail sounded worried.

"I haven't seen Trez except at work in a few months, if that's what you're asking."

"Okay, fine, I get it. Sorry. No need to be coy. That's wicked odd though. Always thought she was into you."

Well, he'd thought so too a few weeks ago. Time to change the subject. "Let me talk this through, try to reconstruct the break-in." Most of the guard security officers had some training on the hardware and software used to secure different areas. He had gotten his promotions by using his head along with his reflexes. At least, that's what he liked to tell himself.

He popped up a holo screen to go over yesterday's events.

"All right, importing the floor plan …" Three additional holo surfaces extruded from the screen. "I don't know, maybe he came in the front door?"

"That what the access logs say?" Vail asked.

"That and the fact that the back door's exit only. No signs of tampering at the exit or the windows. I'll check in with Forensics, since he probably shed some DNA somewhere. But if he used the front door, there's an airlock with a biometric scan. He would have needed to fake credentials there." The holo screen spawned several colored cubes, hovering in the front door area on the map.

Vail traced out several paths on the display. "Well, if he used the front door, all pathways to the lab take him through several doors and elevators." Each lab in R&D 4, which the execs had named Miletus a few years ago, had two heavy-duty security locks on it. Hallways were likewise partitioned with locked doors.

"He could have used maintenance ducts and the stairs to get around some of those." Eric moved the cubes to mark those points on the map. "But I don't see a way for him to avoid the doors entirely."

Vail shrugged. "That's what the Gauntlet's for."

"The Gauntlet might have punched through those locks pretty easily, but the doors … they have a delay before they open."

"Yep. Fifteen seconds. That's a hardware measure. Why not check when the doors were opened, if you still have those records?"

Eric pulled the access logs for all of the doors they had marked. He watched timestamps float above each door on the model. "Something seems off."

Vail didn't answer for a minute. Then, "Do I have to figure this out for you?"

Ugh. He hated looking stupid. Feeling stupid. Even if it was just around Vail. He shrugged. "Something doesn't add up, but I don't know what."

"The access timestamps for all the doors are too close together. It should have taken minutes for him to get to the lab."

Eric flung random cubes at the model in his frustration. They bounced. "What're you getting at?"

"Maybe he's a hacker? Or got a hacker accomplice?" Vail tapped a foot. It was distracting. "Or maybe he had a way to spam the logs or fake access timestamps?"

"How would that help?" He didn't have a lot of practice with forensics.

"I don't know." Vail shook their head.

"But as to hacking, I've no idea about his tech skills. He didn't have a lot of fight training. Just a party's worth of pharma. That's all I've been able to figure out about him." Eric walked to the chrome dispenser and filled his mug with water.

"Well, you do need some hacking ability to really use the Gauntlet."

"Sure. Breaking the encryption on a server is a bigger deal than opening a security lock." Eric compressed his mouth into a line and took several deep breaths. "What I don't understand is how he got the Gauntlet and how he knows how to use it."

"Do you know who it originally belonged to? Maybe he stole it from them. Or maybe it's black market."

"We won't know until we decrypt and analyze the Gauntlet. They're still working on that." Eric's boots thudded on the concrete with his steps. "It's a Klinger S502, which is the most common make and model out there. We use 'em here. I believe they use them at Fairchild and Michaud as well. Can we get any information off it?"

"If he wasn't a total idiot, he would have erased the prior data." Vail smirked. "Though you should never make assumptions about someone's idiocy or lack thereof."

"Point. In any case, I've no idea who he is, how he got there, or what he wanted."

"Presumably data on those servers?"

"Hard telling not knowing," Eric said. "All they'll tell me is that the project in there is security-related, and the servers were kept off-line to help protect them from remote attacks." He made himself stop pacing. When he looked down, he saw coffee stains. "I mean, I think he knew what he was looking for there? Which again doesn't give me anything concrete."

"Do you know if he succeeded?"

"There were perforations in the power supply. So I assume he at least started." A Gauntlet could connect directly through the power cables to any local hosts. Then you could interact with all the fancy security—mazes, he'd heard them called. You could then break most encryption with its brute-force operations. It did take time though.

"I guess you have to assume the worst." Vail began tapping a foot again. Maybe they were more suited to an Intelligence position than Eric.

"If he copied the data he could have beamed it somewhere else. I'm sure there are some Harbor Runners working on finding that data in the wild. If Seymour and her team are even willing to tell them what it is."

"Good luck with that."

Eric had some trouble figuring out whether that was supposed to be sarcastic. He shook out his shoulders. "Maybe

I should start over. If the intruder gets in at first floor from either door, he first has to not get seen. He's going to go up some floors. Stairs or elevator, like you said. The elevator and stairs have the same locks on them."

"Facilities has access to 'em too, for emergency maintenance purposes. Pretending to be a maintenance worker is the one weird old trick that still works," Vail said.

"I checked the access logs. Didn't find anything, but as you said before, someone could've scrubbed them." Eric stared at the holo model. Was there an obvious clue neither of them saw? "We're still not getting anywhere. There's something off, but I can't put my finger on it."

"Well, it's not like we practice this kind of work. It's usually handled by people over in Intelligence. But we could run some sims. Play Ninja," Vail suggested.

"The two of us?"

"Nah, you get better results playing with strikers."

"Then we ask a striker. We can always get a consult on a case."

"Good idea. Why don't you drop her a line?" they asked.

"Who?" Eric kept manipulating the possible routes on his heads-up display, not meeting Vail's eyes.

"You know who I'm talking about. Our coworker? Beatrez Harris? Veteran striker? Has the arm-swords, poofy hair, and killer hips?"

"Trez? I did. She hasn't replied."

Vail's head tilted back slightly. Their mouth opened briefly then snapped shut. "Oh. Well, if you say it's for work, that might get her attention."

———————

Trez sealed her encounter suit over her body. It wasn't a custom job, but she'd had the gloves and elbow pads tailored. The sensation was both that of being tucked in at night and suffocating. Claustrophobes usually didn't make good strikers.

She slipped on her mesh gloves then triple-checked her claws, deploying them to full length and retracting them several times. Titanium alloy inlaid her finger bones, jointed to follow her knuckles. With a straightened hand, she had ten centimeters of metal she could deploy to slash, climb, or intimidate. Harbor cyberneticists had to reinforce her hands and wrists for that one. They'd put a different, less bulky material in the rest of her arms for aesthetic reasons. Heaven forbid she have incorrectly bulging biceps. Her hands already looked something of a mess, warped and padded under the skin.

Now to test her bigger weapons. Arm-swords, Vanchen called them. There was always a slight sting when she extended those. Felt good. Reminded her that she was alive and ready to nab her target. It didn't matter who stood in her way. Her job was to figure out ways through and around them.

She walked past the gun lockers, but didn't open any. The firearms were here for practice and emergencies only. She had sharpshooter training, like everyone in Security, but the rules of Corpfare didn't allow guns on strikes: Shooting to maim instead of to kill left less room for error than melee weapons did. Trez had never been assigned a kill strike, and knew only one striker who had. They'd retired a month after their successful operation.

Some of the new pharma were taking effect. Trez's jitters about how her body might react to them faded. The ceiling lights bled when she moved her head around, but she felt cool, dry, and focused. She didn't need to pace. She could just stand and center herself for a few minutes.

The locker room door opened with a screeching sound. She spun around, startled; she'd had her head so far up her ass that her situational awareness had gone to shit, so to speak.

"Vail?" She hadn't seen them in a while, since she hadn't worked with Eric's division for the past few weeks. "Hi."

"Good evening." They walked straight over to her and ran their hands through their hair. "Haven't seen you in a while, Trezzo."

"Yeah."

"No reason you'd avoid old Vail, is there? Thought we were on good terms."

Trez blinked. Colors swam. "Uh, right."

"Are you headed off for another episode of Corpfare?

"Yeah." She checked her suit's camera. She'd figured out how to make watching replays of the footage during strike debriefs less disorienting. She just needed to convince herself that the person with the suitcam was someone else.

"Trezzo, Trezzo. You can say more than two words at a time, I know you can."

"Sure."

Vail smiled and clapped an arm around her armor-clad shoulders. "Determined to prove me wrong, I see. Where're you headed to?"

"The strike's at a charity event."

"Uh," Vail said. "That's unusual. Won't civilians be there?"

Trez tried to banish the feeling of nausea those words gave her. "Technically, the building is Fairchild territory. So that's within the rules."

"Well, if an exec signed off on it . . ." They pursed their lips. "I guess it's not my business if you traumatize the civvies at a party. But the cleanup for that isn't going to be fun. Especially if any of them get hurt."

"I'll be careful," Trez said.

"If you're not, they'll take it out of your pay, right?"

"Yeah." If there were severe mistakes during a strike, the job could end up paying nothing. Injuring a civilian carried a hefty penalty.

"Decent motivation if you want to retire." They hugged her closer. "But then again, I haven't seen you 'round at work. You been slacking?"

She shrugged, trying to dislodge their arm. Normally she wouldn't mind their friendliness, but she just wanted to get to the strike and get it over with as quickly as she could. "Been resting."

"Resting, huh? Why, Eric ride you so hard you couldn't see any of us for weeks?"

Trez froze. She'd done the riding. "Uh, I . . . Did Eric tell you something?"

"Nah, he didn't tell me. I guessed. You just did though." Vail grinned.

Fuck Vail and their aquiline nose. "It's got nothing to do with him."

"I advise you talk to him. Otherwise he might think you thought him that lousy a lay."

She took two deep breaths. Why were they baiting her? "Look, it's . . . Lots of stuff has come up."

"It's not him, it's you bullcrap?"

That wasn't funny, because it was true. "Don't know that he'd appreciate you asking."

"He can unappreciate all he likes, Trezzo. This is concern for a friend."

"That's nice of you, I guess. We can finish catching up later."

Vail tapped their foot. "Don't keep me waiting too long, or I'll ask him along."

"Asswipe." She strode past Vail.

"I'll remember that!" they called after her.

Trez didn't answer. If Ten's new cocktail did its job, she probably wouldn't remember this conversation.

FIVE

Eric got a notification that the cab had arrived. He'd walk to the station if he'd been going alone, but Sam didn't want to get her costume stepped on. He made one last check that everything was in its proper place, dashed out the door, and locked up. Samantha was wearing a blue garment that he thought was a dress, or a jumpsuit with the widest pants he'd ever seen.

"Looking like one sharp card, mon frère," she said.

He shrugged. "Same suit as last time."

"You don't have to be such a captive to traditional men's fashion though. Plenty of the guests will be in costume."

"I'd rather not draw attention to myself."

"Why not have some fun for once? I know you don't care about transhuman soundscapes or immersive paints, but there are plenty of people to talk to, flirt with, or make friends with."

"You keep assuming I want the same social life you do."

"Well, I know Harbor takes good care of you, but more connections never hurt anybody."

He figured the fine art community had links to politicians and wealthy eccentrics. Not connections he'd feel comfortable making. But there might be other people at the party like him. He should keep an open mind.

The cab stopped at the train station. A mix of costumed weirdos and commuters who worked late shifts crowded onto the car. Sam didn't talk much here, she looked around and people-watched. Eric followed suit. He distracted himself by eavesdropping on conversations about a kriegball team and someone's friend who had just married his eighth spouse.

They got off with other fancy suits and outlandish outfits, a swarm of fashion-conscious ants walking down to Fairchild building 37. If he were on the clock, it'd be enemy territory. Not the most comforting thought.

He distracted himself from his anxiety by looking at costumes: one featured abstract angles in unflattering colors and strategically-cut fabric meant to make him ask himself, he supposed, whether he had a knee fetish. Several gala attendants had welded sculpture onto themselves, one wore antennae, painted his face blue, and presented giant bird feathers from his ass.

Sam saw Eric's expression and laughed. "Peacock. Old bird you can find in zoos and a private collection or two."

"I don't remember peacocks being relevant to Founders Day."

"They aren't. Nah, this fellow's on a mission."

"To get as many gawkers as he can?"

"Nah, he's looking for a sex partner."

"I assume he's not the only one. Is that getup considered hot?"

"Means he's looking for a long-term partner, that is."

"That's ... uh ... certainly a way to declare your intentions."

They followed the glitterfolk into the lobby. Samantha inserted two chips into the turnstile along with everyone else filing in. Impassive doormen wearing button-ornamented coats and shiny hats flanked the entrance.

Sam's knuckles were white. "Need to freshen myself up at the WC."

"You nervous?"

"I'm meeting some prominent artists for the first time and I want to make a good impression."

He didn't have any advice for her there. "I'll wait around here then."

The entryway was set up into some sort of welcoming chamber. Fluted columns a meter in diameter extended from floor to ceiling. Gauzy white fabric inset with something shimmery floated between the tops of the columns. Two young women in sparkling blue sheath dresses were trying to get their arms around one by hugging it from opposite sides. They barely succeeded in entwining their fingers. One of them had her cheek against the column and her eyes closed.

Sam emerged from the WC, smoothing her skirt-pants over her hips. She followed his gaze to the decorations. "Snow, I think. Minimalist. Tasteful. Evocative."

"You think?" He grimaced.

"It could always be an allegory regarding death or silence," she said. "That fits with it. But I know what you're thinking. This party isn't just for art appreciators, so the decorators tend to use more universal themes for inspirations."

"Sure. Everyone here's seen snow. And death," Eric said.

"Some people who come up here from LA haven't," Sam replied. "They've usually experienced it in sim or stimsense though."

"Snow or death?"

Samantha rocked her head in mock disbelief. "You and your thick head."

He liked antagonizing her this way. It kept her from getting too self-absorbed and uppity. "That ... metallic music we're hearing. Snow or death?" When he listened more closely, he noticed all the sound in the receiving room was a bit muffled. "Think they padded the walls?"

"Oh! Of course! That would make us think of snow."

"Let's go."

Sam had been craning her neck a bunch, looking around. "Ah-yeah. I don't think I see anyone here I know."

"Not even column huggers?"

"Column huggers?" Sam raised her eyebrows and scanned the crowd until she saw the women clasping hands, now mouthing syllables. "Oh. No, not the column huggers. Maybe it's art?"

"That, or they got some good pre-party pharma."

"Even so, I don't know if it qualifies. As art, that is."

"You're the creative one." He drew those syllables out.

Sam shrugged her bare shoulders and walked on to the main foyer. Eric noted that more people dressed as some kind of historical European soldiers flanked the entrance. They carried themselves at attention. Decent security for a party.

A large white orb shone at the center of the domed ceiling. Glittery chandelier-like dewdrops coruscated all over the room. The room was dim otherwise, featuring more columns wrapped in gauzy fabric. The far side had refreshment tables with white-and-blue-clad wait staff. Voices were still muffled. "Think they wanted to keep it quiet?"

"I don't know. It's subversive." She bit her lip.

He smirked. "You'll have to explain that one to the uncultured rube."

"There are any number of explanations as to what the silence and winter themes at a celebratory function could imply. Do you truly want to hear my speculations and art theory?"

"Not so much."

"We could focus on your speculation instead then."

"What?"

"With your security expertise, what have you determined about our surroundings?"

"I've counted ten plainclothes—costumed?—guards. That normal for a fête like this?"

"I don't have the same training you do," Sam said. "There could have been plenty of hidden guards at previous events I've been to, and I wouldn't know. Guess it's the first thing you look for nowadays. Instinct."

"Occupational training, really."

"You tell me that the stress comes and goes. How's Vail doing? Still treating you okay?" Sam had been concerned that Vail wouldn't react well to getting passed over for promotion.

"They're a card. Like always." Eric paused. "Maybe they've gotten a bit more nosy which is a pain in the ass, but it doesn't feel . . . uh . . ."

"Malicious?"

"Sure, let's go with that."

"But you still get along? How about your other friends at work? What do you do when you're all stress crazy?"

Eric thought of Trez draped over him in the sparring room, sweaty and smiling. "I needed that more than I knew," she'd said. The hell of it was that he still agreed. Now that he was aware how thoroughly she could blast his brain, he kept thinking of doing it again. But no creepy stalker shit. She'd made it clear she didn't want to be bothered.

"Eric?" Sam's voice pulled him back to the present.

"What?"

"I expected some witty answer involving triple entendres," she said. "Something wrong?"

No point in hiding it. She'd badger him until he gave something up. "I'm worried about a friend."

"Friend in trouble?"

"People have barely seen her 'round the past few weeks," Eric said. "Like she's gone dark."

"Is her job as stressful as yours?"

"Yeah." He was saved from further prying by spotting a couple making a beeline their way. "Who's that?"

Samantha turned. "Ah! Lin!"

The couple gave air kisses to Sam, cheeks touching. "Samantha Greis! Good to see you again!" the man said. He was conservatively dressed like Eric, but his suit looked more pressed. Someone had ironed that sucker. Eric wondered if he needed to do likewise before the next shindig Sam dragooned him into. He'd probably forget to. Maybe he could set up a reminder on his comm.

"Hello, darling!" said the woman. Her brown hair was in a beehive with metal clips in it, and she wore a silver jumpsuit that defined her waist. Various ornaments and devices dangled off her body piercings and rings attached to her outfit.

Why did he even give a shit about how everyone was dressed tonight? Fucking parties. "Yep."

"Oh, Eric, stop that," Sam tapped his shoulder in remonstrance. "Yes, Licia, this is my brother, Eric. Eric, this is Licia and her husband, Lin. She's a visual designer."

"I hear Yavis got funding for his big project. Congratulations!" Licia said.

Sam hadn't told Eric. Or maybe she had and he'd forgotten it in the tangle of twisted thoughts preoccupying him the past few weeks. "That's good. How'd he finagle that?" he asked.

"Don't know how, but he got both Arts Council and someone at Michaud to sponsor it and provide the venue for the installation," Sam said.

"How'd he convince them?" Eric thought of the sculptor as a flake who could barely put on his boots in the morning.

"He said the exec wanted to do research with him on MC Escher," Sam replied. "Something about self-assembling architectures."

Eric shook his head. "Whatever."

"Speaking of installations," Licia said, "Do you know if the den Liu premiere here tonight is set up yet? It's the first Portland opening for a den Liu show."

"I know! I was able to make it to a Boston show once, but it wasn't an opening, so he wasn't there. Now I'll finally get to meet him."

"Samantha, you've been a fangirl for how long? If you want to add an increment to your bedpost, you'll need to be quick about it."

"I just want to meet him, hear what he has to say on stimsense in maze games."

"Quite." Licia smirked.

"I mean, he has such a fascinating mind!"

"You want his abs. I don't blame you. They're nice abs."

"Well . . ."

"I'm going to scram," Eric said. "You all can mack on the guy." He patted Sam on the shoulder.

People continued to file into the ballroom, meandering around and chatting. There hadn't been enough time to get all moxied up, so everyone's hands were steady. More guards milled around in their bad guises as staff. When Eric got to the refreshment station, a too-perky young woman asked him what he'd like to drink. She gave him a slow smile.

"Topaz Twister, on the rocks." He guessed she was cute and curvy, but he wasn't in the mood to flirt. His thoughts kept going over his office troubles, and Vail asking about Trez. If she really was in trouble, wouldn't she have said something to someone?

"Here you are." The server held out a glass for him. Ice floated in fizzy amber liquid. Some kind of algae gave it its color, he knew. Otherwise it looked like dirty water.

"Thanks," he said, taking the glass by the stem. He was going to find a good vantage point and check out the glitterfolk. Maybe all that shallow self-absorption would distract him from worrying about his office and coworkers and Sam's personal life.

He found himself thinking of the event security anyway. The costumes were distracting. Any events with masks were dodgy situations. Systems might catch 'em, but people's brains were so easy to fool.

Guards relying on their eyes would have trouble finding anyone in a more sober suit, because the art weirdos here wore the most eye-catching ... foutaise ... they could find. Eric was loath to call them clothes. They weren't just loud in a visual sense. Several outfits had audible components, and that plus the ambient music and conversation meant you'd have to have your listening device targeted at somebody very close. Also, the costumes disguised gaits. The best way to track a person was to watch how they walked.

Eric leaned against a wall in the least crowded part of the

room, tried to ignore the woman with big red curls sucking face with someone much younger, and sipped his fizz. Lemony alcohol chased by sweetener and acidic bubbles burned his tongue. Eh, passable. He'd never had real lemons, so he couldn't compare. This wouldn't get his buzz on, but he wasn't sure he wanted to get too relaxed here anyway.

That was enough people-watching. His optics would take a while to recover from all that input. Eric browsed his comm for activity on any local security channels. Harbor provided him with a middle-of-the-road scanner for his personal safety. Most megacorps, Harbor included, fitted their security personnel with augmentations to their comms. Eric had gotten his modded so that he could disconnect it from Central. Violation of his equipment contract, but he banked on it not mattering to anyone. Compliance software wasn't worth the money to make and maintain.

He found a signal local to this floor, on the same subnet as the cameras around. He ignored the video feeds and concentrated on the chatter.

When he shifted his weight on the column, he dislodged a garland. White powder/dust came down on him. Shit, they must not have designed these to take a reinforced person's weight. Some flakes floated in his fizz. Since he didn't know the content of the synth snow, drinking it would be a poor idea. His body could filter it out, but it'd be less of a hassle to get a new glass.

"Excuse me, asshole," said the woman next to him. Oh. He'd gotten the dust all over her too, and her partner. The white powder hadn't melted like snow would; it stuck in her big curls, her maroon gown, and her partner's spangled blazer. He looked down at his own suit. The stuff was a bit glittery. Appropriate to the occasion, he guessed.

He shrugged. "Sorry. Didn't know I could do that."

"How am I going to get this snow off?" she asked.

"Uh, you can pass it off as part of your costume? Art or something?" He fought the impulse to tell her to chill. Polite society and all that.

"This ensemble is a rental!" She threw up her hands.

Her partner looked back and forth between them. "Ah . . ."

Eric took the opportunity to flee. He didn't feel like dealing with histrionics tonight; he had other problems to worry about.

He tried to brush off the fake snow, but lots of it stuck or melted into sludge, slightly discoloring his shirt. Marde. He was going to get it cleaned anyway, he reminded himself. Time to head back to the refreshment table for another drink. Maybe this one would actually relax him.

SIX

Eric sampled his wine. The server had told him it was the real stuff, imported from Cascadia. It did taste a little different than the wine he got from the market. Less metallic. He closed his eyes, tilted his head back, and exhaled.

"There you are!" a voice shouted from right in front of him.

Eric caught himself from spilling his glass. He looked slightly downward and schooled his expression into something neutral. The voice appeared to belong to a shorter woman wearing several layers of checked flannel shirts. She had a dense mop of brown hair and a fine-boned face. Her expression was difficult to read, what with her ridiculous flattened dark spectacles.

"You. Eric." She pointed at his chest.

"Uh. Right." He was easy enough to look up, he supposed.

"Kayla Esperes, *New York Times*."

Eric blinked several times. "Good to meet you ... too?"

"Where do you think the heart's blood of the city flows?"

Who supplied this person's chems? "I'm sorry?"

"There's a pulse in every city, an energy pumped through the streets, carrying people in its stream, pushed and attached into its organs. The pathways may be streets, they may be commerce, and without them, the city can't go anywhere. Gets stuck up and explodes. Heart attack."

"Are you asking me for a map?" Was this lady for real? How had she gotten an invite?

"Of course not. I can look up traffic data, but I want your personal experience. As a resident. You look like you could handle yourself. Bam! Biceps. You must be in security or an athlete." Esperes made a flexing gesture, which lacked impact due to the voluminous overshirts covering everything.

The other guests were giving her a wide berth. Convenient for him. He'd rather talk to a crackpot than have to watch his words with a socialite.

Eric gave her a long look. "I work for Harbor, in Security." If she'd looked him up, that information was trivial to get. What kind of game was she playing?

"Yes! A Corp monkey."

Eric shrugged. "Call it what you like."

"So you must need to use those biceps often."

"Well, also the muscles and organs they're attached to."

"And those that those are attached to! Now we're getting somewhere."

"Are you making comments about the use of my body?" Eric found that one funnier than he should have.

"The Corp uses your body for its labor. On that, at least, me and those new anarchists in town agree."

Eric almost spit out his wine. "What?"

"Aha! Do you know anything about them?"

"Anarchists?" Were they talking specific or general? "I know what an anarchist is. Sort of."

She waved a hand in dismissal. "No, I mean local anarchists. The ones right here, right now."

There must be some anarchists in the area, but he didn't know of any. "I don't think I've met them?"

Her eyes gleamed. "You'd know if you did. They're

organized! Ironic, you would think, but no! The history of anarchism contains many coordinated movements."

His week kept getting more surreal. The lemon fizz and wine may have had more alcohol than he'd thought. Had he inadvertently signed up for a history class? "You're the expert here."

"I'm all for free love, it shouldn't have a price, but you gotta admit those early twentieth-century anarchists were all atheists." She spread both arms out wide, palms up. They didn't smack into anyone. The other attendees must be giving the crazy lady plenty of space.

"Uh, so?"

"Well, let's see, not-dancing Security Man. Do you believe in God?"

Eric's thoughts scrambled with the subject change. God? He hadn't thought about that for a long time. "That's a personal question," he said.

Her eyebrows raised, peeking above her absurd plastic optics. "Cagey. Not bad, not bad. But with your accent, you come from the Catholic part of up North."

Sacrament. He stopped himself from saying that. Did he sound like that much of a hick? "I grew up in Athens, flatlander."

"Not the Greek capital, I presume?"

"No." He'd asked to try living with Dad, but neither Maman nor the man himself had agreed. Robert Greis had no use for a kid who couldn't take care of himself.

The look on his face must have been pretty gloomy, because Esperes stopped smiling. "Okay, okay. Not every person with ties to Quebec is Catholic. But how about . . . Do you believe in something more than this?"

"More than what?" he asked. Didn't everyone always want something more than what they had?

"More than all the drugs you can take. Though those do help. More than the world you can touch and negotiate with." Her face relaxed, eyes closing, mouth tilting in a slight smile.

This conversation had gotten harder to follow, if that were possible. But it was still more amusing than any other conversation he'd had today. "If you're asking me if I enjoy my pharma, the answer is every so often. If you're asking me if I go to church, the answer's no."

"That's probably a good thing. The church is very sick. Tumors everywhere. Doesn't want us to be free to love."

"Depends on the church," he said.

"I mean, I guess the Church of the Singularity isn't very picky about love, but they also think that God is a robot we haven't built yet."

The Singularitans were a bunch of kooks. But he supposed there had been stranger cults. "Religious lesson aside ... you were talking about anarchists in Portland?" If there were troublemakers in town, he preferred to be forewarned about it. Maybe it was related to those punks who were harassing Staplehead?

"Oh, yes, anarchists. Libertists! Their more recent history. Well, several decades back a whole bunch of starry-eyed kids wanted to live differently. Locals. Probably all had breweries in their basements. They were unsatisfied, they were sick of it all, they were mad as purgatory and weren't going to take it anymore. They had code words and probably semaphore."

"What?" Semaphore as in waving big flags around?

"Maritime pride. Local heritage. Possibly just loved making flags. Have you ever made a flag?"

"No." Though Sam had. She liked designing flags for fictional countries.

Esperes swayed back and forth. "They had their flags, their slangs, their trends, their ideals." Then she leaned toward him. "This is the way many stories begin."

That rang a faint bell. "I imagine it didn't end well."

"They ended twenty years ago, the Libertist riots. A footnote for any historian, or a superscript in a cyclopedia."

Now he remembered. One of the reasons Maman hadn't wanted him to move to the city was that she thought it was unsafe and overrun by dangerous people. At the time, he'd assumed she'd been being parochial. "I wasn't here, so I don't know the details. From what I remember hearing, they just disappeared."

"Well, they're anarchists, they can only be so organized. Despite what I said earlier." She huffed. "But they didn't vanish all at once. Municipal government made it so life kept getting harder for them. Ordinances got in their way. Everyone got booked and fined. Loan applications were denied. So they started bringing in outside help.

"That help, unfortunately, didn't actually help that much. There were many more voices now, and they were very confused. Did they want election finance reform more, or appropriate taxation? Did they want something to do with their lives, or did they want to be able to set up cafés without getting acquired the moment they got successful? Was this really independence? Did they want something concrete or were they asking questions French existentialists haven't been able to answer after several centuries?"

Eric thought of giving a flippant answer, but by the time he had one formulated, she'd started on the next part of her rant.

"What does it mean to be financially independent in a

corporate-controlled city-state? What kinds of choices do you really want to make? Nobody starves, that's what nutri-paste is for. If you get sick, you get treated. Less than a hundred years ago people here still had to save up to get treatment for a cold. And if you didn't have savings or it was worse than a cold, you'd be stuck owing banks for the rest of your life just because you needed radiation and surgery.

"But no. People didn't have what they wanted. I mean, we never can, that's our nature. You aspire to the highest thing you think you can touch. And so, people got confused and sad and amassed criminal records, and this made some of them angry, so they went boom and got bigger criminal records, and those were big enough to scare them away from Portland. Or stop doing what they were doing. Or stop dreaming. Or both."

"Went boom?"

"They blew up corporate buildings. One of the buildings had people in it when it exploded."

"That's one way to make a stand. And become persona non grata with the general public."

Esperes hummed a few notes. Then her eyes narrowed and she took a long look at him. "What about you? What do you stand for, Security Man?"

"I—" He stopped. "What do you mean?"

Another pointed stare. "Do you buy into the Corp philosophy? Such as it is, I don't think Harbor has an explicit philosophy, I checked. Do you have your own code you live by?"

He took a breath, racked his brain. No words came to his mouth.

"Seems it isn't obvious to you. Well, it isn't obvious to most people. I, however, live by the code of journalistic integrity."

"What's that?"

"It's the search for a truth that has meaning for people. A truth that isn't there to shade them, or angle after the speaker's aims. After my angle. But I digress. What I described isn't a philosophy. But it is a code. A set of rules. You gotta have some rules."

That raised his hackles a bit. "Well, you're not pulling any punches, are you?" He had ethics. He had morals. But putting them into words wasn't happening right now.

"BAM!" She moved as if to tap his nose with a finger, but his hands flew up defensively and she thought better of it. "Be careful where you punch, I getcha, I getcha."

"Do you?" Her question unfurled in his abdomen. Could he really not answer it? If she hadn't put him on the spot, he could tell her how he justified his own life and who he'd take the fall for. He could have said it was complicated, but he wasn't even sure what the complications were.

"Anyway, the Libertists have their code, I'm sure, or maybe multiple ones, it's hard to say with anarchists, wouldn't you be a little worried if a gaggle of anarchists all had the same plan? Would they still really be anarchists? Anyway, they took their banners away and scattered to the four winds." Esperes's gaze went distant for a moment. "But now, I tell you, I've seen that flag here again."

"You sure it's the same thing?"

"Vexillology is not my forte, but I did ask my assistant, a Hawaiian violist Ph.D., to check."

That sounded like an interesting story, but he shouldn't get sidetracked. "Are you on the case then? Will you find their cunning plan?" He had asked the question to himself, but hadn't come up with anything that didn't depress him.

He was going to make something of himself, but that had no moral code.

She shook her head, her shoulders, and her hips simultaneously. "I don't know what they're here for. I haven't been able to pry anything out from any of my sources. All I have at this point are guesses. Maybe they have discovered they were sitting on a giant uranium mine all along and want to mine and sell it on the black market."

Eric couldn't help cracking a smile. "Do you think that's likely?"

"So they're back, and there's a story there, and I'm following that story, but I'm also following something. They have something of mine. I have to find them to get it back. My honor as a journalist demands it!" She made a fist and shook it. "So. If you know anything about them. If you see anything, hear anything, or even hallucinate it! Come to think of it, you, Security Man, are in an insufficiently altered state!"

Eric was reconsidering his earlier thoughts on sobriety. "Working on that." He swished the liquid in his cup. Still half full.

"Hm! This should help!" Esperes handed Eric several unlabeled tabs.

"What're these?"

"Not sure. Probably Velodrome, maybe Glass. Should solve your sobriety problem right fast."

"I'll pass." He didn't have an issue with recreational drugs, but Esperes's uncertainty about the tabs didn't inspire confidence.

"Oh, and my tips line. In case you can let us in on any juicy scoop. We pay in americreds and sometimes pharmaceuticals. Now, where is it . . ." Esperes fumbled around with her comm, getting it to display various menus on a pop-up holo. Eric would bet at least fifty americreds that they weren't helpful at all.

A large-framed man with a nose to match walked up behind Esperes. "Kayla, are you having trouble generating secure tokens again?" the man inquired.

"Token, token . . ." Esperes tilted her head at the screen, and her eyes focused again. "Q-Dave, it's iguanas every-where."

Q-Dave, if that's who it was, patted Esperes's shoulder. "I know those are important. It'll be all right." He turned to Eric and gave a small smile. "You're an information source?"

"Yeah, I guess." This guy at least looked like he still had all of his marbles.

"Here, I've got it." Q-Dave fiddled with his comm and sent a packet which Eric caught in quarantine. "I'd advise talking to her later, when Kayla is a bit less . . ." He put his tongue behind his front teeth.

"High?"

"That's unlikely to happen. Tractable might be a better word."

"All right then. I guess—" The hair on the back of his neck rose. The crowd noise had changed.

———————

Eric tuned into the security frequency he'd found earlier.

"The fuck happened?"

"Guest suddenly attacked another one. Somehow got weapons past security."

More screaming in meatspace. More swearing on the

security feed. Eric looked for the disturbance. Several hundred feet away, people panicked.

"Uh. Got an ident?"

"Harbor Securities."

"Think it's legit?"

"Our idents are pretty hard to fake." All of the people on the feed must be in over their heads.

Eric heard a crash on the far end of the ballroom. Glass shattered. Eric ran to where the screams had come from.

"They're getting out through a window!"

"They're wearing an encounter suit!"

"What the fuck is a striker doing here?"

"I don't know! This isn't a company event! We don't have the security for this! Call FairSec!"

Eric made his way to a cluster of guests. He pushed aside someone wringing his hands and a person making a noise that sounded like the wildlife you saw in documentaries. Three people lay on the floor, unmoving. One of them—some exec-looking type—was bleeding from some deep slices across the torso. Someone else was trying to wrap his wounds with their coat. Cold air came in through the broken window.

Eric stalked his way past more confused and panicking partygoers. Marde on a shingle. This was some kind of strike. A public strike though? That was rare. Random-seeming violence wasn't the best way to bolster trust between Corps and the populace.

Why hadn't anyone told him to expect this? *Because you didn't tell HQ that you were going to the party, Mister Man.* That or the assailant wasn't actually Harbor personnel. If this was some faux striker, he wanted to take the punk down.

But first, he needed to check in with Sam. His comm

showed her location as in the next room. He sent her a ping, and it was immediately acknowledged with an "OK." Nobody else here should be armed, and Sam knew how to handle herself in a chaotic crowd.

The security feed crackled. "Status on injured people?"

"Unknown. One's bleeding, two more unconscious."

"Administer first aid. Emergency response is on their way."

He doubted he could be of use there; he didn't have any aid equipment on himself. He ran to the window as fast as he could and squinted at the hole the striker had left before trying to fit through it without cutting himself on the glass. Getting himself out required some wiggling. If he cared about dignity, he'd be embarrassed. He could tell the art crowd that it was some kind of new dance.

"Someone's following the striker out."

"Man covered in fake snow."

"Ident says he's also Harbor."

"Think he knows anything about the strike?"

"No idea."

Eric caught himself on his hands and feet outside and shivered. He'd left his jacket at coat check. Well, nothing like running to warm him up. But where to? Standard operating procedure dictated that the striker make for the extraction point. They'd need space for a vehicle pickup. Usually a copter.

If the striker wasn't Harbor personnel, who else could they be? Could someone be attempting to create bad publicity for Harbor? Could this be related to the R&D 4 break-in? Well, the perp there didn't have a proprietary suit, just the Gauntlet. Could someone have brought something stealable to the gala? Eric shook his shoulders out. The case was making him jump to conclusions.

The area seemed safe enough—a pretty deserted open

space in a commercial area. Not much traffic at this hour. The sky was overcast, so he couldn't see the moon. Smells of smoke and hydrocarbons rolled in from the docks.

He tweaked his comm to broadcast on several HarborSec channels. "Harbor personnel, listen up." If the striker really was a Harbor employee, they'd get a ping. "Identify yourself." He sent his SIN and hash. That should be enough information to sufficiently vet him.

He got a burst of noise back. That was enough to get a bead on his target, who was weaving back and forth on the street.

He commed HarborSec Dispatch. "Greis here. Do we have a friendly striker at the Founders' gala downtown?"

"I don't have access to that information," they said. "I'll connect with someone at CorpSec. But in the meantime, don't let them out of your sight."

Eric closed so that he was about a block from his target. Street noise was at a minimum, so he could hear his dress shoes hitting the pavement. His traction wouldn't be great with these shoes, but it was better than going barefoot.

He had on moderate protection under his suit, but the striker could still do plenty of damage if the slices on the target at the party were anything to go by. He'd have to get the drop on them. Now if they would only cooperate and move in a predictable direction. Ideally they hadn't picked up his location from the broadcasts. He almost regretted that, but better he knew where his target was.

Eric didn't need infrared to spot the suit. The striker wasn't taking any good covert actions, weaving from awning to awning across the streets. They stumbled and hunched over, limp arms jostling as if operated by two separate puppeteers.

He dashed between buildings, dodging a few bewildered

pedestrians. To his horror, he intercepted his target at the corner of the street. They had doubled back. With all the stumbling, Eric considered it likely that they were disoriented, not checking to see if they were being followed.

The figure's head shot up a split moment before they performed a running tackle. He dove left, dodging a kick. Eric had a moment to get his feet under himself and pushed himself to standing again. Now he could see his target up close. About a foot shorter than he was, curvy figured, a blade protruding from one elbow. His mind blanked for a moment, and he froze.

Piss-poor timing on his part, because she was on him now, trying to attack with her hand razors. His comm crackled. "No," she panted. "No, you're not—" He dodged a swipe at his face.

"Fucking . . . hell . . ." She turned, sped past him, and tried to attack from behind. Her timing was as bad as his though, and he was able to spin around when she closed so that she only grazed him. While she recovered, he trapped her arms at her sides. Her muscles and skeleton might be reinforced, but so were his, and he had the weight advantage and leverage.

He realized he was accepting the obvious now, that Trez was on a mission and he'd interrupted her extraction. "Trez, it's me. Eric."

"Wha—?"

"I'm going to let you go. You should escape. I'm sorry." He eased his hold on her, but she made no move to run. Instead, she leaned against him.

He couldn't see her face behind the black helmet, but it had to be Trez. He knew the feel of her, although her scent was overlaid with bitter herbs and chalk, fear pheromones. Judging from her shaking, she was probably hopped up on several different neurachems. True, strikers sometimes behaved oddly during the comedown from a mission. He hadn't encountered her right after a strike before though. Was this what she did all the time, or was she especially stove-up on this mission? Acid pachinkoed in his gut. None of the possibilities were good. Sacrament.

His comm buzzed. Corpfare Division. "Greis."

"Got the ping. The hell you're doing out near Convention Center?" A dispatcher.

"Party guest. Shit got ill. You have the data."

Trez had gone still against him. She must be listening.

A pause. "Huh. You there with Harris?"

"Obviously. But she hasn't gotten to the extraction point yet, we're technically in enemy territory. She doesn't seem to be able or willing to continue to get there." Maybe that was an exaggeration on his part, but he needed to get her help right now.

The dispatcher said, "Guard her as best you can. I'm going to transfer you to someone actually involved."

Eric began rubbing Trez's upper arms, became aware she was leaning on him. "Hey, stay with me. S'il vous plaît." She made a sound that might have been a groan, muffled by the helmet.

His comm indicated a transfer. "Greis," said a familiar-sounding voice. Jenna Garcia.

"Ah-yeah."

"I'm the incoming pilot. Just headed out on the extraction two minutes ago. Though I don't detect any guards coming after her."

"Je t'entends." Goons didn't always give chase. Maybe there weren't many of them nearby. He glanced down. "Our ace isn't doing well." He had taken more of Trez's weight without realizing it, to the point where he was holding her up. "No pink spray or anything, but she's going to need a thorough detox."

"Shit." Garcia didn't sound surprised. "She stable?"

"For now? Don't know. She's still conscious." Eric removed Trez's helmet. Her eyes were closed, with prominent bags under them. The streetlights gave her face a jaundiced cast.

"I've sent you coordinates for the nearest safe landing zone. Wait for me."

"Acknowledged." He brought his map back up to see the green target several blocks away. "Come on, Trez. Trez, can you walk with me?" He brought her body upright, supporting her by the shoulders.

"Uh?" She rocked back and forth, unable to keep herself steady.

"Can you stand?"

In response, or perhaps not, she went slack in his arms.

Eric took Trez by the waist and lifted her over his shoulder. He tried not to jostle her too much as he made his way through the streets. He listened for her breath. Shallow, but not raspy.

The few people he passed on the street gawked when they saw him. It couldn't look like he intended anything good. His dress shirt was torn and sliced open, and he was carrying an unconscious woman with blades extending from her elbows and fingers. He'd been lucky she was so fucked up, otherwise he'd have some nasty gashes by now. All her reaction times had been off. Most bystanders shrunk away, minding their own business. One young woman in wrinkled clothes stared at him, expression hostile. He made eye contact and sneered until she looked away, muttering to herself. Whatever burned in that woman, he couldn't help her.

The LZ was less than a kilometer away, one of the few

open spaces in the area. It looked safe enough here, but that could change. He put Trez down gently, supporting her head. She groaned. Well, that was encouraging, at least. He almost slapped himself. He'd forgotten the gala security. Well, better check if HQ had taken care of it than inquire directly. He called Dispatch again.

"'Lo. There an issue?"

"I was at a gala with a boatload of FairSec personnel pouring in. Are we being pursued?"

"Oh, the Founders' strike? Nah, they haven't deployed guards to try to pursue Harris. The strike's target is in serious condition, but he's not critical. Reporters are having a field day."

"Just checking."

"It's cool." The comm disconnected.

Eric crouched over Trez, holding her wrist. Her pulse and breathing were too fast, and she was shivering. He didn't have anything to warm her with except himself, so he rolled her to her side and lay down against her back, hoping his body heat could get through her suit. "Trez, what the hell happened?" he whispered. Did he really know her at all?

SEVEN

Blades whirred above Eric's head. He craned his neck from his prone position to see a copter make a bumpy landing ten meters from him. The door opened, and Jenna, who he recognized by her jagged-staircase haircut, jumped out holding a first aid kit.

"Status?" Jenna asked. Her jaw looked tight.

"Still breathing. She's too cold though. I don't know what pharma she's riding, so your guess is as good as mine." Eric disengaged and they tucked the blanket around Trez.

"All right, let's load her in. You got her, goon man?"

Eric didn't dignify that with a response. He rolled Trez's body over and picked her up by the shoulders and knees. She murmured unintelligible words. It felt strange to carry her like this. Wife carrying was a sport in Finland. No accounting for bizarre customs.

"We're going to need to secure her." Jenna indicated a seat with straps.

Once Eric put Trez down, Jenna handed him a tab of Charcoal. "Run basic toxicology with the kit and give her this. Alert me if things go south." Eric didn't envy Trez at the moment. The detoxifier would make her feel like stove-up ass. But better that than her renal system having to handle the drugs by itself.

"What about oxygen?" He fastened Trez in. His hands shook.

"Give her some if she gets any colder." Jenna strapped herself into the pilot's chair. She initiated the copter's takeoff then started plotting a course to the infirmary. "So, you found her collapsed outside?"

"Ah-yeah."

"I wish I could say I was surprised. Little over a week ago, when I picked her up she was pretty fucked up."

Eric pricked Trez's finger with a lancet then disposed of the sharps. The copter shuddered, and he struggled to stand upright. Eric crushed the tablet in his hand. "Come on, Trez," he coaxed. Probably useless, he doubted she could hear him. He pried her jaw open and applied the dust. She tried to bite him, but didn't break skin. Thank God for the polymers woven in his skin.

"You got her?"

"Well, I've given her the Charcoal," he said. He hooked her up to the diagnostic. At this point, with the supplies he had on hand, that was all he could do.

"Keep monitoring her." Jenna let out a sharp exhale. "Some strikers I've handled have a tendency to overdose. I never thought she'd end up being one of them though. Up until a few weeks ago, I thought she had more sense than that."

The lines on the status readout didn't indicate anything dire. "You were saying she was like this a week ago?"

"Yeah. Before that, I hadn't been assigned to her in months. Shlomi would've been on duty, but he was out sick."

"He put anything in her file? Going concerns? Anything strange?"

"No. I asked him about it later. He said she was wicked high, but that's de rigueur behavior for a striker. Seriously?

High is one thing. Not being able to stand is another. I guess he doesn't care because handlers aren't liable for self-inflicted health problems."

Eric kept his eyes on Trez during Jenna's rant. Either the Charcoal was beginning to work, or Trez's chems had overwhelmed her systems. She twisted up the blanket and strained at her securements. Her eyes opened wide and she began to shudder.

"You know how to retract her razors?" He'd rather not get sliced open.

Jenna held her hand level and rocked it back and forth. "I think if you get her to squeeze a fist hard enough, the blades will automatically retract."

He regarded Trez with some caution. Her hands were locked with her fingers spread and stretched widely apart. Eric pinned one of her forearms with his left hand and tried to fold her other hand's fingers in. He gripped her fist, applying force.

Her blades pierced her palm. Blood welled. She made a whimper, and he felt nauseous. He had to keep pressing though. Just when he thought she'd stab through her own palms, the blades collapsed back into her fingers.

"Marde." He needed to open the first aid kit again, but didn't have any hands available for that. "Jenna, can you get me something to wrap her hands with?"

"Sure." Once she'd checked the autopilot and imminent surroundings, Jenna rose from her seat. She retrieved several bandages and crouched at his side.

When she looked at the wounds, her lips peeled back and she sucked in a breath through her teeth. "Keep her hand steady like that." Jenna's arms shook a bit as she wrapped Trez's fingers in place then bandaged around the puncture wounds.

"Think she can redeploy her claws involuntarily?" Trez was trying to throw him off her arm. He didn't want to give her more wounds if he let go of her fist and she sliced herself open again.

"Not sure." Jenna narrowed her eyes. "Why're you doing this?"

"These securements aren't heavy-duty restraints. She could slice them open or hurt herself while she's riding this out."

"I knew that, Greis. I mean, why ... Ugh. Never mind."

He tried to ease his grip on Trez's forearm to attend to her other hand. He couldn't follow through with making her hurt herself more. Instead, he folded her fingers so that the blades extended past her palms. She was going to feel like shit later anyway. If she flailed, he could hold her steady. He could take a few wounds, he reasoned. She had enough to heal from already.

"Anyway, I thought the two of you were ... well ..."

"Were what?" He wondered if he knew the answer to that one.

"Involved? Hotsyncing?"

He ignored the second question. "If so, she stopped her involvement weeks ago. Also stopped talking to me." It still smarted, even though he now understood the situation was more complicated and dire than he would have guessed.

"Not just you. Her avoidance game against me has been wicked good."

The three of them hadn't been in the same place for months. Last time they'd went to a nightclub with some friends. Trez loved to dance. She had good rhythm and he'd loved to watch her move. When they danced together, he felt clumsy, but she never seemed to mind.

"She's still too cold." Eric positioned Trez's arms at her sides and lay down facing her. He pushed them back and fitted his front to hers. He might get some ribbing from Jenna for hugging Trez like this, but he didn't care enough.

Trez's breathing had evened out somewhat, but he could feel her heart hammering hard. He doubted asking Jenna to go faster would get the desired result though.

"How long until we reach med bay?" he asked.

"Give it five. I have to land this rig. But yeah. I don't know what the hell her problem is."

He could only hope Trez would be well enough to cooperate. "She told me it was something personal a while ago. I didn't know if she was letting me down gently." He'd thought she'd been having fun at the time, but people were entitled to have their regrets.

"Nah, she liked you fine. She often said Eric this and Eric that. I told her a year ago she should just jump your bones and see if you were all she'd cracked you up to be."

He squelched the bit of warmth he felt at that. "Well, she could have changed her mind more recently."

"Huh. Well before that. You were saying?"

"What happened ten days ago anyway?" Eric asked.

"Let me land this thing first. Give me a moment." Jenna turned back to her control console. "I have to tell you, holding her isn't a good idea."

He could loop some of the cords around himself, but if it were a bumpy landing he'd have impressive bruises for a few days. "I'll make do." Eric fumbled with the restraints then rolled himself and Trez over. She resisted a little, so he had to raise his knees and cradle her with her side against his chest.

The copter descended to the landing and thwacked the pad. Eric winced. Trez didn't stir though.

"I've called for a stretcher and a medic. Menendez should be on call." Jenna undid her security ties.

"Can you take care of the cords around us while I hold Trez?" She seemed docile for now, but Eric wasn't in the mood to tempt fate.

Jenna smirked. "Kind of kinky, but sure." She released both of them from the harness—Trez by design and Eric by circumstance. "Ouch."

Eric shook his head and untangled himself. "Let's get her to the medic. Her temperature is steady but still low."

"You going to keep her fists all like that on the stretcher?"

"If I have to. I can run with it."

"Seriously?" Jenna smiled. "Well, that's useful."

The medical assistant arrived then, and the three of them loaded Trez onto a stretcher and hooked her up to another monitor. She then secured Trez's hands with metal restraints. "To Menendez?" the assistant asked. Her ID indicated the name Bilodeau.

"Ah-yeah."

The medical assistant started wheeling the gurney away, ignoring them. Jenna and Eric exchanged a look and then started walking after her.

"Anyway, you asked me … before I landed the copter," Jenna said. "Ten days back I picked Trez up from a mission and she was stuttering, stumbling around, completely out of it. I assumed she was sky high."

"I take it that's not normal for her?"

"Usually she'll be shaking some but she'll be able to get into the copter herself. I have to give her some water and sugar before she'll be cogent. Quiet sometimes, but plenty of strikers are after a mission. She tends to talk more the worse it went."

"Ah."

"This wasn't an eventful or difficult strike. It was a straightforward hit, and she executed it without incident. So I don't know why she was so stove-up." Jenna gave him a sidelong glance. "She never tell you about this stuff?"

"Not those details."

"I imagine that's one of the less glamorous parts of the job," Jenna said. They rounded a corner and followed the stretcher into the building. "Not something you talk about with a man you want to impress."

"You think she wanted to impress me?" Eric was skeptical. Trez had never shown any signs of caring about anyone else's approval.

"Ah-yeah. Not that she'd admit it."

Bilodeau stepped into an elevator, selected a floor, and touched her hand to the console to identify herself to the security system. Then she looked up at Eric and Jenna and held the door open. They input their biometric data, and the medic went back to ignoring them. Trez had begun to shiver. Good. It would keep her a bit warmer.

Nobody spoke in the elevator. Unless he counted Trez's incoherent mumbling.

They walked down the hallway to the first intersection, made a right, and then went two doors down to an infirmary. Medic Menendez, a short square-jawed man with a salt-and-pepper afro, was otherwise occupied. He glanced at them when he noticed the stretcher. After a moment, he blinked. "Get her on an exam table, and hook her up to a terminal. I'll be with you soon as I can."

"I'm worried she'll go into shock," Eric said.

Menendez made a clicking sound with his tongue. "In a

gaum again?" He turned to Jenna. "Go get some blankets from the shelf. Make yourself useful this time."

Bilodeau looked straight at Eric. "Help me get her out of this suit," she said. He complied. This was not an ideal circumstance to see Trez naked. She was too thin, and her skin was sallow. The assistant hooked Trez up to a terminal.

"Harris's condition doesn't seem critical, going by the diagnostic data Bilodeau sent. We'll have to oxygenate her blood some." The assistant left, and Menendez went back to looking at his console. Eric snuck a peek. Nothing jumped out at him as a problem. The medic didn't think it serious, but Trez's blood pressure seemed very low to Eric. He needed to stop freaking himself out.

Jenna tramped back over to them with a pile of blankets. "I'll let you tuck her in," she said to Eric. He didn't need her sass, but he took the blankets and tried to fit them around Trez without disturbing the cable connections.

"She'll be okay then?" He couldn't help asking. He took one of Trez's hands and squeezed it. Jenna gave him a half smile then sat on a chair.

"You can never guarantee anything in medicine. Let's see how she responds to the oxygen first," Menendez said. Bilodeau walked back in, carrying a small tank and hookup. She attached it to the box of wires snaking onto and into Trez.

Looking at someone with cables embedded in them always made Eric feel vaguely nauseous. His teammates made fun of him for that sometimes. Worms. They always looked like horrible dead worms that you saw on the pavement after rain. Needles and wires felt like a violation of the body.

Menendez looked over at Eric for the first time since he'd entered the infirmary. "Greis. Why are you here?"

"I was at the Founders' Day gala downtown with my sister. There was a strike. I didn't know that in advance though. When she fled, I followed her."

"I doubt she appreciated that. Are you hurt?"

"Some minor cuts and puncture wounds. Nothing serious."

Menendez turned to his kit. "Have a seat right there." His attention was back on his comm's readout. He gestured to an exam chair without looking up.

Eric sat on the chair and sent another ping to Sam with an OK status. He got the same one back from her, with a request for details. He sent her a "later" message.

Menendez made an inarticulate noise. Eric glanced over again, but still couldn't see the readout. "Get some restraints. She's displaying withdrawal symptoms." Bilodeau rushed off while the medic grimaced at his console.

"You think she'll hurt herself thrashing?" Jenna asked.

"Just a precaution. She already has wounds on her hands."

Eric could cop to that. "Ah, that's my fault."

"I assume you have an explanation."

"Was trying to get her to retract her claws." He tried not to remember the feel of pushing those blades into her palms.

"Yeah, I told him to do that. They are partially mechanical, and I doubt the cyberneticists would have allowed them to be turned against her much," Jenna said, looking away.

Had he hurt Trez needlessly? Irritation flared. "You sounded decently sure at the time," he snapped.

Jenna shrugged and stood up again. "Made my best guess. It worked. Those are minor wounds; I've seen her with much worse."

The assistant returned and began tying Trez's wrists to the bars on the side of the pallet. Eric watched. The woman was efficient, he'd give her that.

"Tie another," he said. "She's pretty strong." Watching her bound to the gurney put an acidic lump in his throat. He wasn't sure how he felt about one of his primary expertises being restraints.

Bilodeau looked up from her work and blinked several times before narrowing her eyes. "Ah-yeah, sure. Got her strength metrics right here. You think you know better?"

"No." Eric shook his head. It felt muddled, as if he were the one coming down from drugs. He took a deep breath, held it for a moment, and began to exhale slowly.

The assistant tapped him on the shoulder. Eric started. "Let's take a look at you." She examined Eric's hands "This'll sting—" she said half a second before Eric's cuts burned.

"Fuck." He closed his eyes again.

Bilodeau finished cleaning Eric's cuts and put some sealant on them then ran a scanner over Eric's back. "Looks like nothing's broken and there's no internal bleeding. You're free to go."

Eric heard some inarticulate swearing. When would Trez wake up? What would he say to her? Would she just try to avoid him again?

Menendez cleared his throat. "We're going to keep Harris here a few more hours, but she can go home after that. We'll put a monitor on her for a few more hours until she wakes up, but I don't anticipate further problems."

Jenna stopped pacing and looked over at Trez, who had curled up as much as she could with the restraints on her limbs. "When can those come off?"

"Give her another hour," said the assistant. "We need to make sure she doesn't behave unpredictably while the chems continue to flush out."

"I'll wait here," Eric said. "I can take her to my place and continue to watch her. I have a spare room." He made eye contact with Jenna, and she started to smile. She giggled. Of all the—

"Yes, do that. I knew something had happened between you two."

"Criss." Vail, Sam, and now Jenna. Why was everyone poking into his personal life?

"Talk to her, she won't talk to me. Maybe you'll have more luck. Or know better interrogation techniques. Tell me what business she's gotten mixed up with."

Eric put his hands behind his neck and kneaded the muscles there. "Fine." He wasn't sure how much Trez would talk about, but he could try.

"I'll give you aftercare instructions then." Menendez cut in.

"Ah-yeah?"

"She came in with low blood sugar, so keep an eye on that. Keep giving her sweet tea or other fluids like it."

"Sure. What about food?"

"She won't want solids for a while. Whatever liquid or pudding you've got."

"I'm still on duty," Jenna said. "I can take you both back in a van when my shift ends."

"Thanks." He continued watching Trez breathe and sleep. He had a few hours to figure out what to tell her and what to ask. Maybe she's just trying to cope with her job. He hoped it was that simple.

EIGHT

Too much light. Trez scrunched her eyes and yawned. She sat up in bed and ran her hands through her hair. A moment of disorientation followed. She was wearing a battered shirt several sizes too large. Big billowy flowers and oversaturated geometric prints on the bedding. A vase with a fabric flower arrangement in it and a decorative doily topped the nightstand next to her. Were those supposed to be orchids? Trez had seen some in the botanical museum, but she wasn't sure if the artist had.

Someone had left a fancy drinking vessel full of water on the nightstand. She managed not to chug it. The liquid sloshed its way into her stomach.

The door slid open. "You're awake." Trez looked up to see Eric at the door. He wore a slouchy flannel hoodie and sweatpants, but went barefoot. Like her, he had no fashion sense.

"Yes." Her head still felt fuzzy, and her voice sounded hoarse. "This your place?"

He raised his chin. "Yes."

Was she in his bedroom? It didn't look like it. She looked around some more, trying to figure out what to say. "I . . . guess I need to report in?"

Eric shook his head. "I don't think it's urgent. They had

a handle on it in the infirmary. Jenna already sent Sloane a comm." His words were clipped.

Shit. The infirmary? She remembered trading barbs with Vail, then . . . "What happened? I mean, why am I here?"

"Jenna and I brought you back." He crossed his arms over his chest.

"Oh. Why?" She didn't know what else to ask.

"I was at the Founders' Day gala my sister dragged me to. Then you turned up on more combat chems than I can name, took out your target, then collapsed during the getaway."

He'd saved her then. Last time Fairchild's CorpSec had captured her, they'd played pretty rough with her. She'd been unable to participate in missions for weeks afterwards. Plus, the bulk of the ransom had come out of her pay.

"After you collapsed I got you to a clinic. You had to detox and rest for a few hours there, then I took you home. You've been out a couple more since then, which should help. You haven't been eating or sleeping properly, or at least that's what I assume. Am I right?" His eyes met hers. She could see the flint in them.

She'd just woken up. She didn't need this now. She wasn't ready, and she didn't know what to say.

"You're hurt, you've lost weight, you've got one grand-motherfucker of a hangover," he continued. "Care to tell me what the hell you're doing with yourself?" Eric paced over to the bed and sat at her feet, pinning her with his gaze.

"I'm sorry," she ground out.

"I don't know what kind of fucked-up shenanigans you're involved in. A few weeks ago, I thought you'd regretted the sex and wanted some space. Fine. That's your prerogative. But then I found out it wasn't just me you were avoiding. You disappeared from everything social and you didn't respond to anybody's comms."

It hadn't been well done of her. "I . . ." She couldn't keep looking at him. Instead, she placed her hands on her own knees. "I didn't want you to worry," she said after a moment. He'd deserved better.

"Trez, that's the stupidest fucking thing I have ever heard you say." His tone had softened though. "I'm not sure whether to yell at you more or give you a hug. I worried anyway."

"I'm sorry." She stared at the vase. Were there fiber optics in the flowers?

He squeezed her hand. "So tell me. Did you develop some random addictions to go with the regular insane lifestyle Harbor provides you? Not enough thrills in your day-to-day life?"

"No. The opposite, really." Everything felt small and stuffy. Her head, her self-worth, her pride. "I'm exhausted," she confessed.

"So then I'm wicked confused about what the fuck's going on." Eric rubbed his hands on his pant legs.

"I don't know if—"

"Work's having me investigate things and play detective, even if I don't know what I'm doing or how to think. Sorry. I need a drink. Can I get you anything?"

"Water," she said. Her cup was almost empty.

"Sure thing." He looked down at his hands for a moment before he picked up her cup then strolled out of the room.

What was he about? He'd begun angry, but then he'd switched gears to amusement. She'd dodged some of his questions, so he'd try to confuse her with levity? Maybe she was too pathetic for him to stay angry? Regardless, she was a captive audience. She doubted she had the energy to leave the flat.

Eric returned with two cups, one for each of them, and plunked himself down beside her.

"Hey. Trez." He put his drink down and made eye contact. He shut his eyes. "I just want to help."

"You can't," she blurted. Her head hurt.

He shut his mouth and his eyes narrowed. "Can't? What can't I help you with? You won't tell me what it is, so how the fuck would you know? Just because we hotsynced doesn't mean you automatically know everything about me."

"No, I . . ."

"Why do you need to keep jerking me around?" He put his head in his hands and rubbed one of his temples. "Shit. You didn't deserve that."

"I'm . . ." She'd already said sorry. "I don't . . ." She couldn't finish that either. "I need the money."

Eric squinted. "What?"

"Ah-yeah."

He growled. "Creds? That's . . ." He clamped his mouth shut.

She shook her head. "I . . . I guess I owe you an explanation." Tears threatened, but she blinked them away. "I guess . . . Where do I start?"

"How's about you tell me what's with the drugs?" Eric spoke slowly now, enunciating each word, maybe to calm himself down.

"Those are so I can keep going with my insane lifestyle," she said.

"Stress?"

Post-traumatic stress disorder. Close enough. "It's . . . gotten tough." The adrenaline rush wasn't enough anymore to make up for the fact that innocent civilians could get hurt. That she had hurt one.

"That's a lot of tough."

She nodded.

"But as you said, you need the money."

"Can't quit yet."

Eric furrowed his brow. Probably doing some arithmetic in his head. "Who'd you piss off so badly?"

She didn't bother correcting him. Linus's problems were hers now. "Makos."

"How'd you do that? Usually they stay well clear of Corp employees. Unless . . . maybe someone tried something funny, then you went house cat all over them?"

"No, no blood shed."

"Okay then?"

"They want money."

"And you're giving it to them because . . . ?"

He was right to be puzzled. It wasn't as if she couldn't take care of herself on the street. "Blackmail," she said.

"Oh." Eric looked sideways at her. "I don't guess you'd tell me?"

Trez pulled her knees up to her chest. The borrowed shirt chafed. "Can't."

"Really?"

She weighed her words. "It's not just me."

He took a moment to digest that. "You're protecting someone."

"Yes. My father."

His eyebrows went up. "Your old man." He exhaled quickly. She watched his mouth crinkle and his head incline. That was his "thinking" face. She had a sudden desire to lean in and bite his lip. The urge grew stronger as the silence stretched. Then he waited. Perhaps for her to spill more?

Trez was so used to keeping her cards close that she couldn't divulge anything unless asked, and even then it hurt almost physically. She was so tired of keeping these secrets. It wasn't her nature to be secretive, but she had too much to lose.

"Yeah," she said.

He smiled. "Don't parents wish for a kid like that?"

"I wish. I owe him." She barely heard herself.

His face came closer. "Sorry?"

"I hate it," she whispered.

Their foreheads collided, and she realized she had leaned in. He put a hand up to her jawline, his touch light. Trez's heart beat faster, but she kept her arms at her sides. His hand was so warm on her face. "I don't . . . I can't . . ."

He pulled away abruptly, and the loss stung. "I'm sorry. Putain." He sounded angry again, but not at her. He stood up and paced.

"No, it's not that. I'm . . . Fuck. You shouldn't have to shovel my emotional shit."

"Trez, it's okay. We're friends."

"I never meant for you to get involved."

He stilled. "I'm sorry. I thought you could trust me." She raised her head. His face couldn't settle on an expression.

"No, not like that. I . . . You didn't ask for any of my personal problems."

"I thought I signed on for whatever drama you could throw at me when I said we should go to dinner together after we had sex."

Trez gave a bitter smile. "There's dinner, there's sex, and there's blackmail by the Makos. If the first two came with the third, nobody'd ever hotsync." The tear tracks on her face burned.

"What do they have on you anyway? Is it something I'd care about? I mean something I'd care about personally."

"Oh." She looked back at him. "Don't think so."

"Can you tell me?"

She trusted him, but the words still wouldn't come. She shook her head.

He put two and two together. "It's something about you and Harbor, isn't it?"

"Sort of." She furrowed her brow and ducked her head. Tension bracketed her mouth.

"Trez, I'm not going to . . . Look." He rubbed his scalp. "I want to help you. A lot of us got . . . problems. Secrets. Issues. Whatever."

"I feel weak, you know. Scared. You did save me, I know that." She sounded disgruntled. "I owe you, but . . ."

"Am I at risk for knowing? The less I know the safer I am or some kind of marde like that?"

"I don't know. I don't like owing you." She didn't like owing anybody. And owing people she cared about, that felt so much worse.

"How about this? You don't owe me."

"Sorry, what?" He wasn't making any sense.

"You can say thank you. That's all. I'd do the same for most of my good friends."

"Rather magnanimous of you," she muttered.

"Really. I'm glad you're not in Fairchild hands or dead from an overdose. That's payment right there."

Trez drew up the covers around her. He scooted away from her on the bed. She couldn't figure him out. He asked questions then gave her space.

Where to begin her story? "My father took care of me for several years. All the family I got left."

"Ciboire. I'm sorry." He reached out to pat her knee then withdrew his hand.

"Nah. We did okay." She smiled, in spite of her general wretchedness and her stomach playing kriegball with her lungs. "I ... It's tough. I love him, but he's not the most, uh ..."

"Unselfish?"

"Responsible, I was going to say. We don't have what I'd call a normal relationship." She fumbled for what she'd say next.

"What do you mean?" Eric's voice was low and soft.

"I didn't grow up with him. My mother booked it when I was thirteen."

Eric paused a moment at that, probably to think through it. "Were you all alone?" he asked.

"Not for too long. Which was good, because I wasn't thinking clearly or coping at the time."

"Did you look him up?"

She shook her head. "He found me. He'd been keeping tabs while I grew up." Eric was silent, his blue eyes soft at her for long enough that she continued. "Took me in. Fed me, gave me a place to live for a few years. Said he wanted to do the right thing."

"Sounds like he did. Better than my pops, that's for sure. Asshole barely acknowledged we existed whenever he came to visit Maman. Why she always waited for him while he did god knows what in the woods for months at a time, I still don't know." He smiled tightly. "Sorry. This isn't about me. Back to your father. You two lived around here, right?"

"We moved around a lot. I found out he got in trouble some places."

"Involved in crime?"

"Stupider than that. He's indigent and likes to gamble. That makes you enemies. Bookies, opponents, houses, whether you win too much or lose too much.

Understanding zipped across his expression. "And now he's ass-deep in Mako shit."

"It's so fucking stupid. IOUs are such a . . ." Her shoulders were shaking. She tried rolling them to relax them. They made a cracking sound.

Eric's comm beeped. "This better be . . . Oh." A woman popped up on holo. Dirty blonde hair striped with pastel pink, square jaw, slightly uneven brows. Definite family resemblance to Eric. "I have to take this. Don't let her know you're here."

Trez blinked.

"I don't think we have anything to hide from the world, but if Sam gets wind of you here the conversation will be several hours long."

"All right."

Eric connected. "Sam."

"There you are." She scowled. "You all right?"

"Ah-yeah."

Sam clicked her tongue behind her teeth. "You were in medical though. Leastaways that's what your status monitor said."

"Minor cuts, scrapes, bruises. I'm healed." Eric shrugged and rubbed his neck.

"You weren't answering comms, so I had to ask around. That was embarrassing. Found out you'd exited the party, probably in pursuit of the ballerina."

"It's fine, Sam. Medical cleared me."

Sam's mouth opened and shut several times. "I don't under— Forget about it. Eric, you say you were okay, but I couldn't reach you for hours."

"I was distracted."

Sam snorted the same way Eric did, with the corner of the mouth turned up. "A pigeon found me."

"Pigeon?"

"Reporter, she said. Little lady with antique optics and retro flannel checks. Said you were having trouble at work with some thieves or something."

"Oh, her." Eric's eyes widened. "High as the space station?"

"Right. Seemed to know what she was talking about, strangely. Guess she found me after asking around. Said she'd talked to you. Mentioned trouble at HarborSec."

"She's a meddling hippie freak. Entertaining though."

"What kind of trouble is there at work? I'm getting worried about you."

"Putain." He shrugged. "I'll explain later."

Dread and levity mixed in Trez's stomach. She bit her lips in so she wouldn't say something stupid. She couldn't begrudge Eric trying to keep the details of his work life from his sister. Some misguided idea of not trying to worry Sam, she was sure. Trez could almost taste the irony.

Sam bristled. "Tomorrow later? Or later as in never?"

"Ah, Sam . . ."

"Don't try to placate me." She huffed. "I say it's tomorrow."

"Ah-yeah."

"All right. I'll see you tomorrow, Eric." She cut off the connection.

Eric took a long deep breath and rolled his shoulders. "Well. Now you've met my sister." His smile looked forced.

Trez nodded, still not trusting herself to speak.

"So that's all great. Right. Okay. Now that's out of the way. You're hot in a toga, you know."

She coughed. He wasn't making anything any clearer. She latched on to a topic that wasn't about their interactions. "You're hanging out with reporters now?"

His brow furrowed. "I think it's easiest if I show you. But, ah, I guess you can get dressed first. Something in the closet should work. Meet me in the living room." With that remark, he left and closed the door behind him.

NINE

Eric downed his caff in two gulps. Sam's bedroom door opened and Trez entered, wearing some of Sam's bleach-spattered overalls in addition to his old shirt. The shirt draped on her differently than him, and reached halfway down her thighs. He smiled. "Drink?" he offered.

"Uh, sure. Something clear."

"I'm going to comm a journalist. She's offered to help me with a matter I've been trying to figure out at Harbor." He grabbed a cup and dispensed melon water. "Here. Sit down and try not to spit this out during the call. I nearly snorted out my drink last time I talked to her."

Trez sat carefully. Her skin was still grayer than he'd like. The sugars in the water should help. She still seemed reticent, but she wasn't making any move to leave. Maybe if he could get her interested in a less personal problem, she would open up a little. He input the one-time key to connect to Esperes over an anonymous proxy.

The channel opened and Esperes, hair fluffed out to the sides, shook herself out before looking at him. "Hello! Security Man!"

"Hello, reporter lady," Eric replied. Trez had tilted her head slightly.

"I've got a scoop for you. Hmm, scoop. They never serve those things anymore."

"Already? A scoop of what?"

"In-for-ma-tion, my good mugwump. In-for-ma-tion." She sounded out the syllables as separate words. Might be worth asking what snake she was riding at the moment.

"You found anything about my little problem?"

"Break-ins aren't little. Neither are you. Unless ... you're sort of a little truck. Bam!"

He smiled in spite of himself and shook his head. "Size of my problems aside, what's your intel?" Eric peeked at Trez out of the corner of his eye. She had perked up a bit, listening.

"All signs point to a sophisticated operation bankrolled by a big pantsed person."

The intruder's possession of the Gauntlet would indicate that. But ... "A big pantsed person?" He heard a muffled giggle.

"Who's that?" Esperes asked.

"A friend."

"Hello," said Trez. She was smiling, but didn't move into the camera's view.

"A security person friend?"

"Close enough."

"I could use one of those," Esperes mused. "I need to hire someone."

"What's the pay?" Trez asked.

"Uh ..." Esperes screwed up her face. "I guess it would need to be an internship."

Trez shook her head, still smiling. "Right now, I'm more expensive than an intern."

"Foiled again!"

He didn't think getting sidetracked any further was wise. "What's a big pantsed person again?"

"Corp, kook, veep, anyone with pants big enough to store lots of untraceable cash in."

"Bien sûr. You got any bright ideas there?"

"Sadly, not yet." Esperes swept her hand in the air. "But! I've got a list of possible culprits and can route that over to you."

"Generous offer. What do you want for it?" He hadn't anticipated needing to negotiate already.

"I want you to share your findings with me. Who sent the break-in artist and why?"

Ah, the kicker. "You want me to find this person for you?" Leaking data to the press would be tough to explain to the higher-ups if they got wind of it.

"Freedom of in-for-ma-tion. Freedom of the press!"

If Esperes had wanted money or connections, Eric maybe could have arranged something. But this was Harbor business. "My employer doesn't look kindly on employees sharing company data."

"You're not going to obfuscate the truth from the people? The people deserve to know!"

Eric glanced over to see Trez folded over in silent mirth. Ostie de tabarnak. He wasn't exactly making headway in the case himself, but how would he explain this to Vail as they continued to work on it? "If I don't, you'll . . . ?"

"Figure it out myself. Scoop you all and catapult your team all the way to Chicagoland. Ask Q-Dave to deploy the Knights Templar."

Not the strongest or sanest of ultimatums, but if there were any truth to Esperes's claims, she wouldn't be the smartest lady to cross. "Will keep that in mind."

"Kay-oh. That done, I'll snort some Glass and hit the clubs. You want to find me in the plaid, I'll be at Abai Bar downtown."

That could be amusing, Eric guessed. He disconnected with a nod and a wave.

Trez was fiddling with her fingers as she digested the conversation. "Huh," she grunted. "That's a rig. Reminds me of Dinoroid Dana."

"Who's ... what's ... Dinoroid Dana?"

"A reporter with what she calls a gonzo style. She has a daily news dispatch."

He chuckled. "I didn't know you followed current events."

"Well, she is funny."

"Were you seriously considering her whack offer?"

"Maybe. She's got ideals. I don't have the time to devote to anyone's ideals, let alone my own, but I think people like her keep us honest." She swung her feet back and forth on the sofabed.

"Us?"

Trez's smile vanished. "Corp-drones. Non-indigents. Haves."

He didn't know what to say to that. He usually tried his hardest to forget that he'd ever been indigent. "Anyway, that's Kayla Esperes. Reporter for the *New York Times*."

"How'd you know her?"

"Met at a party." She blinked. "You know, the one you crashed."

"I was going to ask. What were you doing at that party anyway?"

"Escorting Sam."

Trez's mouth quirked. "Just went up to a reporter and asked her if she could get you some intel?"

"Other way round."

"What?"

"Don't know if she was looking for me, but I was a convenient find for her."

"What does she want?"

"She thinks a security incident I had a week ago is an important story. I was going to ask you for a consult on said incident, actually. Don't know why the *Times* cares about it. I think Esperes is missing a few pinballs."

Trez sipped her melonade. "If you want my advice, then I'll need the details."

"Punk broke into R&D 4 and got into a secure lab. He had a Gauntlet. We fought."

"He any good?"

"He was high and Driving, so downing him wasn't easy one-on-one. Don't know how good he is without performance enhancement."

Trez finished her drink and got up to refill her cup. The yellow stood out against the gray walls. He heard the patter of the rain outside while she thought. She was giving him her back unprotected. It contrasted with her turtling about her ordeal.

She turned around. Her top—his top, really—had slid to the side, exposing a collarbone. He told himself to stop staring at it.

"Problem is, the infiltrator had a scrubbed clean identity. Seymour doesn't want to have this incident looked at too closely by the other execs, so I got some outside help."

"I suppose journalists do have access to information that you wouldn't. But ... don't you want a Runner to help with this?"

Elite programmers who could manipulate the abstract code used in information security were mostly employed by Corps. Harbor paid them handsomely, and Eric assumed other Corps did as well. A few freelanced, mostly with criminal intent. "I don't know any in Security who wouldn't try digging deeper into Seymour's secrets."

"I know an independent Runner. Her name's Vanchen. She's discreet."

"Would you be comfortable asking her?"

Trez nodded and then yawned. "I don't know if she has the time or how much she'd charge, but it wouldn't hurt to ask."

"I'll follow any leads I can." Eric doubted Trez was up for much further discussion. "You need a rest?"

"Yeah. I should go home now."

He stopped himself from telling her to stay. She might spook. "Let me know if you learn anything."

"Will do." She was unsteady getting up from her chair.

He stood as well. "I can—"

"No, I'll see myself out." She frowned slightly.

"Your clothes are all ripped up. You can return these duds later."

"Yeah, sure."

"Will you avoid me at work? Still? You'd better not—"

"I'm off on med leave, remember?"

"You could use the physical company. Someone should check on you. I volunteer myself."

She raised her brows. "You just invited yourself over?"

"Sort of. You can always say no." He didn't want to press too hard.

Trez met his gaze. "Okay, sure. Do that."

He suppressed a goofy grin. "Dinner someday after work then. Wednesday?"

"Works for me."

"You okay to get home?" he asked again.

"Should be." Her boots were by the entryway. She boosted herself out of the chair with his arm and then took a deep breath, centering herself. "Can I borrow a jacket?"

"I've an old one somewhere." He rummaged around in the closet and found a gray coat with matted fake fur around the neck.

She looked bemused. "This getup is . . . something."

"Maybe it's art."

"Hah." She gave him a smile before she stepped through the door. He counted that as a small victory.

TEN

Eric splashed his way through the puddles leading to the racecourse. Oil stuck to his boots. He guessed that the point of a course almost in the willy-wacks was that the authorities wouldn't be interested in policing whatever dangerous activity you got up to. Couldn't exactly have exploding vehicles in the city. Gauche, that.

Presumpscot had supplied the steel for heavy shipping in its heyday. But fifteen years ago, Michaud and Harbor had figured out they could get a better deal buying forged steel from Chicagoland. Some residents had retrained into working in shipwrighting and commuted to Portland proper, others just stayed here and rotted away. Oh, they had food, clothing, and shelter, but their sense of purpose was gone, and there was nothing to keep most of them going. Some people couldn't learn a new trade or, when they couldn't get employed, couldn't cope.

The old factories and warehouses weren't all abandoned; they'd become something of a squatters' haven, with hopeless indigents wandering around zombified. Some with chemical aid, others' minds had just gone. Despite available sanitation facilities nearby, a significant number of people had stopped caring about hygiene and disease. If the world had no use for them that they could understand, why play by its rules? Maman had run off to a zone like this shortly after he'd left home. That's what Sam said anyway. She kept tabs on Maman. He wondered if their mother was still living outside civilization. She had to be alive though. Sam would have told him otherwise.

Several of the older buildings had become flophouses. It wasn't just the natives congregating anymore. Since the suits hadn't bothered to give the derelicts any trouble, folks from all over the Northeast had shown up to live semi-off the grid. How they kept the lights on and their terminals operational, Eric wasn't sure.

Originally a nasscar racing site to keep the steel workers entertained, the park near the warehouses had fallen into disrepair when the jobs left. A few years ago, some enterprising kids had rebuilt the track. Bangor racing came and went as a fad, and it was on the upswing. The result—a body sometimes had to brave angry indigents to watch the crack racers stove-up their cars.

Staplehead's legal name was Agum Kuntoro Kalla, and finding intel on him and his contact details had been easy. He wasn't at the top of the command chain, but he was a trusted lieutenant. Eric hadn't expected that, but he wouldn't look a gift horse in the mouth.

Staplehead had agreed to meet him here as long as he could bring Dorgo. Eric in turn had thought to bring Trez to even the numbers, but she'd been ordered to rest. He doubted having her talk to the Makos directly would result in anything good anyway.

It'd been a while since he'd been to a Bangor race, so named for a joke about the old town nearby and the English banger race. The area smelled of ozone from the recent thunderstorm. The course, not quite a figure eight, wove around a gargantuan pile of compressed trash, the studs of a partially concrete building, a river, and some existing pavement. About forty people clustered outside around the fence wire, entering bets and talking trash. Bangor race followers tended to be youngish and expressive. Loud voices, loud clothing, loud bodmod and upgrades. Were they pretentious? Punk? He wasn't impressed.

Eric saw some thrill-seeking suits mixed in with the kids. Some came to bet on the races, and a few of them drove the carts themselves. Their hired security teams were dead giveaways: men and women wearing neutral colors with similarly neutral expressions and ready stances. Overkill, really. Most of the time all they had to deal with was angry squatters who had an infinite list of things to rant about.

His own gray and blue clothes were the most subdued he could see. Dammit. Misjudged tonight's audience. Was he that out of touch? Thinking over that question soured his mood.

He listened to the banter though really it was all posturing at this stage—boasts and taunts he overheard from the kids gathered around the racecourse. Best he could hear, some of them had hands in designing or building the skimmers. The skimmer pilots were in there somewhere too, trading barbs about their skills—something about wheelies and Ka-furies. Eric couldn't make sense of it. Maybe he was too old.

"Lug." Staplehead hailed him with an exaggerated wave. The Mako was dressed in some kind of trash grunge that might be all the rage right now, along with the fauxhawk. He fit in with most of the attendees. Dorgo's jacket was closed, covering up his top. It probably didn't say "BITE ME" this time. The jacket's rainproofing needed reapplication. Wet streaks darkened patches of the fabric.

"That's me." Eric roused himself off the concrete.

Staplehead walked over, his gait loose hipped. "So you're a Harbor man."

"Ah-yeah." No point in hiding that. Easy enough to find him.

"Whatcha want with good old Agum and Dorgo, mon ami? Samurai lifestyle not all it's cracked up to be?" He chuckled a little. It wasn't unheard of for Corp personnel to moonlight, so long as they were discreet.

"Who tried to run you off the road?" If Staplehead wanted to be direct, Eric could follow suit.

"Pardon?"

"Last we met, you were sculpturing the Anupam's Synth Sweets storefront with your bike. Then I had some fun with a few disreputables. Who were they?"

"What's it to you?"

"I'd like to know who I pissed off. And as I said, I like the neighborhood just as it is."

Staplehead turned his skinny studded neck to Dorgo. "Good enough for me. I say we let him know the score."

"Boss may not like us meeting with Harbor goons," Dorgo said.

"Boss has bigger problems. This is fine. The guy covered for a stranger until I phoned you and got a bunch of those punks off me."

"Keeping this on the down-low?" Eric asked.

Dorgo shrugged. "Doesn't make us look like we've got a handle on things."

"He's already seen me in a pretty embarrassing situation. Anyway," Staplehead said. "Far's I knows some of them always been here, doing their delinquent gig. Making graffiti, petty theft, nothing to worry about."

"AR graffiti or the paint?"

"Whatever. People get bored when they got nothing to do." Staplehead probably also had too much free time, judging from the head job and the tacky tats. "But these days, they're starting lots of shit. Making statements, taking names."

"Setting fire to skimmers," Dorgo added.

"Is your bike next?" Eric asked.

"I, uh, I hadn't thought about that." Kalla reached up and scratched at the staples on his head. Eric couldn't help wincing at that. Skin growing over stitches was gross.

Dorgo cracked his knuckles. "Past two months, more kids show up. Start causing trouble on a bigger scale. Then we find out they're packing colossal heat. Unlicensed guns, several vibroweapons," he said. "I think that with more resources, they got more confident."

"Knocked down some stores?"

"A smash and grab or two, sure. But that's not the thing." Staplehead rubbed at his neck.

"The thing?" Eric arched a brow.

"Thing is, they got Runners."

Well, it wasn't like there weren't plenty of amateur hackers out there trying to make names for themselves. But Staplehead sounded concerned. "Good ones?"

"Well, these aren't jokers just fucking around and jacking in."

Must have run afoul of the Makos' online activities then. "Stove-up a bank job of yours?" Eric tried to suppress his smirk.

Dorgo covered Staplehead's mouth with a massive bony hand. It didn't match up with his lean body. Staplehead waited a few seconds before sighing and removing Dorgo's hand from his face. "You think he and the Corps don't know what some of our business associates do?" He shook his head and rolled his eyes at the same time, a feat Eric found impressive.

"No, but your trap flaps too much," Dorgo said.

"And you're making us look like ungrateful oafs to mon ami here."

Eric's smirk broke through. "My opinion of your kind of fish hasn't changed from meeting you two." Criminal enterprises, especially successful ones, required a few bodies with brains in their heads.

"Fish in Lobstahland." Kalla elbowed Dorgo. "Whatever powers your hotsync."

Time to get this conversation back on track. "You were saying Runners."

"Right. Judging from the damage they've done to our servers, the troublemakers have recruited at least a few Runners with decent rigs."

"Runners and Architects sometimes go where the money is. You think these fuckers are foreign?"

"Have to be imported from somewhere. Near or far, I don't know."

"Even if we did know, I'm not sure how useful that information would be," Dorgo said. "What I want to know is where all the creds came from. Someone has a plan, but fuck if I know what it is."

"They gotta be calling the shots," said Staplehead. "The someone bankrolling them, that is. Like Dorgo said, you don't throw that much money around for shits and giggles."

"And you don't know who that someone is?" Eric doubted they'd tell him if they knew, but it didn't hurt to ask.

"If the boss knows, she certainly hasn't shared that with me." Staplehead had visibly relaxed. Dorgo, however, was still giving Eric major side-eye.

"I don't know who and what they're hitting besides us," Staplehead mused. "With the expertise they probably got, they could Run the Corp servers too. Have you heard anything about rogue intrusions?"

Like the break-in at Miletus? Could it be linked to these guys the Makos were tussling with, or was he jumping to conclusions? He'd have to investigate on his own. "That's above my pay grade to know. If they are, I guess Harbor doesn't consider it a security threat." He could get back to Staplehead and Dorgo once he knew more. "But why're they picking on you anyway?"

"I'm guessing we're softer targets than, say, Harbor," Staplehead said. "You want a foothold, you don't try to take on the big boys first."

"Ah-yeah. Don't have any other ideas, myself." Drizzle beaded on Eric's boots.

"Anything else? The races he bet on will start soon." Dorgo worried the closure on his vest.

Eric tipped his chin at the racetrack. "You a fan?"

"Ah-yeah," Kalla said. "I race too. These karts handle differently than a bike. You have to think farther ahead."

"Seen a few races, but never tried it myself." It could be an expensive hobby, and Eric had enough adrenaline spikes at work that he didn't need to risk his neck any further. Plus, if you got hurt while off duty it wasn't optimal for your career.

"I'd say you're missing out, but I don't think everyone agrees with me." Staplehead elbowed Dorgo, who grunted. "Well, don't slip the wind, mon ami."

"Likewise. Good to talk a bit, Sta—Kalla." Eric got a funny look from the Makos for that one. "I'll see you around."

Dorgo made a dismissive gesture as he walked away. Some sort of goodbye. The two chatted a bit as they headed closer to the track, Staplehead filling Dorgo in on some details of the upcoming races.

Eric closed his eyes and exhaled slowly. He heard a crunch of metal off to his right. He'd come to talk to the Makos to distract himself from the R&D 4 case. The lead he'd uncovered this morning was a bunch of suspicious bank transfers to the office accounts. Was somebody in the department in on it? Was it someone he cared about? The thought made his chest tight.

He stayed and spectated another hour, watching the wreckers go after the rodders. He turned over his thoughts about what to do with Trez, the lab break-in case, Seymour, and how to keep his job. They tumbled about, but it felt like they were on an inescapable rat wheel.

ELEVEN

Eric would have wondered why Trez had chosen to live in Gastown if she hadn't told him about her money problems. Brutal concrete complexes with doors and windows placed to remind him of eyes and mouths. The place smelled of old rain and petroleum products. Poor drainage and unpatched potholes meant he had to make his way around several puddles.

Faux-leaf ornamentations on the outside of the windows distinguished Trez's apartment building from the others. The building was partially paid and partially public housing. A teenager with disheveled hair sat on the steps. The kid gave him a long stare. Eric bared his teeth in response. Sam had bought these clothes for him: a green-striped shirt with an intact collar and pants she'd tailored to fit him closely. They marked him an outsider, but he wanted to present himself as having his shit together.

The punk took several pulls of a joint then slinked away behind a corner. Trez still hadn't come down or buzzed him in. She'd said dropping by this evening would be fine. If she wasn't home by some chance then he'd bloody well wait for her to get back. Like some creepy stalker, or an infatuated suitor who would promise the moon to the object of his affection. He didn't want to analyze how close he was to either of those.

The entrance opened, plastic doors swinging outward. Eric opted to take the stairs up even though he saw an elevator. There wasn't any art or graffiti on the walls, but the steps were stained with splotches of ink and scuffed so that the ledges were no longer sharp. Every so often, Sam talked about how your living environment affected your outlook. She'd say this place leached hope away from anything there. Not wretched, but bleak enough to heap more stress on you every day.

Trez lived on the third floor. Someone had thought to carpet the hallway to protect it decades ago. It should have been ripped out; Eric was sure many undiscovered species made it their home. The units didn't seem to have any distinguishing differences from the hallway, so he was glad he knew which one to knock at. He waited a long minute before the door opened and Trez gestured for him to come in.

She looked somewhat improved from yesterday. Still had dark circles under her eyes, but she wasn't shaking anymore. She wore plain green sweatpants, a faded tee, and a wrinkled scarf in her hair. Her feet were bare, and she wasn't wearing any cosmetics. He tried not to dwell on that thought. The door closed behind him.

"I have water, tea, coffee, and synthade. Can I get you anything?"

"Water will be fine." The living room was also the dining room and kitchen, so he could watch her go through the cupboards and dispense drinks. He had his choice of chairs—some overstuffed microfiber cushions or cracked plastics. He decided not to take his chances with the plastic chairs.

She handed him a mug and sat across from him. She was sipping something warm, according to his IR readout. "Cold?" he asked.

"I guess."

Stupid question. There was a blanket on a small foldout couch opposite the apartment's terminal. If she was cold, she could have wrapped herself in that. This was not a good opening to the conversation. He searched for another topic. "Feeling any better?"

"Yeah." She continued sipping her ginger-smelling drink.

He shifted in his chair. The foam stuffing was lumpy. "I came over to see how you were doing."

She didn't respond except by staring into her cup.

"Don't shut me out." Where to get his footing in this interaction?

"Sorry," she said. Her hands were folded in front of her, and she had taken an interest in how they flexed. Not very well, apparently.

"If you're really sorry, look at me," he said, as gently as he could. She raised her head, expression neutral and eyes blank. He'd have to get her riled up again to get anything out of her. Trouble was, that would wind him up too, and he wasn't sure he liked the tactic. "Still hiding?"

"Maybe." She broke eye contact.

"I'd thought you braver than that, ace." He hadn't tried going after her pride yet.

She didn't take the bait. "Look, I'm sorry. I'm tired."

How did he readdress their discussion at his place? She'd been less guarded then. Maybe he could try a display of vulnerability. He'd rather eat half a kilo of sauerkraut, but he knew Trez had her head up her ass and would ignore subtlety.

"We've known each other years now, right?" He couldn't remember how many. Seemed as long as he'd been working with Vail, he'd noted Trez's presence.

"Four? Five? It was after I joined the strike division." She pursed her lips, perplexed. Well, if neither of them could recall, that was less embarrassing.

"Well. Few months ago, I realized I had a thing for you. Thought I'd ask you out. Time never seemed right though." Had a thing? That line had sounded better in his head. Sacrament.

"Ask me out?" She raised her brows, and he tried not to take offense.

"Like an old-fashioned ... date thing." This sounded so stupid. Sure, people dated or hotsynced casually, but it felt strange to talk about a setup encounter with a friend.

"Like dinner and vids? Even though we hung out plenty?"

"Ah-yeah. Dinner and entertainment. Caff or a concert or something like that. But I was trying to figure out how it could work."

She smiled again, and he felt lighter. "We could make dinner and bitch about our coworkers."

"Anyway, I dragged my feet because I thought it'd be awkward."

"I've never known you to hold back in speaking your mind." She sounded pleased, and that helped him continue.

"Higher stakes, you know?"

"I told you you were hot before."

"That's one thing." He'd remembered her frank appreciation on a day three months ago, when they'd met for dinner in the mess hall as usual. He'd had his mind on something else that had seemed important until she uttered those words.

"But that's not going out or even hotsyncing. Plenty of hot people I don't want handling my tender bits." There was his brain getting in the way again.

"Guess we were headed toward it though." Trez flexed her fingers again. He couldn't see her expression.

"Do you regret it?" He inhaled slowly, bracing himself mentally and physically.

"I regret that it got you mixed up in my extracurricular shit." She met his eyes again for a moment, then had to turn her face away.

Not a direct answer. Another apology. "I would have gotten mixed up in your shit, like you say anyway." She wrinkled her nose at him. "I care about you." It came out more combative than he'd intended. Well, daring to care about Trez was decent perilous anyway. He put his hands on her knees and massaged them for a moment.

He was momentarily amused when her eyes went wide and her mouth bracketed, then relaxed. Her face went through several almost expressions as she tried to figure out how to respond. Maybe she'd thought of apologizing yet again then discarded that notion.

He didn't know whether he was coming or going. Well, not coming, he thought. Not like he'd want anyway. The heat of her thigh transferred through her pants. Touching her skin was a tempting thought. This had his feelings tied in knots. Angry currents plus tenderness, and he wanted to laugh at their awkwardness.

"So tell me then. Why did I have to save your fine ass on a strike? Why're you popping tabs of everything under the moon? Why did you stop talking to almost everyone? If it'd just been me, my ego could've taken it. Not great, but we rushed into things without any promises or discussion beforehand. I'd deal, somehow. No, you've been taking pharma that could end your career or kill you. Why?"

Trez's mouth compressed for a moment. She shook her head then inhaled audibly. "I didn't want to remember their faces anymore," she said.

Eric didn't visibly react. He let the words hang and drift in the air. He inclined his head. "Whose faces?" he asked.

Trez rubbed her arms and hugged herself. "The mission collateral. The civilian woman's. And then the Fairchild guard."

He waited more. His patience hurt. She'd gone over this with the counselor Harbor assigned to her, but Eric wasn't someone professional who was paid to listen to her.

She straightened her shoulders. "I screwed up a while ago. Offed someone during a strike who shouldn't have been there. She'd been dressed all dark, like the guards." Trez took a deep breath to steel herself. "I had a feeling something was wrong when I first saw her at the site, but I didn't process it until after the strike. She wasn't wearing armor." She remembered the sensation of sinking her blades into unprotected flesh and shivered.

"How high were you?" It wasn't a rude question. The worse a mission went, the more drugs a striker ended up doing, and Eric knew that.

"I wasn't Driving too hard, but I wasn't sober."

Eric cracked his knuckles. "How'd the debrief go?"

"Far as the suits are concerned, all right. Didn't catch much flak for the pink spray. 'These things happen,' Sloane said.

'One of the hazards of Corpfare.' I guess they have actuaries to deal with the damages."

After the debrief, she'd had the shakes and couldn't sleep for hours. Maybe because she hadn't felt anything at the time, and wasn't she supposed to when she'd murdered someone? She'd tried to think of herself as just a tool and pass off the emotional responsibility to Harbor, but that hadn't worked.

"So your boss bailed you out?"

"Mostly. They had me see a headmed."

"Any good?"

"I don't rightly know. She said it was okay to have nightmares about it. But it's not like I would have told anyone else."

Eric nodded. "From what I've seen, the culture's decent macho," he said carefully.

"Pretty much." You had to keep up a facade of robotic efficiency. If another striker sensed weakness, they'd try to poach your assignments to make themselves look better.

"But it sounds like you had more than nightmares."

She took a deep breath, held it for a moment. Pushed it out fast. "I thought I saw her everywhere. Made me jumpy all the time. I'd be on strikes and the guards would have her face. Started second-guessing myself. Took a performance hit." She had never admitted that out loud before. Apparently it showed, because Eric took her hand under the table and squeezed. She started, but after a moment a latch in her guards opened. "Then a job went bad and I got captured."

"I remember that." He didn't let go. "It took a few days for the ransom to go through."

"Wasn't the first time I got captured. I knew what to expect. They weren't cruel. No nose and ear violation like Mihai got a year ago."

"Nose and ear violation?" His eyes were the widest she'd ever seen them. He might be accustomed to brutality, but he could be squeamish about the most random things.

"They had a glass wand. Got creative and used it on him until it broke. Doc Julio got a lot of shards out of his nasal passages. Perilously close to the brain, he said. Even the mesh we get installed up there lets tiny particles in."

"That's not okay." Eric had paled. His hands gripped hers too tightly.

Trez let herself laugh, that bit of release a relief. "No, it's not." The callused texture of his hands anchored her to reality. She used that to continue, to go past the mental wall she'd constructed for herself. She'd promised herself that she'd answer Eric's questions. It wasn't right to go back and forth on him, to play the mystery up. Even if that was unintentional.

"I lost my shit when I woke up after the strike. You're supposed to not antagonize your captors. They hadn't gotten the memo about my implants, I guess, because I tore somebody's face open. Sloane gave me a lecture about that afterwards."

"Criss." He shook his head. "No, I ... I'm not judging you. I'm just still in not-in-the-face mode."

"Reasonable." Somebody else acknowledging her ordeal made her feel like she was less of a crazy person for thinking about it so much.

"I got a bad beating when they tried to subdue me, I think. Don't really remember. But afterwards, I kept dreaming of those two women I'd savaged like they were the same person. Their face would open up and suck me in. Or they'd melt and break open and I'd be stuck wrestling with all this fleshy tar. It would cling and I'd be helpless and know something was coming for me."

"Something? Like a monster?"

"If you want to call it that." Lately, the monster had worn Santorini's face. But she wasn't ready to cop to her momma issues out loud. That was an older wound, and she only had so much of her own blood to spill at a time.

"You talked to a counselor about this?"

"About the lady's ripped open face? I only vaguely remember attacking her or seeing the damage. As for the rest ... all the mental exercises can help. Sometimes. But not under stress, on a mission. That's why I use the anesthetics." They induced a semi-trance, and she wouldn't accumulate any more memories.

"How does that help? You'd have to be as high as ..." He grimaced. "As doped up as you were, sure. But even that ..."

Even taking more than her prescribed dissociatives hadn't been enough. "Well, I got someone to cook me up some anesthesia."

"Painkillers?" Eric's voice came to her over a dull roar.

"That's a side benefit. You know how when we get surgical upgrades we're awake but don't remember anything?" She'd blurred all the enhancement procedures together in her mind. The memories all had the same kind of hazy fidelity, like she'd only seen them through a wall of fog, not lived them.

"Ah-yeah, the stuff that fucks with your short-term memory and ... Trez, that's both wicked brilliant and wicked fucked in the head."

"The memories were beginning to pile up. Jobs blurring together. With the pharma I wouldn't remember anything that went down during the strike." The confession made her shiver.

"But how did you ... Your mission reports must have been interesting."

"I wasn't as honest as I could have been with the medics. I

figured the data feed they got from the suit would be enough." She had to wrap her arms around herself.

"And you strikers are usually total messes after a job too, whackheadjobs or no. Color me impressed." Eric's smile faded. "Do you really not give a fuck whether you live or die?"

Trez's shoulders slumped. "It's not like I didn't know the dangers. I just . . ."

"Thought you could get away with it?" Where had he gone? His voice sounded so far away.

"Look, if I can't pay off the Makos and they expose me, I'll be jailed for life with my assets seized." While that wasn't death, nobody would be able to protect Linus. If she died, her will took care of him. She rubbed her temples. She'd gone over the risks so many times in her head that she didn't know what the correct calculations were anymore.

"You never told me what they had over you."

"I'm sorry." She had to stand up and pour herself some water. "I'm so used to keeping it all in that it doesn't come naturally, you know? It's like its own evil ball of black goo stuck in my chest. Tumorous. I try to keep it apart from everything else."

Eric turned his head slightly, so he looked directly at her with one eye. "Doesn't change the fact that you're playing Russian roulette."

"Maybe I'm more like my father than I thought," she said. "Gambling that I can pay this off before the gun that's firing at my head has a loaded chamber." Bile burned in her throat.

He looked a bit lost. The same kind of lost she felt. "You're all right with me, you know," he said.

Tears blurred her vision. "Even though I went all AWOL on you?" She couldn't look at him.

"Even though you're going demolition racing without a helmet or brakes." She heard his chair rasp along the floor.

"Some friend I am." This was why she tried not to think about him, about anyone close to her. She couldn't ... His hand was on her jaw and he tipped it up for a kiss.

Eric's mouth was warm and firm, and she felt hers part in response. He kissed her as if he had hours to kill, waiting with each brush and change of pressure. He nibbled her bottom lip slowly while cradling her face in one rough palm. She wondered if she was getting tears all over his face.

A mixture of shame and relief had her chest hurting, and she grabbed his free arm and dug her nails in, as if to channel that pain from her body into his. Shit. Her claws weren't out, but he hissed a bit but didn't try to remove her hand or stop kissing her. He brushed her tears away with one hand, and she felt close to begging. She removed her nails and tried simply holding on to him.

When he lifted his head, his eyes seemed an even brighter blue than usual. Clear.

"I'm sorry, Eric."

One side of his mouth curved. "Sorry for what?"

"Everything?" She wiped her face dry.

"Well now, I don't think everything's on you."

"I ..." What on God's gray earth was he talking about? "What?"

"The recent economic downturn—"

"That's not what I meant." But what she did mean eluded her right now.

"Oh." His eyebrows rose. "Well." His smile was smug. "I didn't exactly stop you in the sparring room."

"About that ..." She wasn't sure how to say it. She wanted

to forget herself with him again, was sure he'd be happy to oblige, but she was so afraid. What did he want from her? To be fuck buddies? No, he'd already said what he wanted, hadn't he? She went back to hugging herself.

Eric widened his eyes and fluttered his lashes. It should have been ridiculous. "I believe I enthusiastically consented." He waited for her to finish her sentence. Why did he have to be so sweet? Damn him. The memory of his "yes" against her mouth inflamed a dull ache in her gut.

"I don't know if I can do this," she confessed.

He put his hands on her shoulders and bent until their eyes were level. "Well, much as I'd love to, you don't have to now."

Too much had happened too quickly. Trez didn't have the space in her head to hook up with Eric when she knew he wanted to court her. She'd just fuck it up and disappoint him, then he'd leave her. She tried to shake away that thought and the pit it opened in her stomach.

"Besides, I came here to hash some details of my case with you."

Wait, what? Trying to process that statement made her dizzy. Was he dropping the subject? "Really?"

"Well, I wouldn't complain if we danced horizontally. But I thought I could use your perspective on this."

"You think my brain's actually useful for critical thinking right now?"

"Can't hurt. Also, it might—never mind."

She couldn't keep up. "Never mind what?"

"It would have been a joke in poor taste." He waved a hand and turned away. Began pacing. "We have two working theories about how the intruder got in. Both require some prep and maybe a glass cutter. We think he staged a distraction to divert most of the guards to another floor. Even with a Gauntlet, getting past security takes time."

"Huh." She passed her cup back and forth between her hands, sliding it a few inches across the table. Reconstructing this wasn't going to happen tonight, but maybe Eric talking through it again would help him.

"Nobody else was on the floor except Vail. Someone had called in a false alarm on the ground floor, and Security all got orders to go investigate." He paused and blew his bangs out of his eyes. "Vail and I took him down, but I don't know how he or whoever he works for got in in the first place."

"Know what he was after?" She'd missed that earlier, if Eric had even told her.

"Other than that, it was in Miletus's second floor incubation laboratory, I'm not sure."

"What's in the lab?"

"There are several prototype devices in there, but I don't think he touched them. I think what he wanted was on the servers there."

"Live servers?" Why bother breaking in physically?

"Nah."

"What's on 'em?"

"That data's above my pay grade. I could ask Seymour." Distaste inflected his voice.

"I assume the Fairchild strike at the gala was related somehow," she said. "But I did think it was strange. Edgy thing for Seymour to ask for. Within the rules of Corpfare, technically Fairchild territory, but . . ."

"Tres gauche."

"I've never heard of a strike at a public gathering before."

She'd thought she could handle having civilians around, but she had been lucky not to hurt anyone more than bruises. Physically anyway.

"I think I should ask Vail. They have a different pair of eyes. Might see something we're overlooking." Eric looked at Trez.

Trez yawned. She was done for the night. "Sure."

"I'll let you sleep some more. You've given me some details to follow up on."

"Uh, you're welcome." Another yawn. "I . . . Do you want to come back tomorrow night?" Her own words surprised her. What was happening to her caution?

"I would love to."

TWELVE

Eric had invited her back over to his place tonight. It was two train stops normally, but tonight she felt like walking.

It took a moment to find the moon when the night was this overcast. Trez wasn't an astronomy buff, but she liked the glow's contrast to the city lights; it gave off a gentler energy than the buildings full of worker bees. Not that all the lights were on in this district. Some residents were likely out, and a few places abandoned. She stopped by the area whenever she wanted dessert. Although the last time had been over a month ago.

The door to Eric's apartment complex slid open. Eric was at the entrance to greet her personally. "Glad you could make it."

"Thought I . . . well. Meeting in person is one of the more secure channels," she stammered.

"Anyone around here give you a hard time?" Eric cocked his head.

"Ah, no. Why?"

"I'll get to that in a minute." He led her to the elevator. The up and down arrows were a bit scuffed.

"People don't tend to bother me on the street."

Eric gave her an appreciative look. "It's in your stride."

"What?"

"You take long steps. Sort of lope with your shoulders forward."

"Like a wolf? Don't they have four legs?"

"It's predatory. Our supposed reptile brains can recognize it. I think it's hot."

She couldn't think of a cogent response to that, so she followed him out of the elevator silently.

Eric IDed them into his apartment and gestured extravagantly. "Welcome back," he said. She hadn't paid attention to the common area last time. It was rather nice, she thought. Funky, sturdy furniture. Not all black and gray like at her studio.

The kitchen area had cups already out on the table, one full of steaming tea. "For me?"

"Didn't want to presume, so your cup is empty. What can I get you?"

"I'll have what you have here. The minty-smelling stuff." It was strange how little rituals like getting someone a glass of something to drink could take on intimacy. "I can serve myself though—"

"Uh-uh. Save your energy. You still got bags under your eyes the size of a baby's fist."

She thought about protesting, but she had no real reason to decline politeness. Even if it came with some unflattering commentary. She took off her coat, gloves, and boots while she waited.

He must have heard the thunk of her boots, because he turned from the drink dispenser. "Oh. Hah. You can put your jacket and gloves on one of the chairs. Don't have many coat hooks. That I have more than zero is Sam's doing."

"How is she? Still worried about you?"

He snorted. "Sam's in a tizzy about some career marde. I know her team has a deadline for an installation they're doing."

He pushed her cup to her and she noticed his hair was slightly damp and wavy. She stopped herself from reaching to touch it. She sniffed at her drink instead. It was still hot enough to burn her tongue. "You expected I'd run into trouble on my way here? Have I acquired more enemies?" She hadn't felt like anyone was watching her, but she was off her game. She'd need to be more careful in future.

"Nah. It's not you, it's that there's some trouble going down here." He sat and his chair scraped. She started for a moment and nearly knocked her cup over.

"Last I checked, the Makos claimed this area as territory." She'd worried a bit about running afoul of them, but remembered that all her payments had been on time. They'd no reason to rough her up yet.

"Seems there are some new fish in town."

Trez groaned. "You've been waiting to say that one, haven't you?"

"Ah-yeah. But it seems like the interlopers are giving the Makos trouble. Welcome news?"

"Huh. I don't know." If the Makos didn't have all the neighborhood shit handled, they might be distracted and ignore her. Or they could panic and come down hard on her. "You got anything else?"

"To continue with the horrible puns, these aren't small fry." His eyes danced.

"If you keep doing that, you're buying me some seafood at the waterfront tonight," she threatened. "Maybe even the real stuff." Coated and breaded enough it could be hard to tell, sometimes. Not like she could splurge though.

"It's a date."

"You'll be the one paying."

He shrugged. She had a few moments to try to infer his thoughts on dating and the cost of real fish before he said, "That Runner friend of yours. Vanchen. Wonder if she has any data on this." His eyes narrowed, almost crossed. "Could you ask her if she's heard any gossip or encountered any other hackers online lately? If that's not too personal."

"You think these new guys are wiremonkeys themselves?"

"Intel I got says they've multiple Runners getting in everyone's grillface. Don't think the Makos quite know what to do with that."

That sounded more serious than all the fish jokes. "Everyone's?"

"Corp, Makos, who knows what else. Vanchen may know more than Staplehead."

Trez blinked. "That seriously what he goes by?"

"Fuck. Keep forgetting that it's not." He cracked up a little at that. "I may have been a bit judgmental when I first saw him, before his name got into my HUD. Now I just ignore it, because it's too funny. Drink your tea."

She gave him some side-eye for that. "You're a medic now?"

"I don't need to be a medic to know your tea will get cold."

"Maybe I want it cold."

"Hey." His tone had changed. Probably noticed her distraction.

"What?" It came out more snappish than she intended.

"Don't 'what' me. You okay?" He leaned across the table until his eyes were level with hers.

"I'm ... Fuck. Now's not a good time." She shifted in her chair.

"Is there ever a good one?" His gaze softened. "Trez, you're not okay. It's all right."

She stared back incredulously. "Uh, no." He didn't know the half of it.

Eric backed off at that. While she drank her tea, he filled the silence with idle commentary, gossiping about office drama. When she finished, he took her cup and put it in the sanitizer.

"I'd better be going," she said. "Seeing a parent."

"I could walk you there."

She shook her head. "That won't be necessary. Thanks for the offer though."

He didn't push, and that made her want to both hold him close forever and scream at him to run as far away as possible. "You keep in much better touch with your folks than I do." Half of his mouth smiled.

What were Eric's parents like? They probably weren't local, otherwise he'd talk about them as much as he did Sam. "I'm not sure that's a good thing," she said.

Eric walked her to the train station entrance before saying goodbye. "Have fun." He squeezed her hands.

"I wouldn't call it fun."

"Well then, we can have some fun once you're done with your business."

She would probably need a distraction after she talked to Santorini. "I'll ping you when I'm free."

"I look forward to it," he said.

Trez walked up a metal ramp onto the pier. March was still early in the season, and the eateries all closed at eight.

Nonetheless, odors of shellfish and beer mixed into the smells of motor oil and garbage. Rubber tires and spare coils of rope were stacked up on the edges of the boards.

Santorini had agreed to meet her here. There usually weren't people around at this hour, and being outdoors made Trez a little calmer.

They had kept their communication to audio, so she wasn't quite sure if Santorini had changed her looks in the past two decades. All her memories of Santorini were a bit faded. Trez avoided looking at old family photos.

There was a smell of rotting fried food coming in with the ocean breeze. Her ribs felt tight, like she was tensing for a blow. She tamped her ugly tangle of emotions down. She wanted to talk to Santorini like a rational adult, not a bitter child. And Santorini always kept her composure.

Santorini stood on the pier, one hand against the rail. She was wearing hand-me-downs several sizes too large. Baggy, but they didn't swallow her. She had a few more wrinkles than Trez remembered, including a worry line between her brows. Otherwise, she seemed unchanged. She still wore her hair in a dozen braids, her brows still pointed down and in toward her nose, and she still carried herself slightly forward, as if to share a private conversation with the next person she met.

Her heavy tread announced her presence. Santorini looked up as Trez took a step forward, then stopped. She took a look around her, making sure that besides the pigeons, they were the only souls around. Then she peered at Trez for a moment before her face softened in welcome. Trez raised her chin in response.

"Hello . . . Trez, is it?"

"That's what I go by now."

"All right then." She peered at Trez. "Are you well?"

Trez fought not to squirm. "No," she said flatly. "You?"

Santorini chuckled, though when she stopped, it sounded more like a hiccup. "I'm managing."

Silence stretched between them. Finally, Trez asked, "What is it?"

Santorini frowned. "I wanted to talk to you, now that I'm back in town . . ."

Trez swallowed bile. "You didn't contact me for years. Said it was too dangerous."

"Now is different. Now I have a good team with me."

Trez's eyes narrowed. "What's that supposed to mean?"

"We have a Runner now, and enough resources to cover our tracks. I don't think anyone will find us as long as we keep a low profile." Even so, Santorini's gaze darted around.

"Who'd you get to follow you this time?" Trez was unable to stop herself from suppressing all the barbs that came to her lips. She grabbed a length of rope someone had left tied to a nearby post.

Santorini leaned forward. "Levin's here, you remember him. But it's not like I'm in charge of everyone. There are a few of us who run things. It keeps the movement from becoming a cult of personality."

Trez tried to concentrate on the roughness of the nylon rope under her hands. "What brings you back to Portland?"

Santorini's eyes widened. "We're gearing up for a big operation. We've been spending years gathering resources for this, and now we can pull it off."

"Does it involve checking who's in the building before you blow it up this time?"

Santorini averted her gaze. "Accidents—"

"Never mind." Trez reminded herself that she wasn't here

to provoke the woman. She tightened her hands on the nylon rope, sinking her nails into the fibers. "So where do I come in?"

"Oh, you. Yes. You've gone into the Corp's world."

"Been keeping tabs on me?" Her fingertips tingled. She tried not to pay attention to them.

"It was dangerous to contact you, but . . ." Santorini shifted against the railing. "Once I found out your new name, it was easy to see where you'd gone."

Trez opened her mouth to stretch her jaw. "You going to give me grief for that?"

Santorini shook her head slowly. "I guess I shouldn't have been surprised. You were always resourceful."

"You think I betrayed you?" Trez had wanted to lash out in some way, after Santorini abandoned her—to do what her ma would least approve of. Working at a Corp had seemed the biggest middle finger Trez could raise.

"No. I think you were trying to make the best of the situation I left you in." She plucked at the neckline of her sweatshirt.

"Oh?" Trez kept herself from sniping. The less Santorini saw of her daughter's feelings, the better Trez would feel.

"You were so upset by Morrison's death."

Morrison had played video games with Trez when she was bored and Santorini had been too busy to pay attention to her. Trez's claws deployed. She hoped Santorini didn't notice. "Morrison died because you got all three Portland-based Corps to actually cooperate in order to crush the Libertist movement. Getting civilians killed with your tactics will do that. Surely you weren't surprised that they came to our safe houses and opened fire."

Santorini nodded. "I understand that losing people hurt you. Linus got upset about that sort of thing too."

Anger blurred Trez's vision for a second. "That sort of thing? We're talking about people dying."

"Don't you kill people? Isn't violence your job?" Santorini's voice was gentle.

"I've never been asked to kill someone." Supposedly the execs could order a striker for a kill instead of a down, but Trez had never heard of any actual kill strikes.

"Maybe not, but as I was going to say before, accidents happen," Santorini replied, unruffled.

"All execs know it's a risk. They literally sign up for it." Did Santorini know about the civilian woman Trez had killed? Trez wished she had a litany of sacres to go through. Maybe Eric could teach her a few.

A frigid breeze blew in from the water. Trez watched Santorini shiver. This was why the docks weren't a popular walking spot in March. That didn't stop the gulls from patrolling the area for scraps though. Little bastards. No doubt they'd committed far more murders than the two women had.

"In any case, I have a proposal for you."

"A proposal for a Harbor Securities striker?" Trez forced her hands to uncurl from the now-shredded rope behind her.

Although Santorini remained calm, she glanced around a few times. "You can't be happy with your career. I'm here to offer an alternative. You would help our cause a great deal."

Trez giggled, too loudly, high pitched and fake sounding to her own ears. Santorini might be correct that Trez wasn't happy with her career, but it wasn't because Trez found it too corporate.

Santorini lifted her arm to outstretch her hand, but stopped halfway and took it back. "Trez, I know you're in trouble."

Trez's stomach dropped. All of a sudden the cold bit right through her jacket. "Excuse me?"

"Our Runner found out that the Makos have you on their books. I don't know why though." Santorini's eyes were guileless.

If the woman knew that much already, there was no point in hiding the rest. "Pa has giant gambling debts."

"Oh." Santorini's face fell. "Oh no." Santorini had often worried about Linus's impulsivity. It was one reason they'd never stayed together for long. "You took them on, didn't you?"

"Yes." Trez stifled another inappropriate giggle.

"I see." Santorini brought up her hand and nibbled on her knuckles. "I could try to have your records erased."

"Think you could do a better job than I did?"

"I don't know who you hired. But our Runner, Yang, is top-notch. They used to work for a bank in New York."

"You have a Runner with your crew." Well, that was different. Santorini had bemoaned their lack of a good hacker decades ago.

Santorini nodded. "If you are willing to work with us, we will do the best we can to make the Makos not your problem."

"That's only half the problem. The Makos found a friend of Linus's from decades ago. He confessed to knowing that Linus was involved with a criminal. You."

Santorini cocked her head. "We can track him down. If the Makos have him we can probably extract him. With your help, that is."

"The Makos are not small potatoes."

"It's risky. But we'd do it for you, if you joined us."

"What makes you think I'd be interested?"

Santorini took a moment before she answered. "Aside from the offer of helping you with your money problems? You have an edge to you. You seem unsatisfied. You could do something else here. Something that does more than soothe someone's corporate pride at the expense of their guards' health. When you were six, you told me you wanted to make a difference in the world. Find a way to matter."

Pretty speech, but ... "Do you think you know me?"

Santorini didn't meet her eyes, but played with a speck of lint on her sweater. "I'd like to think I could make a good guess."

"I'm very busy these days. Do you think I have the attention to pay to politics?" She decided not to mention Dinoroid Dana.

Santorini cleared her throat. "I believe your character is strong. Otherwise, you wouldn't have taken on Linus's debts."

"What do you think I could do for you?"

"Put that training of yours to better use. Physically infiltrate building security systems for us before we commence demolition. Yang is excellent, but there's only so much we can do remotely. We have new muscle to clear the way for us, but they're not security specialists."

"Ah." It made sense that they'd want that. "Breaking and entering. Clearing the way so you can blow shit up. Might be an upgrade, but it sounds like the same MO you used twenty years ago to me."

"We've tried other things." Santorini raised her head. Her gaze was somber. "Different things in different places. Different tactics. Demonstrations. Holding up traffic. But what we've learned is that nothing talks like money does. Nothing gets the haves riled up like breaking their wealth machines."

"You said you'd tried other things. I guess you haven't perfected the art of blowing up buildings yet?"

"Please. We could really use you."

Could she do it? Even if she didn't kill anyone herself, she'd be enabling operations that were more cavalier with human lives. When the Libertists had bombed a Harbor building with people in it, adolescent Trez hadn't known how she felt. Santorini and Morrison had told her that people dying was an unfortunate accident, and she'd accepted it at the time, though something had still felt off. She didn't want to be responsible for others dying anymore. Maybe that's why she'd lost her edge.

She wasn't in a position to dictate terms, like checking if someone was in a building before demolition commenced. Even if she got that promise from Santorini, would everyone abide by it? Trez took a deep breath and changed the subject. "Where are you hanging out?"

"I'll tell you more if you join us," Santorini said. "Sorry. Professional courtesy."

"I'm surprised you don't already have someone doing my job, if you have the resources you've been hinting at."

Santorini looked over at some of the pigeons, who had decided to fight over something, if the squawking was anything to go by. "Independent Runners exist. Independent Corp-trained infiltrators, not so much. We'd prefer not to settle for less experienced operatives."

"You're asking me to completely upend my life. This is insane." Trez tried to keep her voice even. She kept making sure her breaths were deep enough. She didn't want to feel anything.

"I know." Santorini shifted. "But we would both benefit from it."

"I would need time to think about it. I may be in a situation where I couldn't do you much good." There, give herself an out. She stifled a frown of uncertainty. She would need time to actually think about what was going on here, without looking at Felicity, without the sound of her voice.

Shit. She would confide in Jenna or Eric, but she didn't want to answer all the questions about her past. What could she tell them? Did she want to tell them anything? She had to think for herself first.

"I understand. You understand, however, the sooner you decide, the sooner we can work on getting your records erased."

"All right. I'll ... contact you if you give me another private key."

Santorini beamed Trez the key from her wrist-comm. Trez couldn't tell if she was disappointed. Well, what did the lady expect? Just show up and get welcomed and Trez would throw the life she'd built away?

"How is your father? Aside from the obvious?"

"I would think the obvious is enough to take up his entire life." Maybe he'd forgiven Santorini for leaving and saddling him with Trez. He'd never complained about her ma.

"If you see him ... you can tell him you saw me. But that might be too dangerous. He might do something foolish with that information."

Santorini was right, Pa wasn't exactly reliable. "I won't tell him." She didn't know how she'd explain this to Linus anyway.

"Thank you for hearing me out," Santorini said.

All the graciousness in the world wouldn't make Trez feel more at ease. "I gotta go. I'll talk to you later."

Santorini waved, but made no move to leave the pier.

Instead, she watched a seagull dive-bomb the group of pigeons. They scattered.

————————

Trez managed her brisk walk away without looking back. But from the way she felt, she thought she'd need to burn off some of her anxiety before she headed home. She kept her eyes on the ocean to orient herself and followed the coastline. She counted her breaths, keeping her stride slow and deliberate.

Rocks dotted the coast, either to shore up the land or for decorative purposes. The dock floodlights made the minerals in them glint. At one inlet she saw a moss slick floating on the water's surface. A flock of gulls landed on an assortment of buoys. She was far enough away that she couldn't hear their bird calls though.

Trez replayed the conversation with Santorini in her head. Despite her efforts to keep her mind clear, questions assailed her. What kind of impression had she made? Should she have said anything differently? Santorini had seemed to take her seriously.

Did Santorini really believe they could work together again? That she could simply resume their relationship and have everything be like she'd never severed it? That she could crook her finger and Trez would jump to obey?

Maybe she should have rejected Santorini's offer flat out. But even the thought of saying no had made her chest tighten in anxiety. What if Santorini had tried to persuade her to reconsider? Her thoughts had been jumbled enough that she doubted she could commit to a decision in the face of that.

By default, Trez still wanted to do whatever Santorini said.

Old habit. Even if she didn't want to get tangled up in those feelings again, even if she didn't want to desire Santorini's approval, the desire still tugged at her. She didn't have much practice saying no to that voice.

Since they were no longer talking, Trez allowed herself to think of Santorini as her mother. It had been as awkward a mother-daughter reunion as she'd anticipated. They didn't know how to talk about their feelings with each other. At least there hadn't been any tears. Neither of them were normally watering pots, but Trez knew she didn't have the best handle on her emotions the past few months. Old anger stirred and beat in her pulse. She still couldn't forgive her mother for leaving her behind all those years ago.

Her stomach roiled inside. She needed to run somewhere, anywhere, until she no longer felt like punching something. She activated her in-ear implant and connected to her comm. She turned on one of her favorite old Dinoroid Dana audiocasts, an exposé about the pirates in Providence and the city's history of organized crime. Maybe the Makos were an offshoot of the old Providence mobsters. She didn't know if it was true, but it did sound plausible.

She ran until she got shin splints. Then she kept running, feet thudding into the ground, until endorphins kicked in and she didn't care about the pain. Someone catcalled her at one point, but their words didn't register.

Half an hour later, she tired and had to slow down. The atmosphere reeked of stale hydrocarbons instead of fish guts. When she got her bearings, she found her feet had taken her to the neighborhood she'd lived in right before Santorini left her.

The two of them had lived in Morrison's apartment. It

beat living with the squatters on the outskirts of the city. He'd inherited it, so they didn't need to pay rent or register as tenants. His family had some money, so he'd gotten in-person schooling instead of at-home stimsense and reading. Morrison had studied journalism after his grade school, and he'd become a big fan of Dinoroid Dana. He had shown young Trez the *Fake Tales and Other Dignities* long vid, and she'd become a Digger herself.

Trez wondered who lived in the building now. The city must have rezoned it; now there was an appliance repair shop on the ground floor. The sign said "Scolides." A Fairchild subsidiary then. She turned around to see several bars across the street grouped together. Their concrete façades had murals or graffiti on them. They'd faded enough that she couldn't tell which. Her throat was dry. She briefly thought of going into one of them, but she didn't want to risk being around other people. Someone might want to talk to her, and she didn't have the wherewithal to deal with social conversation right now.

She'd tired enough that anger didn't haze over her mind anymore. Ma's offer to erase her criminal record in exchange for Trez joining the Libertists—how would that even work? Santorini was a pretty good judge of talent, and she didn't exaggerate. If she said this Runner she'd recruited could make Trez's criminal record disappear, Trez believed it.

Harbor would likely keep tabs on her if she up and quit. If they connected her to the Libertists, she'd likely end up serving several life sentences for insurrection and conspiracy. She'd need to keep as low a profile as possible and pretend everything was normal. Santorini's Runner could cover up Trez's participation in any operations. But the skills she would probably employ for the Libertists were rare. There were only a hundred active strikers in all of Portland, and several hundred more retired ones.

With property damage would come police investigation. She would have to be careful with her words. Random details could implicate her or arouse suspicion, like when she would be away from home. Harbor could look at the apartment building's security damage.

She couldn't tell Eric or Jenna about working with the Libertists. They wouldn't sell her out, and that would mean they could get labeled as accomplices and face criminal charges if she were ever caught. Jenna had a spouse and a toddler, and she was the income provider in their family. Trez didn't want the kid to grow up with their parent incarcerated. And Eric had worked hard to get to his current level at Harbor. Even if he was found innocent, his career would go nowhere. But she was thinking too fast and borrowing trouble.

Trez started to walk again, beginning to head home. She played another Dinoroid Dana audiocast, one she hadn't heard before, to distract herself. Every person on the street has a story, Dana claimed. One just had to dig—sometimes in places that nobody would guess, sometimes places where it hurts the subject, or even you. This series was called *Millions of Stories in the Naked City*. Today's subject was a municipal worker in Philly who ran a side business creating obstacle courses for squirrels, charging for tickets. All to feed their old currency-collecting habit.

What would her story be about, if she was one of Dana's subjects? Probably not bizarre enough for that though. She left the audiocast on but didn't pay close attention to the contents. Dana's patter made her feel less lost, even when Trez didn't know what was actually being said.

What would working with her ma and the other Libertists

be like? Decades ago, Trez had been the errand girl, the courier, the odd-jobs person. She'd answered only to Santorini, and she rarely had needed to work with anyone else.

She'd liked Morrison, but Morrison was dead. She was acquainted with Levin, but they'd never warmed to each other. They'd recruited a Runner, some muscle, and probably some energetic young people with big eyes and the desire for the world to be simple and make sense. This time, instead of the gofer, she'd be one of the most valuable people in the org. The idea didn't give her pleasure. She'd have to cooperate with the hotshot hacker and impressionable kids.

She'd never learned how to work consistently with the same set of people. A strike "team" consisted of a striker, a Runner, and their handler. They all signed up separately for strikes, so the personnel changed almost every strike. The handler's job was to evaluate and mix the data and physical security situations she got from each of them, so Trez had rarely needed to communicate with the Runner.

Trez tried to visualize a typical operation working with the Libertists. She couldn't picture any future for herself that wasn't a black abyss. She'd been trying to live a day at a time for long enough that thinking ahead made her break into a cold sweat. She removed her jacket. A mix of feelings continued to assail her, tangled enough that she couldn't identify all of them.

Her head pounded. Meeting with Santorini had taken all of her emotional resources, and the run had exhausted her physically. She should make her way home and rehydrate and take a caffeine tab. She should also eat, but nothing seemed appetizing.

Her apartment was not a long walk away, so she took it

slow, procrastinating her arrival home. It would feel emptier than usual. She should call Jenna or Eric, just to hear their voices. She needed to keep Santorini's offer a secret from them, but she could manage that for now. Even if she found the weight of her secrets getting heavier every day.

THIRTEEN

Eric got a comm from Trez while he was poring over security logs and trying not to get distracted by dirty thoughts about her. He picked up instantly. As soon as he saw her name.

"Hi. I, uh . . . I just called to hear your voice."

He couldn't help smiling in response. "You're hearing it now. Anything you'd like me to say? Something in French? I'm out of practice, but I can try."

"Oh." Her voice sounded a bit higher than usual, flustered. "Just . . . I don't know. How are you doing?"

"I'm all right. Tu es merveilleuse juste comme tu es."

"What does that mean?" She sounded puzzled. He'd meant to flatter her, but now that felt awkward. He didn't want to sound like he was making fun of her.

"It's a compliment. I'll let you look it up."

"All right." She paused. "Did I catch you at a bad time?"

"Nah, it's nothing. Your calling is a welcome distraction." She sounded worried. He wanted to see her and see if it was true. "Hey, what are you up to?"

"I was taking a walk out by Lunts Corner. Heading home now."

"That's not far from here. If you want to hear my voice, you can do plenty of that if you head over." He kept his tone light, so she wouldn't feel pressured.

"You're free?"

"I am now." Oof. Maybe that was laying it on too thick.

She didn't call him on it though. "Okay, I'll see you soon."

When Trez arrived at his apartment, she went straight to his armchair and plopped down.

"Something on your mind? Other than the usual fear of going to prison and your foolish dad starving without you?" he asked.

She lifted her face to meet his eyes and their mouths almost touched. She exhaled, her breath warm against his lips and then drew back. "Augh. What are we doing?"

He smiled. "Following up to the interlude in the sparring room, I hope." He touched her nose briefly with an index finger.

"This isn't a good time—"

"Will there ever be a good time? I think you could use me now more than ever." He wasn't sure exactly when he'd decided he wanted Trez as a fixture in his life, but the idea of regularly working off his work stress with her had become his go-to fantasy. Sometimes he daydreamed of coming home all stove-up and grumpy, and she would hold him and try to get his jokes. The second part was a more dangerous fantasy. "Seems my problems are tied to your problems. We're already intertwined, no going back there."

She didn't dispute that, so he laced his fingers with hers. Sacrament, the woman had a grip. She'd been able to hold on to the wall when she rode him. Awareness of the pressure of her ankles on the outside of one of his registered. He placed his free hand at her collarbone and traced the line of her top. Eric hooked his fingers in and caressed her an inch lower, ghosting over her skin. She stared at his hand as it moved.

She started, then shook her head once she realized his intent. "Wait, what? You think sex is going to solve anything?"

"Nah, but we'll feel better afterward. Then I'll get dinner and we can do our best to relax."

"Are you fucking serious? I mean—yes, no, ugh!" She frowned, but she didn't stop his fingers from tracing patterns over the top slopes of her breasts. Convenient that the green material was rather giving. "What if—"

"What if we're as awesome together as we were last time? Then we'll just have to repeat the experience as much as possible."

Her voice rose in pitch. "I can't commit to fucking anything until this nightmare is over. You know that. Don't make me hope for things when I don't know if I can wade through this mess."

"I'll make no bones about it. I want a more permanent arrangement, but we'll take it as it comes." Calm settled over Eric. She was worth the risk. They were, together. He couldn't get this feeling from a promotion or more creds. His relationships before had always taken a backseat to his career. Was he getting old? "As for hope, seems to me it's a feeling you could use more of." He smiled and shrugged. "You can always hope we have sex again." He got a dirty look for that. "Just enjoy me for now," he said. He realized he hadn't gotten a clear confirmation from her. "At least, if you can enjoy me. I wouldn't want this to be one-sided."

She traced the contours of the outside of his arm. "I'm okay, Eric." She closed her eyes.

"Good," he muttered. He could have waited, but he'd really rather not. He inhaled a scent coming off her skin—some kind of fake cucumber mixed with something warmer. "Is that a yes?"

He waited for a moment. Her breath came a bit faster, and her heart thudded against his fingertips. He didn't think he'd overplayed his hand, but dread pooled in his stomach anyway.

"Yeah," she said. She was a bit quieter than usual. Well, if she changed her mind, he'd stop. Much as it would suck, he'd stop. He had all the time he needed to warm her up. Last time had been far too quick.

Having solidified her decision, she was staring at him with naked hunger, but she didn't move. He moved his hand up to where her neck met her shoulder, caressing lightly there before tracing the outline of her ear. Her hair tickled his knuckles. "Now, what would you like?"

She licked her lips and he felt an answering tug in his groin. She swallowed. Watching someone's throat had never gotten him going before. "Kiss me."

"Facilement." He kissed her smooth neck first, making little nips as his mouth traveled up and over to her lips. She continued to stay eerily still. He took her mouth gently this time. Now that he'd figured out how they fit together, he could do it with more finesse. Her mouth parted and he kissed her even deeper. Her response was hesitation, so he didn't try to speed things up. He continued to lightly skate his mouth over hers, switching angles to see if anything could unlock her sudden tentativeness.

Eric lifted his head. Her eyes were big and bright, and she didn't close her mouth. "You all right?"

"Don't stop," she whispered.

He didn't cheer in triumph, because that would be tacky.

Instead, he went back to kissing her, then slid his hands under the back of her shirt and spread his fingers wide. She was all supple muscle here but for the indentation of her spine. "Off?" he asked.

Trez smiled and raised her arms. He inched the top up with care and fumbled at the sides to unfasten the supports. She didn't try to help him. He'd never seen Trez so passive, and it was a bit worrying. She kept eating him up with her eyes though. He pushed her shirt up and off then put one hand on her shoulder before using the other to cup a breast. Her skin pebbled under him and he looked up to see her still watching him, her face tight with need.

He urged her to lie down by pressing back on one shoulder. Then he lowered his mouth to her chest, kissing her sternum first. She gasped. "You like that?" he asked, looking back at her face.

"Please," she said. She watched him closely, so he kept his head tilted up, meeting her gaze as he laved one of her breasts with his tongue. Trez made a little noise at that, so he redoubled his efforts. She was such a beguiling combination of smooth strength and soft skin, decorated with her scars.

"I'm wearing too many clothes. Help me out." He put her hands on the hem of his top and she complied, causing a moment of awkwardness when she tugged and the fabric caught on his chin. He had to take his hands off her for her to finish the job. He grumbled and he thought he heard a short laugh. Good.

She hugged him to her then, her arms wrapping around him. "Don't leave me," she said.

With her bare against him, he thought he could feel her heartbeat. His was thudding hard in answer. She didn't let go, digging in with the pads of her fingers. Fuck. He liked the threat of her nails too much.

Eric shifted so he was lying over Trez. Her hands went to his slacks, palming his ass as she eased them down. The waistband got caught on his erection and he had to shift his hips to help her get his pants off. She squeezed his thighs, and he clenched his jaw.

"Yes." She pulled him up against her, lining up her body under his to press against it. He needed to feel her skin now, so he pushed her slacks off, following each inch he uncovered with his mouth. She was panting and making more of those little noises.

A contented hum came when he discarded her pants and she pulled him back up to her mouth. He resisted a bit, wanting to put his mouth on her thigh, but she put enough strength in her wordless request that he complied and kissed her. The heat of her body was distracting. He thrust his hips against her involuntarily. She harrumphed into his mouth and he laughed back into hers. That was a new, exotic sensation—sharing a joke that way. Tenderness tempered his desire.

All that strength, that resilience . . . He could lie full weight on her and they could fuck each other as hard as they cared to and be none the worse for wear. This was an advantage to hotsyncing with other enhanced people. He didn't have to be too careful with their bodies and they could both just be masses of hammering flesh and yowling. But right now he wanted to take care. He let his hands explore her sides while the rest of him lay still on her. They had time, and he could savor the burn of unfulfillment. The anticipation made him harder and their combined musks sharper.

"Please," she said in between kisses.

"Please what?"

"Argh. Touch me."

Eric thought of telling her that he was touching her, but she likely wouldn't be amused. He pushed his hand between them to her pelvis. Was she ticklish? It was her turn to buck against him involuntarily, and he smiled. He found where she was wet and explored with his hand. He hadn't had a chance to do this last time.

Experimentation informed by the inarticulate sounds she made told him what she wanted right now: a firm circular palm on her clit and teasing fingertips on her outer folds. It was a little awkward with his arm trapped under him, so he sat back on his haunches. Trez took that cue to grab him and his eyes rolled back. Apparently she wasn't in the mood to tease. "This how you want it?" he asked when he could connect his speech centers again.

"Slow and hard," she said, tugging. "But first, I want to do this." She leaned forward and caught him with her mouth. He felt his muscles go slack as she licked him then engulfed him with her mouth and sucked hard. Sacrament de tabarnak. She obliterated any thoughts he had on his plans for her. He didn't know how long he lay mute, breathing hard, at the mercy of her mouth and her hand on his hips while the other traced in between his legs, pressing up against his perineum.

Trez released him before he reached the point of no return and guided his hand down to her crotch. "Feel what that did? I'm ready." He felt giddy. He'd been worried at first by her passiveness, but she was most definitely with him now.

Eric traced her lips, learning the different textures of her flesh. "Lie back." She scrambled back onto the couch so they wouldn't fall off, and he spread her thighs apart to get a good look at her center. "Beautiful." She laughed, and that made her belly quiver. "Don't agree?"

"I don't . . . I guess I'm not one to know the aesthetic merits of different women's parts down there." When he looked up at her face, it was free of strain. That felt like his greatest achievement in years.

"I have special equipment that tells me you are," he said, deadpan.

"Your brain?"

"More or less." Trez lay back, smiling, naked and open to him. Eric didn't think he'd ever seen anything more beautiful. He pressed a kiss to her center and she gasped. Emboldened, he used his mouth to lick, suck, and kiss around her clit while she made those noises again. Suddenly, she went still, then her body seized. He had to hold her in place to continue ministering to her while she cried out her release.

She lifted her head. "Please."

Eric grinned wide enough that his face felt odd. He kissed her thigh. "Please what?"

"Please now."

"Now what?" Teasing her never got old.

Trez sat up, her eyes wide and a bit wild. Her hands went to his shoulders and he felt the sting of her nails. "You are horrible."

"I just made you come," he noted.

She pressed her lips together. "I will end you." She easily hauled him up against her. Her belly ground into his arousal.

"I look forward to it," he said between kisses. She circled her hips, angling them underneath him so that she lined up with him, and his eyes slid shut. Dieu. She was still wet and soft against him there, and he couldn't wait any longer without killing off brain cells. He lifted his hips and pushed into her slowly until he was fully seated.

That moment was one he'd remember for a long time. He savored her closed eyes and slightly open mouth, the press of her inner thighs around his hips. All her senses opened. He slid out of her partially and thrust back. "You said slow and hard?" She nodded.

This was the kind of sex that he had to be fully present in, absorbed in her, in his movements, concentrating on her responses. He didn't know how long he could do this, every sensation skittering down his spine urged him on faster, but he held on. More pleasure for her that way.

One of Trez's hands drifted between their bodies and she stroked herself, the sensation causing her to tighten around him. Tabarnak. There was no way Eric could last like this.

Her hands and the flutters of her muscles around him brought him over the edge. It was his turn to scream, or at least make some sort of animal noise as he became one nerve, one exploding star. He was aware of her coming beneath him as his vision went white. The clasp of her legs, arms, and sex hard as she squeezed everything he had—thoughts, senses, come—out of him.

He panted for a few seconds as her grip eased and the fog cleared from his head. Had he been a bit rough? "You okay?"

Razor-sharp nail tips tested his shoulders again. "You ended?" Her words were soft and warm with pleasure, and her limbs were still wrapped around him.

He had to laugh. "Fin. For now." He lifted himself off her, and she made a little moan of protest. Encouraged, he rolled onto his side, flush against her body.

"I won't break," she muttered.

"I know."

"Heavy bone and muscle weave."

It wasn't only each other's bodies that they could break. He shoved that thought away. "Maybe I want to look at you again," he said, trailing his fingers up her bare side.

"Fine." She turned her head to him and narrowed her eyes.

It was just short of petulant, but it somehow struck him as funny. This was the afterglow he'd wanted—not frantic, instinctual, and through a haze of adrenaline. Sometimes working for your pleasure made you realize what it was worth.

FOURTEEN

Eric disengaged himself from Trez and went into his bedroom. When he returned, she'd burrowed her head into the couch. He tossed a blanket at her. She reacted by tussling with it in surprise until she figured out what it was. She tucked it around herself and peered at Eric. "This your way of saying you don't want me to put clothes on?"

"Thought you might get cold while I made dinner."

"I get to lounge on the couch while you prep?"

"Unless you want anything fancy." He was feeling magnanimous, but all the generosity in the world wouldn't improve his cooking skills.

She yawned. "Guess I don't feel much like going out."

"It's a cube night then. I'll also make dessert if you want it." He pulled his pants back on and whistled while he went to the counter.

The dehydrated cubes were easy to cut, heat, and prep. He could watch her shift around, all sleepy and cute, while he plated the food.

"I should put my clothes back on before eating," she said.

"Why? I like the view." He waggled his eyebrows.

"Because I'm cold, like you said." Trez sounded as if she might fall asleep before dinner. Well, he'd let her rest once he got some food in her.

"Blanket's not enough? Fair." The thermostat didn't go above fifteen; he hadn't paid for that feature.

She dressed and made her way over to the table with the blanket wrapped around her. She brought up a private screen on her comm. Maybe she didn't feel like talking right now. He didn't want to press her, so he pushed the food in front of her and waited for her to notice. When she did, she ate absently.

His doortone buzzed. Who would— Sam must be letting herself in downstairs. Of all the times to stop by . . .

"Who's that?" Trez asked.

"Just Sam. Ignore her."

Her brow furrowed, but she looked back at her comm. "If you say so."

Samantha opened the door. Eric wondered what impression she was getting from finding him shirtless with Trez here. Probably the right one, he concluded. Her hair was scrabbled back in a brown ponytail, and there was a smudge of grease or dust on her neck. There had no doubt been more on her apron. She'd come directly from work then.

"Yo," he said.

"Bonsoir." Sam kicked off her boots, which had gray spatters on them. Eric didn't think those were for fashion. Her jacket had dark patches on it, and one of the sleeve cuffs was fraying. She tended to dress drably at work to save money, and because work clothes would get easily ruined. "Oh, hey. You're . . . Trez, right? Eric talks about you."

Trez looked up from her display and blinked. "Uh . . . yes. And you're Sam."

Sam looked up and down Trez. "Ah . . . yes. Keeping Eric company?"

"You could call it that," Trez replied. It sounded more like a question. She avoided eye contact with Sam.

Time to step in. "What are you here for?" Eric asked.

Sam hung up her jacket. "Left some tools here. Thought I'd pick them up."

"Go ahead." Eric got up from the sofabed and followed her to the guest room. She stored a lot of random art supplies in the closet.

Sam poked around a bit before moving some boxes out of the closet. She unearthed a container at the bottom and set it aside. When she opened it, Eric saw an assortment of implements: knives, spatulas, brushes, screwdrivers, wrenches, all-in-one multitools. He'd never been able to figure out why she needed multiple all-in-ones.

Sam took out several knives and spatulas then winced. "Tabarnak de câlice. These are old and dull. Well, guess I'll use what I've got until I get the little bastards working again." She put the tools aside. "You got a bag I can borrow? Wasn't quite expecting needing one today."

"Yeah, there should be a few in there somewhere." Probably, anyway. Somewhere buried in all his random shit.

Sam muttered a string of sacres while trying to root around in the boxes. There wasn't much space for her to maneuver.

"Get out of there, I'll find it," Eric said.

"No, I've ... ostie ... got it," she said. She had wedged herself into the closet. "I think I see one."

"Suit yourself." Sam didn't like accepting help from him, especially when she considered it trivial. But it wasn't like it was any trouble for him to lift and move and balance the heavy stuff.

"Tea before you go?" he offered. It would help with the damp chill outside.

"Good idea." She placed her supplies in the bag then followed him back into the common room. Trez was fidgeting with a mug. Sam helped herself to tea and leaned on the counter opposite Trez. Trez looked up at her, eyes darting back and forth. Eric didn't remember the last time he'd seen her that nervous. Was she worried what Sam would think?

"Did you find it?" Trez asked, her voice a little hesitant. He shouldn't find her awkwardness so adorable.

"Ah, yes. Needed to find my spare tools." Sam took a swig of tea. He was never sure how she did that when it was still hot.

"All of them?" Eric asked. How many tools had she broken at work today?

"Almost. Enough that I'll need to replace my spare supplies again."

He thought about possible ways to get Sam more liquid creds so she wouldn't have to worry, but he didn't make any offer in front of Trez. "Did something happen?"

"Ugh, yeah." Sam put her tea on the counter. "My tools got iguana-ed."

Eric took a moment to rack his brain. "Iguana-ed? Like, as in the lizard?"

"Not real iguanas. Robots. It's the installation I'm working on." Sam sighed.

"Robot lizards? That could be fun," Trez said.

Eric vaguely remembered discussing Yavis's project with Sam at the gala. "Oh. Now I remember. Something about architecture and interactivity." He tried his best to remember the details of Sam's work, but art concepts usually sounded like bizarre practical jokes to him.

Sam uncrossed her feet. "Right. These little putains are robot lizards that have full navigation and climbing capabilities. They're programmed to interact with unpredictable elements."

Trez inclined her head. "Why iguanas?"

"Fucked if I know," Sam said. "Maybe because they're funny looking. Yavis said it's important they be unique. So not only are they funny looking to begin with, they have to each be designed a little differently. Both aesthetically and behaviorally. We're supposed to demo them as a feature in some Bangor races. There's a new investor who wants to spice the races up. Make betting more interesting."

Eric noted Trez was still watching his sister intently, as if Sam could strike at any moment. The idea was preposterous; Sam was full organic and had no combat training.

"Cheaper than adding more demolition elements to the track?" he theorized.

Sam made a moue. "The iguanabots are supposed to be able to grip the karts. So they adhere to what the karts are made of—titanium anodized alloy. Unfortunately, lots of sculpting tools are made out of the same metal." Sam hefted her bag. "Anyway, all my tools are currently occupied by iguana."

Trez squinted at her. "Occupied?"

"Well, I need to sculpt the iguanas to customize them, right? Problem is that the robots think my tools, especially the blade edges, are karts." She blew on her bangs. "Getting the fucking lizards off the tools so I can actually use them takes hours. And it's crunch time."

He picked up one of the knickknacks she'd left in the house and brushed the dust off it. "Won't your spare set have the same problem?"

Sam grimaced. "I'll try coating these tools with other metals and try to make do. I think we can still get it done by launch."

"When's that?"

"Ten days from now." Sam wiped at her cheek. "If we work fourteen-hour days, we can probably run a few test races and calibrate some of the settings. If I have to work overtime to fix iguanas physically and tweak their inputs a lot, well, I've dealt with worse."

"I hope you're successful." Trez's attempts to sound optimistic fell flat.

"You'll get exposure either way," Eric said. "If you can spin the publicity right, maybe you can do something about it if things go south."

"I'm not sure I have those kinds of political skills." Sam shrugged. "But I don't know what the audience will think. I don't think most race spectators are art critics."

"Where are you showing?" Eric asked. He only knew of a few tracks.

"Up near Presumpscot. We're not live yet though."

Eric couldn't contain his mirth. "Hah! Staplehead will probably be a fan of your work then." Both women looked at him, brows raised.

"Is Staplehead what he actually goes by? Or is that another of your crank nicknames?" Sam asked.

"I call him that, but mostly in my head," Eric admitted.

Sam snorted. "That's got to be an interesting story."

"Pretty simple. He has obvious staples on his scalp. Or he did last I saw." Eric tapped the equivalent spot on his own head. "I'm guessing he ran out of funds for surgery at a cut-rate chop shop. Or he's a poseur aping the actually dangerous thugs. Even odds."

"You're rather judgmental of a stranger's aesthetic choices." Sam narrowed her eyes at him.

"Why do you care about my opinion of some mobster? You're not giving me the benefit of the doubt," he said.

"Course not. I know you too well." She turned to Trez. "If I remember right, you could kick his ass all the way into his thick head."

"Uh." Trez opened her mouth then shut it.

"I saw one of you strikers working a few weeks ago and it was not an experience I'd care to repeat. You're all supposed to be super ninjas. If you got the drop on him, you could totally take him, size difference or not."

"Well . . ." Trez sat with her shoulders braced. She didn't look at either of them.

"You should do it. He deserves it sometimes," Sam said.

"What?" Trez's voice rose and she blinked. "Why would I . . . ?"

"Do it for me, because I sure can't," Sam said.

This was not a time he was glad to have a sister. "Sure, give me all you got," Eric said. He didn't think Trez would actually try to damage him.

"Uh, I . . . I don't really go around . . . Fuck." Trez cut herself off. Seemed she realized that she in fact did go around kicking people's asses because someone thought they deserved it.

"When he least expects it," Sam instructed. "Then you take him down a peg or five."

"Five?" Eric protested. He knew his attitude needed work, especially when he was tired, but he wasn't sure how much Sam was joking.

"At least," Sam said. She put her cup in the sanitizer and picked up the bag with her tools in it. "Thanks. We'll catch up again later. Probably after this lizard race project premieres." She tugged on her boots.

"Don't let the door hit you on your way out," Eric said.

"Hardly. Have a good one." She waved as she left.

Once the door shut, Trez relaxed in her chair. "I've been

meaning to ask. You have an entire room for your sister? That's generous of you."

"She used to live here, actually. The landlord hasn't raised the rent much over the past ten years, so it's still cheaper than market rate for a one-bedroom. And it's here in case she hits a rough patch and has to move back in."

"The decor is ... something else." She gestured to the wall opposite the futon. A big collage of paint, iron filings, and old-style photographs hung next to a vidscreen currently displaying nature photography.

"That's supposed to be the Taj Mahal. Sam was able to show it at a gallery for a while and got some interest from someone who later connected her to Yavis."

Upon closer inspection, Trez could make out a large domed structure. But only if she squinted. "I'm not sure I see the resemblance."

He laughed and walked to the back of her. "I don't dare show it to Gramma Rachna. She wouldn't be amused."

"I didn't know you're Indian."

"A quarter," he said. He nuzzled her shoulder. "Gramma was born in Montreal though, still lives there. She didn't come south with Maman, and I haven't visited her in ages."

"My ma's folks are in Chicago," Trez said. "We've never been close though. Linus's parents are local. They're doing all right, I think. He doesn't talk to them much. Grandpa used to be a musician. He played the guitar for a band called Happy Monday."

"Let's forget about grandparents and postmodern art for a while," he said. "We should cuddle some more instead."

She brought a hand up to his chin and caressed it. "You're demanding."

"What, you don't like good old-fashioned snuggling?" He pouted slightly.

Her fingers traveled to his lips and she tapped them lightly. "I haven't done that in ages," she admitted. "Okay, you're right, that does sound like a good idea."

He blew a kiss into her fingers. "That's me," he said. "Full of good ideas."

She stood and looped her arms around his neck. "But I'm lazy." Was she enjoying teasing him?

He put his hands on her waist and hoisted her up. "Luckily, I can work with that." He carried her back to the futon and then put her down gently before lying down flush against her. "This good?"

"Yeah," she said. "Better than good." She fell asleep within minutes, but he stayed awake longer, savoring the feeling.

FIFTEEN

The comm woke Trez from her nap. She took it without thinking, she'd already filtered out any senders she didn't need. Priority only. "Pa," she said. She saw herself in the video preview then realized she must look wicked tired. Too late. She'd turned on visual.

"Bee." He was smiling, but she could see the strain around his eyes. "What are you up to?"

This wasn't a usual time for him to check in with her. "Lazing about."

"Taking care of yourself?"

"Enough." She hadn't let Linus know about the strike at the gala. She spent the time since resting or talking to Eric.

"Your shoulder has a bad bruise."

"Some bumps and bruises are part of the job. There's a reason it pays thirty times more than chauffeuring for HarborSec."

"You didn't get hurt driving the execs around."

She had. But it had been easy to hide those from him. "I know you're unhappy with the way I support us, but I need a way to occupy myself. And I'm good at this." Chauffeurs often ended up doing some security duty. A few suits had recommended her for other positions in Security after she'd gotten them out of a scrape or two.

Linus didn't have anything to say to that. He furrowed his brow then frowned and looked away.

He needed some prodding, most likely. "How about you? Still enjoying Cape Elizabeth?" That came out with more bite than she'd intended.

Linus rubbed his palm through his bald spot. "Me and Steph, guess we don't see eye to eye on lots of things. I don't know how much longer I'll stay there."

Seemed like they were both bad at communication in all of their relationships. "Are you safe though?" It bore asking. He'd clammed up. Trez doubted his romantic difficulties were the entire reason for his comm.

"Ah, about that." His face turned even more grave. "I got a call from Withers's people."

Her stomach sank. Hearing Withers's name invariably made it do that. "What about? They must have gotten the last transfer. I got a receipt."

"No, they got it. That's not exactly what it's about."

"What was it then?" She picked up her book reader from her nightstand.

"They got to step up the payment schedule, they said." He continued to stare at a wall she couldn't see.

"What?" He couldn't mean what she thought he meant.

"Two hundred fifty grand this Friday, another two fifty next week."

Her fist opened. She heard a thud.

"The lady said something about external exigencies and that this would lessen the total amount due." Linus gave her a watery smile.

"Oh." She couldn't get her bearings. She couldn't think.

"I, ah, I don't got any ideas. Even if I try to find some work, I don't think . . ."

For that much liquid cash? She didn't have any valuable possessions to sell. "I don't know. I'll ask around." The Makos were the best source for less-than-aboveboard loans. But they were the ones she owed money to.

Trez closed her eyes. "I think I can do the first payment if I empty all my accounts. As for the rest, I'll look into it. Figure something out." She couldn't inflect her words.

He winced. "I didn't want to put this on you."

"I know." He meant well. Linus always meant well. She needed to sit. Where was her chair? She shuffled to her sofabed.

"Bee, I feel awful. I don't know what to do."

"I know." Her mouth tasted sour. How many times did they have to go through this? When she opened her eyes, he looked like he'd aged in the past few minutes.

He looked as sick as she felt. "I'm sorry, Bee." His voice sounded far away.

"I've . . . got work to do. Ta." Trez cut off the comm. Rude, but the news had ripped all her manners from her.

She logged in to HarborSec's strike postings. Letters and numbers swam before her, and she had to wipe her eyes to see clearly. There weren't enough listings. Mihai had taken the big Fairchild job this upcoming week. Could she beg him for it? She didn't want to make him curious. He'd always been competitive with her. No. She entered the waitlist for that assignment. She accepted two more unassigned jobs. Wasn't like the details mattered.

Her stomach roiled, and she doubted she'd be able to get

back to sleep. God. The first one was in two days. The medic had told her to take it easy. But what else could she do? She couldn't see any other options.

She should comm Eric. He deserved to know. He wouldn't like it, but he didn't have to. This was the only way forward.

———————

Eric paced across his office at least fifty times looking for a breakthrough in his investigation of the Miletus security incident before Trez commed.

"Ah-yeah?" He couldn't help smiling when he saw her.

She sat on her sofabed. "Hey." She rolled her shoulders back. "I've bad news."

"Well, I guess it's good to keep things interesting." He tried to sound optimistic for her sake.

"You'll be angry." She picked up a pillow and kneaded it. "Oh?"

"I signed up for a strike. Happens in two days."

He'd thought her wiser than that. "Trez, you're going to kill yourself like this. For what?"

She drew her knees up to her chin and shivered. "The Makos want their creds faster."

Sacrament de tabarnak. Ice formed in his gut. "How much?"

"Half a million. Half of that due Friday. Other half, end of next week."

He grimaced, closed his eyes, and thought about his last credit transfer to Sam. "There's got to be a way I can help." Shit, he should go over to her. Not like he was getting any closer to figuring out how the Libertists got into R&D 4.

"You have any ideas to make a quick few hundred thousand bucks?"

Not offhand. "Maybe not, but ... you're not recovered yet," he said.

"Doesn't matter."

"Didn't the medic say to take it easy for a few more days?"

Trez's voice rose. "Don't tell me what to do." The words were compact and clipped. "I already accepted some jobs."

"Hey," he said.

"No. There's nothing you can do." She'd withdrawn further into her curled-up position. He couldn't see her face.

"Don't shut me out." He wasn't sure whether he was commanding or pleading.

"Look, I at least commed you. Didn't fall off the grid." Now her voice was flat.

Eric remembered looking over her still body with the IV in it, her eyes closed and her hands clammy. He thought of her twitching and disoriented as she came down from the drugs. "I don't want you to do this."

"Look, I fucked you. That doesn't mean you're my keeper."

Ouch. Way to go for the gut. His jaw tensed. "Don't be like this."

Trez flinched and looked up at him. "You can't help me, okay? Just let me be!"

He had to find a place to sit. Figure something out. "Trez, don't—"

"Why don't you just leave?" Her voice was too hoarse to scream. Her face twisted again.

Her wretchedness defused his anger slightly. "That's not going to happen."

Trez punched her pillow. "I can't do this. Can't fucking—

I'm out of ideas and I don't want you to get fucked over by my problems."

"You've said that before, Trez. Trust me to handle my own worries, thank you much." Maybe he didn't have the power to do anything here that could solve her problems or make her happy. But he could at least be an adult about this. "Look, I'm not going to argue further about you doing your damnedest to kill yourself. But since you're committed, you can do me a favor."

"What do you mean?" Her head popped up, resting on her knees.

"Jenna's your handler, right?"

"You mean Jenna Garcia?"

"She can view your suit feed and comm with you while you're running a strike."

"Well, she talks sometimes. I don't really respond during a strike."

How best to phrase this? "I'd like to shadow her during your mission." He couldn't go with her on a strike, but he could be on standby. Ready to help if matters went south.

Trez's brows drew together in bemusement. "I don't know, that sounds ..."

"It'd make me feel a lot better." He rubbed his jaw. "It's not like we're violating any company policy."

"Well, you'd have to clear it with Jenna," Trez said slowly.

If Jenna had the authority to ax the strike, she would have shut it down already. Eric was pretty sure Jenna would welcome the help. "I think you should be the one to ask her. It's your strike."

"I guess." She looked down at her toes. "It's uncanny, having a handler. Nothing's private with all the feeds and the video I see later, and I know someone up higher monitors things, but knowing you'd sort of be there with me . . . feels strange." She was waffling.

"I've seen you during and after a strike. And more." He wasn't going to tell her this would make her safer. "Please?"

"You're right, but, I just . . ."

"Talk to Jenna. I'm going to get back to work." He didn't know if he could talk to Trez any longer without getting either maudlin or angry again.

"Bye." She closed the comm.

He exhaled noisily and rolled his shoulders. They made crunching sounds. He needed to let off some steam. There was an exercise room a few floors down. Shouldn't be too busy at this hour.

Eric grabbed his gear and took the stairs. The scale of money Trez needed . . . he definitely couldn't get that kind of loan. But there was always something someone wanted. Something that could be exchanged for money. He just had to figure out what.

He sparred with the dummy until his arms felt heavy. He wiped sweat out of his eyes. The Makos were fighting the Libertists. What resources did he have that they didn't? There must be a way to leverage those to save the woman he loved before she destroyed herself.

SIXTEEN

Trez looked up at the side of the edifice she was going to scale then checked her encounter suit monitors one more time. Her biometric data displayed all her vital signs as within operating parameters. She tested her Gauntlet then sent a ping to Jenna on that channel to verify the connection.

She'd had the nightmare again, the one where she found her mother and tore her face apart with her finger-blades. Trez almost hoped it was because her body hadn't cleared the pharma she'd taken on the previous strike yet. She'd called Doc Ten. He hadn't been sympathetic. Said she had to make do with some low-impact stims and painkillers. She'd thought about obtaining other chems, but Eric would probably make her regret it if she did that. He'd sent her a comm. So they couldn't disagree every sentence, she supposed. He'd said that he was there for her, but she couldn't afford to be sloppy; that'd just leave her stove-up and bankrupt.

The strike suit had gotten looser in some places and uncomfortable in others. She'd need to get it re-tailored if she was going to continue this line of work. That or eat more.

The building wasn't heavily guarded on the outside. She should be undisturbed until she could break into a window. She molded herself to the outside wall to get a feeling of its texture. The material was slightly porous. Trez attached her gecko grips to the gloves and boots on her suit. Once acclimated, she began to scale the concrete.

Tonight's target was Aliki Gunnarson. Executive vice president for strategy in Fairchild's manufacturing division. She was currently scheduled for a business lunch with an internal client. Her dossier said she had three dedicated guards with some experience.

Gunnarson may have a fancy title, but with that came a loss of control over her day-to-day life. Others scheduled her meetings for her, brought her food, decided how many children she could have and when. Her power was abstract; she made decisions that pushed ideas and credits around, changing their amounts and forms. Execs floated ten thousand meters up, high on attention-focusing chems and the size of their bank accounts.

Trez couldn't think of why she would want that job though. It seemed disconnected from everything. She may not be bettering society or realizing her ideals, but at least she had the satisfaction of violence. Sure, strikers got mentally numb to every blow whether given or received, but the physical sensations were still there and a small part of her savored them. Maybe that joy was animalistic, but it felt more real. At least, more so than the automated financial transactions that Gunnarson might get to tweak a few settings on once in a while.

Her shoulders burned as she progressed. Her muscles hadn't recovered from her last strike. Cost of getting older, she supposed. Every hurt lingered longer. Trez bit the inside of her cheek to stop herself from audibly swearing.

When she found the window, she extended her finger-blades. She carved a circle in the glass polymer. Her suit vented cool air as it tried to slow her heart rate down to normal.

The circle of glass fell into a room with a thud. Trez pitched herself through the window and rolled to her feet. She donned the Gauntlet on her left hand and triple-checked that it worked.

She'd need to climb a few floors indoors. The Runner assigned to this strike, Flaherty, sent her a real-time tactical map and confirmed that her cloaking was still up.

Flaherty hadn't found any heat signatures in the hallway, so her stairwell access was clear. She clamped her Gauntlet to the lock and followed the prompts on the screen. The door slid open, and she raced upstairs. Her footfalls echoed on the stairs despite her best efforts.

Four floors up, she exited to a featureless hallway. Her nav told her the breakroom's entrances were the fourth and fifth doors after taking the right turn at the end of the hallway. Six heat signatures in there. Flaherty had already hacked the doors; he'd open them on her signal. She administered the stims to herself as she advanced to her target.

She inhaled and took a moment to ground herself. Her helmet released the scent of lavender. The room's doorway whooshed open just before she barreled through it. Trez saw Gunnarson and three civilians seated diagonally from her around the conference table. The guards had been facing the door, and they froze for milliseconds before sounding the alarm.

She noted potential obstacles as she charged: heavy office furniture, supplies, the few other meeting attendees. The noncoms scattered and Trez leapt over the table, burning her actuators and unsheathing her arm-swords. The female guard interposed her body to catch Trez.

Trez abandoned herself to thousands of training exercises and muscle memory, going for gaps in the armor with her finger-blades. Her opponent wasn't as fast as Trez, but she wielded short batons that packed a decent wallop. After a few hits, Trez felt painkillers feeding into her body.

Incoming projectile chair. Trez managed to get most of herself out of the way, but her thigh caught some of the blow. She made eye contact with the guard. Even through the helmet, Trez could see brown eyes. She blinked and continued stabbing. Blood rushed through her ears noisily. The guard fighting her crumpled into her blows. She felt her arm-blades penetrate after some resistance. Someone screamed, and it echoed through her helmet.

The other guard took advantage of Trez's distraction, tackling her. They tumbled to the floor together, trading blows. She registered the impact of his knee to her helmet and sliced at him until he stopped moving. The screaming continued.

A persistent beep cut through the sound. She glanced around. No Gunnarson. The "ABORT MISSION" sign flashed on her HUD. The target must have gotten away, and Security had entered the building. Trez's vision swam with black fuzzy spots.

An escape route lit up on her map, back to the stairwell. She dashed out of the office, following the glowing blue line on her HUD. It took her up several flights of stairs. The painkillers were beginning to wear off. All her muscles burned, even the ones in her throat.

At the top of the stairwell, she stumbled and smacked into

the exit with her shoulder. She fell onto the floor. Jenna was saying something on the comm about someone waiting for Trez, but it was hard to hear her above the screaming. Why wouldn't it stop?

Her legs shook as she picked herself up, bracing her body weight against the exit door. She saw a person standing against the overcast sky. The person was coming toward her. She'd been waiting. *Felicity?* Trez limped over, her ears rang, and she collapsed in her mother's arms.

Eric caught Trez in his arms. She was whimpering, little agonized cries he hadn't heard her make before. "I got you," he said to Trez. He doubted she heard him.

When the awaiting copter's ladder unfolded, he slung Trez onto his back and levered them both up into the copter. Criss. He was almost glad when she slumped into unconsciousness, because her sobbing made his chest hurt.

"Gonna get us out of here first, then we can look at her." Jenna yelled to the back of the craft. Fairchild Security would be swarming the roof in short order.

Jenna only gave him a moment before the copter lurched up. He fumbled with the fasteners and secured himself, before fastening Trez to him with the belaying cord. He kept a close eye on her vitals during the flight.

Neither of them spoke until Jenna landed the craft. Trez twitched, but didn't wake.

"We should be out of pursuit range by now," Jenna said. "Get the medical kit."

"Should I get her out of the suit?" He didn't want to disrupt any of the suit monitors.

"Let's get the helmet off, at least," Jenna said. She found the strap and popped off the helmet.

Eric affixed several electrodes to Trez's head. "Adrenal fatigue," he read out. Well, he didn't need to be a trained medic to figure that out. "Water next?"

"You got it."

Eric got the hookup out of the kit. Jenna grabbed it and secured Trez's head, immobilizing it against the seat. She only took a second before plunging the needle into Trez's neck. Eric turned his head aside.

"Gah." Trez came awake with a sputter.

"Trez," Eric said. He felt his shoulders slump a little.

"What . . ." Trez blinked and then moved against her bonds a little. "What . . . where?"

Jenna held two fingers up. "How many fingers?"

"Ugh. Two? Ma?" Trez's body tensed. "Where's Ma?"

"What are you talking about?" Jenna looked at the aid readout again.

"Where is she? We were on the roof . . ." Trez went quiet. The echoes from the small craft made her voice sound breathy and hoarse.

Eric took her gloved hand with his. "I got you there, remember?" What the fuck was Trez talking about?

"She was waiting for me." Brown eyes, big with fright, focused on him. "After so long . . ."

Jenna wiped her palms on her pants. "Sorry to say this, but the only other person on that roof was lover boy here." Eric spared her a dirty look.

"She won't stop screaming," Trez confessed. Her eyes squeezed shut.

Eric and Jenna shared a long look. Had Trez flipped her gourd? "Honey, it's Eric. You're safe. You're okay. It's quiet."

Her eyes opened again, somewhere between luminous and glassy. "Eric? You . . . I'm so sorry. I can't. I . . ."

Jenna scowled at Eric while he shushed Trez. "Let's get her to medical."

"Noooo," Trez murmured.

Trez would be furious that he'd seen her like this. Funny, he'd taken care of her when she was tweaking, exhausted, wounded . . . but she'd probably see a mission failure and psychological meltdown as a new low. "Comm Menendez and tell him to expect us."

"You're assuming he doesn't already. But I'll order a stretcher." Jenna's hands went to her comm. "Secure yourself in again. Trez, hijo de puta. What the hell are you doing now?"

Jenna vaulted back into the pilot's seat, cursing more as she secured herself. Eric kept his hand in Trez's, his gloves wicking away his sweat. He cradled her cheek as they lifted off. "It's okay." Meaningless words, perhaps untruths. What else was he to say when he didn't understand? His gut churned. He was pretty sure her bosses would furlough her or relegate her to noncom duty.

If he could figure out what the Makos needed, or at least thought they needed, maybe he could give Trez some breathing room. Her future depended on it.

They landed with much less of a jolt this time. Jenna helped him haul Trez out of the copter to the waiting gurney. They belted her in and pushed her down a familiar route: to the medical wing and up an elevator. The halls looked empty to him. He didn't have to dodge any other doctors or patients.

When they rolled up to Menendez's wing, the medic barely glanced at them. "Bring her in," he said, taking some time to adjust his diagnostic display.

His lack of urgency baffled Eric. "Uh, where?"

"Next to bay four." He glanced up at Eric and Jenna. "She isn't in imminent danger, but we'll need to run some tests."

"Menendez, you aren't worried? Isn't this the third time you've seen her this month after a strike? Isn't there some kind of problem with that? Repeated traumas and all?"

"Traumas?" The medic swiped through his display holos. "This seems like a less severe case, although the patient isn't awake. Her injuries will need treatment. But again, there's nothing critical about her condition, and possibly nothing serious."

He turned back to Jenna and ran a hand through his iron-gray sideburns. "The usual pattern with these professional idiots," he waved at Trez and Eric both, "is that problems escalate. I would have expected some kind of overdose. But that isn't the case." He peered at Trez and began a manual scan. "Mm-hmm. Help me get her out of this contraption."

Eric began to unfasten one side of Trez's encounter suit. "You really don't think this is serious?" Removing Trez's suit revealed some ugly bruises. He'd seen her sustain worse injuries, but they still made him wince.

"The data you sent, the readouts I'm getting, and my own senses all line up," Menendez said. "I understand you're worried about Harris, but right now what she needs most is rest."

Trez made a tiny moan. She opened her eyes when Jenna placed a blanket on her. "Wha?"

Menendez nodded, satisfied. "Good, you're conscious now. I'm going to ask you a few questions."

Trez's eyes went wide, and her hands moved out from under the covers, seeking something. When she parsed that

Eric was there, she seized his arm and looked up at him as if to verify he was real.

"What's the last thing you remember before you woke up?" Menendez asked softly.

Trez gasped. "Oh God. Ma. Ma was ... Where is she?" she asked. "Did you find her?" Her finger-blades erupted and punctured Eric's arm. He hissed, more from surprise than pain. "Oh God," she said again, snatching her hand back and staring at the blood on her blades.

"I don't know what on God's gray earth you're talking about, but you're safe now," the medic said. "All right. You're in medical, Harris." He turned, opened some swabbing from a nearby kit, and handed it to Eric. "You're going to be fine. Thanks to not being chemmed out of your mind this time."

Eric frowned. "But ..." Something was still wrong. "Your diagnosis, doc?"

"I'd say shellshock, which I'm not qualified to treat. She'll need a psych."

Eric took his eyes off Trez for the first time since he'd found her on the roof. She shouldn't see that he was scared. Their future, if they had one, might have more nights like this—when he couldn't get any responses from her because she was locked in her own private hell.

"I can schedule the psych for her," Jenna volunteered. "Last time she didn't get around to it herself."

Trez made another weak sound and lay back down, leaving her hand on the side. She tilted her head up at Eric. He concentrated on cleaning his wounds.

"Get some rest," Jenna said, pulling up her covers and smoothing back Trez's springy hair. None of them spoke until her breathing evened out and the monitor indicated she was asleep.

"I don't anticipate any big problems, but given her recent history I'm going to keep her few more hours for monitoring. Then recommend she be put on medical leave for a good long while."

Eric tried to keep his voice even. "I can stay with her, if you think that'd help."

The medic nodded. "Good. If she gets too agitated, we can give her some aromatherapy." When Eric stared at him, not sure if he was joking, Menendez cracked a slight smile. "I wouldn't muck around with tranqs. She's taken more than enough of those in the past month."

"Who the fuck takes a heavy dose of tranqs when they're on a strike? Adding them to stims and hormones seems like it wouldn't be effective. Wouldn't it just make you feel like garbage?" Jenna said.

It wasn't Eric's place to give that game away. He was thankful that Menendez saved him from having to say anything. "These strikers, they'll try anything. And the rest of you in Corpfare, you're hardly any better." He waved dismissively and went back to scrutinizing his monitor. "I'll be on my rounds. You good to watch her?"

"Ah-yeah," Eric replied.

Jenna tapped him on the shoulder after the medic left. "I've work to get to, but comm me if anything changes." She smiled. "She's lucky to have you."

Eric snorted. "I wouldn't say she has the best of luck." Let Jenna take that however she wanted. She'd gossip anyway.

"Other strikers might start fucking up their jobs the same way if it got a side of beefcake to take care of them," she said.

"I don't think strikers lack for masculine attention."

"Or any other kind, come to think of it. You're right." Jenna shook out her hair and rolled her shoulders. "All right, I'm out. Let me know if things go south, like I said."

"Will do." He wasn't up for further conversation anyway. He stared at the Gauntlet on his lap for a long moment and began turning it over and over in his hands.

SEVENTEEN

"You're lucky I had a break in my schedule," Doc Ten said. "I know I said I wanted you to check in with me soon, but this is wicked short notice." He had dark circles under his eyes. They still didn't compare to hers.

"Well, I'm pretty flexible right now." Trez lay on the examining table. Looking at the holos on the walls made her dizzy. She closed her eyes.

"Hm." He raised her right arm, put pressure on her wrists. "Does this hurt?"

"Nah."

Ten continued manipulating her limbs and palpating her extremities, testing her range of motion and asking about discomfort. "Why all of this physical therapy?" she asked.

"I'm not a kinesiologist," he said, "but the substances you've been taking can cause muscle problems. Didn't you listen to that lecture?"

"Sure, but I didn't know that would mean you'd try to push my knee into my chest."

"I'm also checking for pain. I have devices for so much else, but pain, that's subjective." He grimaced.

"Well, everything hurts right now. Especially my head, which tends to drown the rest out."

Ten frowned. "Get me a urine sample and we'll go over your results together."

Trez went to the restroom. Her comm buzzed several times. Eric was calling. She ignored it for now.

When she emerged, she found Ten massaging his temples. "Here." She waved the sample in his face.

He started for a moment before he took the container from her. "Oh. Okay. Yeah. Got it." He deposited the container into his diagnostic equipment and brought up several diagrams and numbers on his comm.

Trez returned to the exam table. "You have my records?"

Ten's attention was on one of his diagnostic screens instead of her. "Yes. I'm putting it all together now. You're on leave at work, you say?"

"Until further notice. Staff medic's orders," she said.

"Sounds serious. What did they say?" She was thankful he didn't bring up any clown-related jokes, or asked what kinds of clowns had staff medics.

"Said I should get some rest, fluids, and go back in two weeks. I gave you the codes he put on my patient record." How risky would it be to tell Ten everything? He'd keep her medical privacy under normal circumstances, but what if he worked with the Makos? Or the Libertists? Or her rivals at work had found her out and paid him off? People did unwise things with information when they were desperate.

Ten frowned at his display. "You'd better follow your medic's orders," he said. "Though you probably don't have any intention of doing so because you're a dumbass and wanted to see me to see if I could keep you going somehow. Tell you that the first doc is wrong."

"I can't lie around for two weeks."

"The children can wait for their entertainment," he said.

Ugh. She couldn't summon her sense of humor right now. "I'm not paid while I'm grounded," Trez said. "I need the money."

"This where you tell me it's a matter of life and death?" He had the nerve to smile slightly.

"Thought I already did," she snapped.

He looked back up at her, eyebrows raised. "Look, I do take some parts of my job seriously. And I'm not going to do anything that I think will kill you. Your results are, well . . . let me verify . . . What did you take when?"

"Three days ago, some stims and painkillers." At least that's what she thought. She couldn't remember it very well, even though she hadn't used anesthesia.

"And before that?"

"The mix of tabs you called Pharma Cocktail A. The slower-acting one."

"I'd hoped adjusting the formula would tax your system less, but your kidneys are still working far harder than they should. Take a look at this." He projected his screen onto the wall.

There was a lot of red and bold text on it that she couldn't parse. She tried to focus on the screen, but only saw blurred splotches. "So . . . ?"

"I'm not prescribing you anything until you've flushed everything out. And your organs have recovered fully. Thank God I didn't give you extra formula." He shook his head.

He might as well have dropped an anvil on her chest. She doubted she could run another strike clean and succeed. And she didn't have enough time for psych rehab. She searched for words.

"Hey," he said, his voice softer. "I know you're in some kind of trouble that you can't tell me about. Or won't, anyway."

"Stop worrying about me. Worry about someone else instead," she said. Her voice came out in a monotone. Her personal fiasco wasn't really his business anyway. She paid him well, and he kept her going so she could pay others well.

"I wouldn't suggest trying to replicate the formula yourself by combining other drugs either," Ten said. "I never gave you the proportions of each chem. You're not a pharmacologist, and I'd bet you can't find another one that understands your situation who can see you anytime soon." He didn't sound snide or cynical. His voice stayed soft, which hurt more somehow.

She'd gotten this far by dealing with one thing at a time. When she tried to think ahead, she only saw a terrifying blankness. "So you won't do this anymore," she said. Her eyes were wet. She tried not to blink.

"I'm sorry, Kufo. I won't be responsible for your death."

She stood up too quickly and had to sit back down, putting her head between her knees. "That's that then?"

"My office is still open to you. But I'm not giving you any more enhancers or pharma cocktails until all your systems are functioning normally."

She rose again, this time bracing her hands on the chair. "Well then, that's everything. Goodbye." Trez paused a moment before she let herself out of the office. She didn't want to see Ten's expression. There might be some pity in it, and then she'd want to do violence. Even if it would be useless.

Once she left the building, she wiped her eyes and scanned her perimeter. Seemed safe enough, so she checked her comm. Eric had left a message: He could come to her apartment anytime to keep her company. She held her comm close to her chest. What was she going to do with him? She couldn't stop herself from wanting to hear his voice. Her mouth twisted.

What a fucking stupid time to realize she loved him. It should have made her smile. Instead, she muffled a scream. She felt her dread grow with every step as she approached the train station.

———————

Once Trez boarded the train, she zoned out. She missed her stop. And the next two. Instead of walking across the platform to take the train back, she walked. She could hear her heartbeat in her ears. Drizzle grayed out the sky and softened the edges of the cityscape.

Santorini's offer hung in the air, a possible lifeline. If she seized it, how would her life change? Could she hide it from Harbor? She would need to make as few changes as possible to her life to avoid arousing suspicion, but she should make sure she could disappear fast if she needed to.

Thankfully she didn't own a pet or many precious objects. There were a few gifts she kept for sentimental reasons. Tiny blue stud earrings from Linus. A stuffed bear from Jenna, named Howie. Her photography collage by Dinoroid Dana and her art print of a cybernetic dinosaur. She might have to leave the collage behind; it wasn't the easiest to transport. The idea made her chest ache, but she'd deal with the potential loss when or if the time came. She'd have to break her lease. But by that point, owing money on a broken contract wouldn't rank as one of her top ten concerns.

By the time she got to the pier, the drizzle had strengthened to heavy rain. It made the wood more slippery. She had to concentrate on her steps, on her balance. Keep her thoughts focused, to the here and now, to her body.

Trez plodded along until she found an unoccupied dock. Someone had spilled a large patch of polymer oil onto it. The smell of rotting seaweed combined with the chemicals made her head swim. She had to lean against a railing and look down at the choppy ocean. Mercifully, she didn't vomit.

Was joining the Libertists her only way out? She'd exhausted her alternatives. She couldn't get a loan without it showing on her employee record. She didn't have an "extraordinary circumstance" she could list to pull from her retirement fund. And her med leave was involuntary; she couldn't strike even if she felt up to it.

The building the Libertists blew up twenty years ago had been a Harbor building, so she very much doubted Harbor would be inclined toward leniency if the Makos exposed her past. The best she could hope for would be life in prison for her and Linus. If the Makos didn't decide to kill him to set an example for their other debtors, that was.

She had to cut Eric and Jenna loose. Eric especially. It would be better this way. She'd charted her own path for years, only to find herself alone and helpless. She couldn't rely on anybody else. Her mother had abandoned her and Linus had gotten himself into a mess that he needed her help to get out of. Eric would inevitably get tired of her baggage. Better she drove him away before he could leave her.

She commed him before she could second-guess herself, her hands shaking.

"Eric. I—" His image popped up. The waves made an incongruous background for the hologram. She'd caught him at the kitchen table, a slab of protein on his plate.

He smiled in greeting for a moment, then his face fell. "You don't look good. Everything all right? Have you eaten?"

She closed her eyes for several seconds, gathering courage. "I can't see you anymore."

His spork clanged on the table when it fell from his hand. "What?" His eyes narrowed.

"There's something I have to do." Her stomach sank further, which she hadn't thought possible. "I don't know what else to say. Thank you. For everything."

He blinked several times before he grimaced at her. "Wait, what? Seriously?"

Trez cut the connection. There was nothing else she could tell him. She tried to distract herself by looking for fish in the murky water. She'd forgotten her rainshield, and she sneezed from the dampness. She couldn't summon the strength to get out of the rain, so she rubbed her arms for a bit of warmth.

How did she really feel about Harbor? She'd observed coworkers and execs for years. Grunts, execs, and the glorified in-between that she fell into. They played their roles, filled their functions, as dictated by hierarchy. They had their jobs because their jobs couldn't be automated.

Harbor wasn't cackling and evil. The board of directors simply didn't think any further than what made their share price go up. She had no illusions that she was more than a numerical asset to them. Lots of her coworkers used their careers to give their lives meaning. She had tried that, but it didn't banish the feeling that she wasn't fulfilling her purpose in life. Unfortunately, she didn't know what her purpose was.

Corps qualified as persons, but they were incapable of empathy, unlike humans. The only reasons Corps did anything empathetic were for PR reasons. A pacified populace meant a more stable market. The Libertists didn't bother with abstractions like the market. Instead, they worked to realize their beliefs. That seemed a better purpose than indirectly making somebody's profits go up.

She needed to call Santorini and accept her offer. But not yet. What if she didn't like Yang, or any of the Libertists? That was fine, she didn't like any of her coworkers that much besides a few friends. But if she ended up disappearing from her apartment to live with them, she wouldn't be able to put her job aside when she wasn't actively working.

She didn't need to believe in the Libertist cause to work for them. It was a lost one anyway. Harbor had tanks and antiaircraft missiles, for anything's sake. The Libertists were risking their lives but Harbor probably saw them as bozos who'd happened to get their mittens on some dangerous toys. If they posed enough of an actual threat, the Big Three would simply crush them again. And probably do a more thorough job this time. So she was still going to be risking her life.

She tried to think of the upsides of working with the Libertists. She'd be more than a cog in a big machine. She'd be uniquely skilled. And she liked being around Santorini. Her mother had a way about her; she made people feel good about themselves. Harbor tried to make their employees feel committed to their workplace. Employee positivity seminars. Meditation rooms. Cocktail hours. None of them had made her feel cared for like Santorini had.

Trez felt the railing shift under her with extra weight. She started and looked to her side.

Eric stood beside her, his jaw set. He didn't move to touch her. He opened his mouth then shut it. He shook his head, perhaps rejecting what he'd been about to say.

"Eric?" How long had she been standing on the dock? "How did you find me?"

"It was a video call. And I could figure out which dock from the landmarks in the background." His voice was flat.

"Oh." She couldn't even give someone the kiss-off without mucking it up. Embarrassing, but nowhere near the top of somewhere she thought she should feel embarrassed, but that emotion was too far away right now.

He drew closer, so that his rainshield covered her. She was already wet, so she almost told him not to bother. But she was too exhausted to reject his presence. They stood in the rain, listening to the wind, the city noise from inland, and the vicious gulls harassing other birds.

"Something's bothering you. I mean, something new, something that I don't know about, is bothering you," Eric said slowly. Then he scowled. "You know better than to call a guy and dump him over the comm."

She hadn't wanted to do it in person because then . . . they would argue. She didn't want to argue. She wanted to make the break as clean as possible. He would be less likely to get hurt that way. "I can't see you anymore, I told you."

Eric winced. "Ouch." When he squeezed the railing, the metal flattened slightly.

"I . . ."

"No matter your reasons, ouch. I'm trying to be charitable here. I know you're going through a lot. But please." He opened his hands. "What's wrong? I'd like an explanation."

"It's nothing you did."

"I would say that's a relief, but don't give me that marde." His words were clipped, and he held his shoulders stiffly.

"It's safer for you this way." She regretted it as soon as she said it. The last person who'd said something like that to her had been Santorini.

"Really." His voice was quiet, but it came through his teeth.

He had every right to be angry. Trez didn't have any words to defend herself. She still couldn't let go of the railing. All she could do was wait for him to finish venting. Then he would go away and be safe without her.

He stood up from the railing, but made no motion to leave. "So you think I'm better off without you? You say something you're keeping secret is dangerous? You think I can't take care of myself? I'm an adult, thank you very much. Don't assess the risk for me. I thought you trusted me."

"It's not that I don't trust you, or your judgment." It was her own she couldn't get a handle on.

"Oh?"

"The fewer people know, the better." The words sounded weak.

"Okay. So you're talking nonsense now, and I can't make heads or tails of it. As I said before, I want an explanation. You don't owe me one, but I'd appreciate it."

Wetness stung her eyes. She shuddered. "I can't … not here. Anyone could hear."

"So let's go home. Get out of the rain. You're soaked."

She couldn't hold out against the patience in his voice. "I said, I can't see you—"

He exhaled sharply. His patience must be dwindling. "Sacrament, Trez. Breaking up with me can wait an hour or so. Can't it?"

She couldn't say no. Not honestly. Dumping him so abruptly, without explanation, had been cowardly and thoughtless. She'd known that, somewhere. "All right." She shivered. Her face was wet with hot tears and cold rain.

"Is your place good?"

The thought made her feel cornered. She shook her head.

He gave her a curt nod. "Then, we'll go to mine." He shrugged out of his jacket. "Take this for the trip back."

She fumbled with putting his coat on and sealing it, her fingers stiff. When she was done, he held out a hand to her. She was afraid to take it. She didn't want to give him hope.

He withdrew his hand and put it in his pocket. "Let's go."

She followed him off the dock, her steps stiff and slow.

EIGHTEEN

Eric guided Trez forward as they exited the subway station. Their footfalls echoed in the stairwell. Her face was drawn, but at least she wasn't crying anymore.

He still wasn't sure whether he was more shocked or insulted by her comm. Being dumped always felt personal, but he told himself not to throw a fit just yet. Once she got more comfortable and less sixes and sevens, he could suss out what bee had crawled into her bonnet.

When they entered his apartment, she shucked his wet coat and looked around, at a loss for what to do with it. He took it and hung it on the bare hooks right in front of her.

"You'll need a clean shirt," he said. Hers clung to her skin. That would have been hot if it weren't for her fifty-kilometer stare.

"What? Oh."

"And a towel, I'm guessing?"

She blinked owlishly. "I think so?"

Câlice de sacrament. They'd get nowhere like this. "You're soaked and chilly. Go take a shower. I'll get some clothes for you."

"I—"

"Get yourself warm and dry, and then we can talk." Then he would have more time to try to calm down and think. He hoped he didn't sound too angry. "I'll leave some clothes on the bed for you."

His own clothes reeked of damp birds and hydrocarbons, so he threw them into a pile and changed to sweats. He folded his oldest softest pajamas for Trez before remembering she would drown in them. Sam would have something closer to her size, so he ransacked her dresser for casual clothes.

When he returned to the kitchen, he poured a mug of water, as cold as the dispenser could make it. Trez wasn't trying to hurt him. He didn't think she'd thought that far. But her words still stuck in his craw.

He downed the frigid water in several gulps and shivered. She'd said she was protecting him? He liked to think he knew danger well. He risked his body for a living. For others' sake too. She knew that, so what had her so spooked? He tried to think of everyone they knew and why they might have frightened Trez. The Makos? A coworker of hers? Another corp? Jenna? The Runner friend? The municipal police? None of those sparked any revelations.

Overthinking everything wouldn't bare her secrets. He should wait for Trez. He filled another mug of water, this one for Trez. She might be hungry. He'd forgotten to ask.

When she came out to the kitchen, she looked very small, drowned in several layers of flannel and wool. Her eyes seemed clearer and more awake though. She didn't say anything before she sat on the futon and began taking little sips of water.

"Can I get you anything else?" he asked.

Trez shook her head. "My digestion isn't great."

He let her finish her drink before he softened his voice and said the words he'd been mulling over since she'd told him they should break up. "Can you tell me what's wrong? If you really want to cut ties with me for your own sake, then we can do that. But I don't want you ghosting me just to protect me without telling me why. That isn't fair. We know I can take care of myself."

"I don't know if I can—"

"You worried about my safety? I appreciate your concern, but can't you let me judge the risk myself?" Putain. He hadn't meant to interrupt her.

She shook her head again. "I don't want you targeted."

"By who? You don't think the Makos will go after me, do you? I've no idea why that would happen."

"No, it's not that. It's Harbor."

That didn't make any sense. "What the hell are you talking about?"

"I know I can trust you with any of my secrets, but you could get in trouble for obstructing justice or conspiracy or some other crime like that—"

"Wait. Slow down." This was making his head spin. "Start from ... start from what's changed since yesterday."

She looked down for a few seconds then exhaled slowly. "Harbor put me on medical leave for three weeks, and my medic cut me off."

"Doc Menendez?"

"No. Someone else I was seeing. For the extra pharma."

"Ah." A part of him was relieved that she couldn't damage herself that way for now.

"Doc Ten ... he said more chems would likely do irreparable damage. But I can't strike successfully without it. Look at the last strike."

He'd been meaning to ask her about that. "You started screaming incoherently during the fight. I still don't understand what happened there."

She spent several minutes inspecting the cacti on his windowsill before she closed her eyes and shook her head. "One of the guards there reminded me of the civilian woman I murdered."

No wonder she'd lost her marbles. He kept his tone light. "That was an unlucky coincidence."

"You think there's a way for me to specify that any strike I sign up for needs to be clear of medium-height women with dark curly hair?" She compressed her lips. "That's not possible."

The deadline for her to make the final payment was in less than two weeks. "So you need another way to get the money."

"Yeah." She rubbed the back of her neck with both hands and grimaced. Then she stared out the window and experimented with putting her fingertips on the cactus spines.

Maybe she was screwing up the courage to say something. He put his hands in his pockets so he wouldn't fidget and tried to keep his expression regular. If she really didn't want to tell him, she could just go home. He wouldn't stop her. He hoped she knew that, but he stayed quiet so he wouldn't distract her.

Eric programmed the food printer to make them some pudding. If her stomach was acting up, tapioca should be bland enough.

Trez finally spoke up after several minutes. "The Libertists. They said they'd get my criminal record erased if I worked for them. As an added benefit, they'd chase the Makos out of the area, so Pa and I would be safe."

The Libertists? The word sounded familiar. After a few moments, he remembered his conversation with Esperes at the Founders' Day gala. But he couldn't have heard that right. "Ah, Libertists as in the goons who blew up a bunch of buildings several decades ago?"

"Yes. Them." Her voice wavered.

"Why would they approach you though?"

"Well, I used to be one of them. That's the dirt the Makos have on me."

It took more than a moment for that to sink in. Eric swallowed and lowered his forehead to the countertop, bracing himself on his forearms. It was his turn to be at a loss for words. How was what she was saying even possible? He did some arithmetic. "Wait. Several decades ago. You must have been a child."

"I was young, but I don't think Harbor would care much about that."

The printer beeped, signaling its readiness. What had he been doing? Making pudding? "Wait, they recruited kids?" He couldn't keep the disbelief from his voice.

"Not usually. I mostly ran errands. Acted as a lookout. My ma was one of the people in charge."

Her mother? She'd said her mother had abandoned her as a kid. But if she'd grown up as an anarchist, how had she become a Corp worker? The countertop remained a soothing coldness, so he didn't raise his head. He concentrated on the feeling of the smooth surface while he tried to put his thoughts in order. "You went from aiding the Libertists to striking for Harbor? How does that work?"

"After Santorini and the rest of them left Portland, it wasn't like I had anything I could do on my own."

"Santorini's your mother?"

"Yeah."

"Well," he said. He levered himself up from the countertop

and turned to face her. She held herself stiffly, awaiting his judgment. "Give me a moment to get my head around that."

"I'm—"

"Are you going to apologize? Don't."

She blinked. "No. I'm thirsty. I would like some more water." She pulled the blankets up, thoroughly ensconcing herself in flannel.

"Oh." Right. He shouldn't have assumed. "Sure thing, I'll get it for you."

Trez had never volunteered information about her childhood. He'd learned she grew up with her ma before the lady skipped town, but he couldn't picture her as an anarchist. Then again, he had trouble picturing any anarchists. The closest he could think of were street toughs with loud hair and colorful words. She didn't have the chip on her shoulder—sometimes literal microchips—he expected from a street tough or rebel. Maybe she'd had one and had grown out of it? If she had worked for an anarchist cell, how did she feel about Harbor?

He retrieved her cup. She brought her knees to her chest and curled into a ball.

When they had first met, Trez had smiled when she said what she did for a living. He'd asked her if she enjoyed high-adrenaline commando action, and she'd replied that it suited her inclinations. And she knew megacorps were the only employers who would offer it.

But over the past two years, he'd noticed some ambivalence. She hadn't wanted to talk about her strikes anymore. It must feel strange to depend on a Corp for her livelihood, given her history.

Almost a year ago, they'd met up with Jenna and one

of Jenna's acquaintances for a vidconcert. Trez hadn't volunteered her what she did for a living. She'd only said she was Jenna's coworker. At the time, he'd thought Trez was having a shy moment or felt that she didn't have anything to prove to this new person. Had she been reconsidering her life path? Did she disapprove of what he was doing with his life?

He began to pace. Hopefully Trez didn't have any more bombshells for him. "These Libertists. You think they can make good on their offer?"

"Probably. They have some hired muscle and a Runner, so if Ma thinks they can take care of my and Linus's records, I believe her."

If she believed it was possible, he'd believe her. "I assume knowing about this puts me in danger from Harbor because I could be in trouble for not turning you in?" The carpet cushioned his footsteps.

"Yes. That's what I'm afraid of." She shifted around in her seat.

"And you tried to dump me because you think I'll accidentally let something slip about your activities with the Libertists if you join them?"

Trez gave him a pained smile. "I don't think you would. But if someone knew to investigate me, you'd be one of the first people they'd question. It's one thing to not report someone's past misdeeds, it's another to not say anything about known criminal activity."

"True." But he needed to ask her the ten-thousand credit question. "But do you actually want to join them?"

She furrowed her brow and stared at him. "What do you mean?"

He stopped pacing to watch her and try to figure out her feelings. His anger wasn't gone, but confusion and concern had pushed it far back enough that he could try to reason this out. "Are you doing this because you want to or because you think you have no choice?"

"Huh." She wet her lips. "I hadn't thought . . . What does that matter?"

"Because I want to understand where you're coming from. Explain it to me like I'm five." When she didn't immediately speak, he drew up a chair opposite her. Slowly, so she didn't bolt.

"When I was little, I wanted to please my mother. I learned all the big words from the historical anarchist texts she had me read." Her eyes met his. She waited for him to nod before she continued. "But there was more to it than that. I'm not sure. As a kid, you like to think in terms of things being good and evil, right?"

"In North America? Sure." He pictured little Trez, skinny and big-eyed, making notes on a learning text.

"It's easy to buy that the corps are giant evils that brave people must fight against. It's the narrative I was given."

"Pays well though." That had not been the funniest thing he could have said, but he got a nod from Trez.

"I was taught to believe that we had everything we needed, and luxuries were just that—luxuries"

He whistled. "So did they get you to believe that growing up poor was somehow glamorous?"

"A little. I never knew anything else. I mean, we had access to all the food, clothing, and medical care at the municipal centers." Her voice went soft and she brought her blankets up to her chin, snuggling in them. "We had many secondhand things—clothes, furniture, electronics—and Ma and I would come up with stories about their lives with their previous owners."

He'd grown up with the same standard of living, but the way she said it sounded more fun. "Sounds like you weren't upset about it."

"Most kids grow up without money. I just had a religion telling me it was a good thing. Once Ma left, Pa took me in. I was so grateful to him, I thought maybe if I supported him, he would never leave. I started working as a delivery person so that he could have a few nicer things. Then after a while, one of my frequent customers took a liking to me and recommended I work at Harbor like she did. She sponsored my employment application. So that's how I ended up a Corp driver. The rest you know.

"A small part of me wants to join them. I may hate what Santorini did to me. But I loved being around her, once upon a time. When we were together, life seemed bright. But it might be childhood nostalgia, and that would be the wrong reason to work for them."

"Would there be right reasons?"

"To risk that much? Perhaps. Maybe if I believed that the Libertists' actions would actually have the results they wanted." She worried the carpet with her bare toes.

Even when cornered, she tried to remain principled. People like that were rare and should be protected. What she'd done as a kid didn't matter. And if she'd wanted to join the Libertists because she genuinely desired to, he'd have been devastated, but he wouldn't have stopped her. But she shouldn't be forced into a lifetime of hiding. She may have been cagey and secretive with him, but she'd had good reason, and she'd never lied. He loved her, and he would find a way to fight for her.

What a clusterfuck. And she was in it because she tried to take responsibility for those she loved. "Does your dad know about any of this?"

She shook her head. "I don't want him to get involved. He would sympathize, panic, and somehow get us into deeper trouble." She yawned.

He would have to trust her judgment on that. "You're sleepy?"

"Yeah."

"You can sleep in Sam's room."

She blinked at him. "You sure?"

"Ah-yeah. Thanks for telling me all of this. We can talk more once you're rested." And once he had more time to plan. Thankfully she didn't suggest that she go home.

She rose and shook her muscles out. He wanted to kiss her good night, but he wasn't sure where he stood with her right now. Risking more rejection wouldn't do either of them any favors. "Sleep well," he said. It was late afternoon, but the bags under her eyes indicated that she might crash for more than a nap. "If you wake up while I'm asleep, use the kitchen. Make yourself at home."

"Mm-hmm." She shuffled over to Sam's room.

He stood looking at the door for minutes after she closed it. He needed to put his thoughts together; he'd have to pull a rabbit out of his hat in order to give her a real choice. Where to start wasn't obvious, but the best course of action would be to collect all the information he had and try to organize it.

There was still a lot he didn't understand, but he had to put his feelings to the side. He wanted to ask her at least a hundred more questions. If he wanted to offer her a way out that didn't fill her with the same dread, or have her constantly looking over her shoulder, he'd need to keep his head cool and his heart cold.

NINETEEN

Trez woke with her usual headache. She got up to silence her alarm before it rang and stubbed her toe on a chair. She stumbled, then sat back down on the bed. Why was the door in the wrong place?

Also, what was with the flower vase and doilies? Oh. This was Eric's sister's room. She'd passed out around five, but the sun was low in the sky. She checked her comm. 7 a.m. She'd been unconscious for fourteen hours.

Eric had said to make herself at home. He had the same municipal-issue food printer and drink dispenser she did, so she made herself tea and oatmeal. While she waited for her breakfast to be ready, she took another look at the apartment's funky decor. The electronic display had changed. Maybe before last night, but she hadn't noticed at the time. Instead of photographs of the American Southwest, it showed footage of baby penguins in their nests.

Eric must not be awake yet. Maybe she could creep home. The door would auto lock behind her. She'd told him about what she was grappling with. He knew there were things more important than their feelings and relationship.

But he'd clearly wanted to continue the conversation. She still felt guilty and wretched about trying to dump him via comm. That had been stupid and unnecessary, and she'd hurt him. Instead, she would have to convince him that the only way to avoid Linus getting killed and her sent to prison was for her to join the Libertists, and that meant them not seeing each other anymore.

Would he understand why she was so fearful? She wasn't sure. He'd said how much risk he was willing to take on, and she trusted that he wouldn't tell anyone else her secrets. Now that she'd exposed him to that risk, she might as well tell him the whole truth. If they were done with each other, neither of them would wonder why they couldn't make it work.

He wandered out of his bedroom, pushing his hair out of his face. "Morning," he said.

"Hello."

"Let me get some coffee. You're eating? Good." He fumbled around for a mug, eventually picking a dented one with "HARB R SEC RITIES" printed on it.

Trez watched him operate the dispenser. "Thanks for letting me stay over," she said.

"Of course. Why wouldn't I?" He had deep shadows under his eyes. Had he slept poorly, or just not enough?

"It's what you're supposed to say when you didn't plan on it, right?"

Eric yawned and brought his steaming mug to the table. "A spare room is there to be used. So I'm glad you used it. You sleep okay?"

"I feel like I slept a week, but I still feel groggy. Maybe I should have woken up earlier."

"You probably needed it."

"I guess." She spooned some oatmeal into her mouth. It was bland, a little thin, and overly sweet.

Eric didn't press her further and turned his attention to

his coffee. He yelped and made an undignified face at the first sip, then blew on his drink to cool it down.

"I had some time to think," he said. "And it sounds like you're thinking about all this"—he made an expansive wave with his hands—"like you need to go it alone. And I get you trying to do everything by yourself. You've come really far on your own. You grew up indigent and became a Harbor striker. That's not something just anyone can do."

"I . . ." She was flattered, but she had difficulty believing him. As a rule, she tried not to think about her life's path to corporate commando. But the events of the last few weeks had made it clear that ignoring her history wouldn't stop it from biting her in the ass.

"You look skeptical. I know you don't like to ask for help But you know, this mess with the Makos and your pa and your ma and your job, why should you have to handle it all yourself?"

She'd kept up her guard so much that even though she'd told Eric, she hadn't thought to lean on him. "I guess I thought getting other people involved was too risky."

He held his pointer finger up and wiggled it from side to side. "Ah-ah. Can't I make decisions about what risk I'll take on?"

Trez shrugged. She could have argued, but he was probably right.

Eric tapped on the table. "We have about a week and a half for the payment still. I assume that your offer from the Libertists doesn't expire soon?"

"What do you mean?"

"I'd think it would take some time for them to get your records erased. How much time do you have before you absolutely must make a decision?"

"About a week."

"All right then." He leaned forward, his voice gentle. "I'm asking you for one week. A week where we can try to figure another way out of this. Together."

What could they accomplish in one week? Where was he getting this optimism? "And when we can't figure out anything together?"

"If we can't, you do whatever you need to do. Cut off all contact between us, because I'm a known associate of yours. I won't lie, I don't want that, but I understand where you're coming from." He leaned in closer to her and put his hands over hers. They were warm from the coffee mug. "Just, please, don't leave me hanging like this. Without even trying."

She'd begged her mother not to leave her behind, years ago. Santorini hadn't taken Trez with her because she wasn't up to keeping a kid safe while she was in hiding. But Eric was an adult. If she rejected his request, wouldn't she be abandoning him without really trying to consider his wishes? Trez felt a rare flicker of sympathy for her mother. Had Santorini agonized like this?

"All right," she said. "A week to try to find an alternative solution."

His shoulders relaxed. He smiled. "Thanks." He stood up with his mug in hand. "More tea?"

"Yes, please."

"All right then. Let me get my notes." A hologram screen popped up from his comm. "There's a lot of guesswork here. Preplanning before the planning? Something like that. It's what we have to go on right now."

She looked at the screen. The words Sam, Esperes, Vail, Vanchen, and Staplehead were printed under a heading labeled Resources. Vail had a question mark after their name. "These are people who might help?"

"Yeah. I'm not sure yet how we can leverage these connections. I don't know what Sam could do to help us, unless it involves getting invited to an art show or cultural demonstration. But I listed her anyway because ... maybe I'll think of something. I don't want to discount her."

"Esperes has access to a lot of information. But why would she help us?"

He perked up. "We have something she wants. Information about the Libertists."

She had to take a few moments to digest that. "Are you serious?"

"When I first met her at that shindig you crashed, she chatted me up about some anarchists in town. She wanted any information I might have on them. At the time I didn't know that they had any connection to you."

"All right ..." she hedged. "Can we trust her to keep things confidential?"

"I think it's a personal beef. Besides, she works for the *New York Times*. Outing a source or even putting one in danger would be a career killer."

"Good point." She looked back at the display. "Why does Vail have a question mark after their name?"

Eric frowned. "I have suspicions about them, but I'm not sure that they're accurate. So, would your Runner friend be able to look at some security logs from the R&D 4 break-in? I also have some questions about bank transfers."

"I'll ask her and tell her it's urgent."

"Basically I want to both investigate Vail and implicate the Libertists in the break-in. They masked the IPs they used to disable the building's security system, but I'd like her to do a trace and see if she finds anything."

"Why do you want to look up information you already know?"

Eric shook his head. "I'm not going to tell Seymour that you told me whodunit and how you know about the Libertists," he said. "If I'm going to report anything, better I have a record of paying Vanchen."

He stood up to get more coffee. It wasn't the best idea to make major plans when they were so tired. But what else could they do? It wasn't as if they had time to rest. Maybe she should drink something stronger than tea. But her stomach still felt queasy.

"Now, about Staplehead. I don't know exactly where he is in the pecking order, but he may be able to help us. He owes me at least a few minutes to hear us out."

"Perhaps." She put her hands behind her ears and rubbed her neck. "Everything we've come up with involves us talking to people and attempting to negotiate."

He sat back in his seat. "And I think of us as people of action, not words. But hopefully we can use our musclehead credentials as a bargaining chip. The Libertists want your commando skills. You know, the Makos might too. Have you considered working off your dad's debts by working for the creditors?"

"No. I had hoped to keep my nose clean in this whole mess. I didn't want to have anything on my adult criminal record." Trez ran her hands through her hair. "But ... it seems the only alternative that keeps Linus alive and me out of prison or worse is terrorism, and that's a bigger crime than dealing with the black market or local protection rackets." She looked back at the penguin chick vid. A claymation pelican had arrived while they'd been planning. The bird opened its beak wide and snarfed up a chick whole. "Oh my god. That's appalling."

Eric turned his head and recoiled at the sight. "Putain. I told Sam to take that sequence out of the film."

"Do they really do that? That is not okay at all." She had the urge to laugh. It was both absurd and a relief to be horrified about something so trivial.

"Pelicans will eat anything they can fit in their bills," Eric said. "That's what I read, but using clay for this seems odd. I'm sure it's some kind of artistic statement."

"Anyway, we don't have to commit to anything yet. We should talk to the others first. But those are the people I could think of. Do you have anyone to add to this list?"

She racked her brain. "Uhh ... there's Doc Ten. I don't know who he associates with though. Anything from indigents in need to execs who want to try out new performance enhancers just for thrills. I don't actually know."

Eric started tapping on the table again. "Could we rush people to him in a medical emergency?"

She blinked. "Oh. Possibly. He has general medic certification, and he sees patients at odd hours. But I don't know his exact schedule."

"Could we put him on retainer?"

"I don't know," Trez said. "I can comm him and ask."

"Great." Doc Ten's name appeared under Vanchen's on the holoscreen. "Who else?"

She didn't want to say it, but she had to. "There is Santorini." Her voice was low.

Eric sat back in his seat. "What can she offer us, without the condition that you join the Libertists?"

"I think she'd be willing to answer some questions. She also has a Runner working for her but ..." Trez twisted her chapped hands together. It hurt a bit, but the pain blended with all of the rest of her dull aches. "I don't think she's willing to spare them for us. She has them busy with whatever espionage they need to do for their anti-corporate operations."

He snorted. "Do they really call them anti-corporate operations?"

Ironic, when it sounded like sanitized corp-speak. "Yes."

Eric angled his face away so that he wasn't quite looking at her. His knuckles went white on the sofabed's arms. "So. She'll only go so far for you."

The truth of that rankled every time she thought about it. "Unless I do what she wants."

He stayed quiet for a moment before he turned back to her and forced a smile. "And you don't want to involve your dad."

She slurped her tepid tea. "Right."

"Fair enough." Eric touched the names on the screens to color them, going by whether they were affiliated with Harbor, the Makos, the Libertists, or none of those. "How about your coworkers? Jenna?"

"I don't know how she could help, but at this point I guess I'll ask anyway." Jenna already understood some of Trez's predicament. Trez could tell her about the blackmail and Makos without mentioning the Libertists.

"So we need to talk to the people who aren't affiliated with either the Makos or the Libertists first. From there we should be able to get a better picture of everything."

"Sure." She was exhausted already. Or rather, she had never stopped being tired, and all that critical thinking had depleted what remained of her energy.

He took a long look at her, his expression soft. "Need more tea?"

"Just water for now." His kindness hurt a little. What had she done to deserve it?

"Need more sleep?"

"I slept plenty. I'll manage."

"I'll comm Sam. You comm Jenna and Ten. Do you want to talk to Vanchen, or should I?"

"I'm on her trusted contacts list. Send me the message you want to send her and all the logs. I'll forward them."

"All right. We'll talk to Esperes together after we comm everyone we listed above the screen."

"Sounds good." Everything was moving so fast, and she still didn't see a way she could stay out of prison without going to the Libertists. But Eric was trying so hard to help her. The least she could do was believe in him.

TWENTY

Eric checked the time again. He tapped his foot while he waited. Sam liked the decor at this bar, but it just looked chaotic to him: wall art of foxes made out of triangles, purple-lacquered tables, retro keyboards on all the vending machines. Abai had good drinks, but its real attraction was the low-grade EMP field that interfered with most network activity and surveillance. Never hurt to be extra cautious when you were discussing sensitive information.

Vail arrived a few minutes late. At the door, they gave one of the regulars a grin and a slap on the back in response to some small talk. Eric wasn't sure if they'd seen him yet. He looked for signs of distress and distractedness in Vail's posture.

They ordered a Long Island iced tea and rubbed their side. When they spied Eric, they ambled over to the soundproof booth. Vail sat with a grunt, adjusting their lean frame in the seat until they were comfortable.

"Been a few months since we've gone for a drink together," they said. When they'd first partnered up with Eric they'd met for drinks every week, but those meetings had gotten further apart the last few months.

"Thought it was time."

"Time. It keeps marching on." They rubbed their hip.

"Ah-yeah. You thinking of retiring soon?" That would give plenty of reason for what Eric had found. One he hadn't considered before. He'd been too focused on his own job and his dissatisfaction, then too preoccupied with Trez. His foot started tapping again.

"I'm forty-one and have a bad replacement leg. I may be good another few years, but I can't count on it." Vail smiled, but it didn't reach their eyes.

Eric knew that his body didn't bounce back like it used to, and you could only safely down so many painkillers. The antiaging treatments helped some, but they didn't compensate for the number of injuries he'd had. He didn't like to think about what shape he'd be in five years down the line. He'd always been a bit in awe that Vail was still up and running, as it were. "You could transfer to another division in Security."

"Office work? Instruction? Maybe. I've thought about it."

"Don't get the hazard pay though."

"Nah. Not so much." They took a brief look at the bar.

Eric waited for Vail to take their first sip. "So speaking of money." Vail raised their eyebrows but didn't otherwise reply. "I don't know how else to ask this, but why've you been getting money from break-in artists?"

Vail swallowed, paused, and looked Eric in the eye. "Please elaborate." Their face didn't give any fear away, but their jaw was set.

"Putain. You want me to spell it out?" Eric had ruminated on Vail's motives, but they still didn't make sense. Vail had been a good report and boss, and had seemed genuinely happy for Eric even though he'd been promoted over them. "Fine, maybe you can give me another explanation." Vail made a little noise of assent. "I brought in an outside contractor on the Miletus case. Did some investigating in my off time."

Vail swirled their drink around in the highball glass. They still didn't look away.

"The outside help looked into the intruder. He's associated with some other interesting shady characters. All of them with more identities than I can count. But the contractor managed."

"All right." Vail's patience was admirable.

Eric was beginning to sweat a little, as if the burden was on him. Perhaps it was. Innocent until proven guilty, right? "Then we went through their recent financial transactions. Some of them were deposits that could eventually be traced in your accounts."

Vail steepled their slim fingers and waited a few more moments. "So, you're saying some people who might be acquaintances of our Miletus perp have sent me money."

"Ah. Right. That."

"Anything else?" Conversations around them had fallen a bit quieter. It made Eric want to drum on the table.

"I went over our security logs. Investigated the emergency call that took the other guards off our floor. Found out you'd placed it."

Vail shrugged. "There was a genuine bomb threat."

"So why leave us understaffed?"

Vail's mouth pursed, and they spoke slowly. "You wouldn't be saying all this if you weren't confident, and you wouldn't have come to me if you just wanted to report it. What gives?"

"I don't know." Eric stared at his reflection on the table. "Maybe because I thought you could make this all make sense."

"Eh?" For the first time, Vail seemed uncertain.

"You've always had that knack. That's why I always ask you questions."

Color appeared on Vail's cheeks. "That's kind of you to say." They leaned forward a bit, cupped their chin in their hands.

Seemed he had to talk in ever-increasing circles to find the center of what happened. Without that, he wouldn't be able to go forward. "You're changing the subject."

"Guilty. Of that, anyway." Vail seemed to find something over his shoulder interesting. Eric's first instinct was to look behind him, but he hadn't heard any movement or seen anything that could have gone into his blind spot.

"Are you saying you didn't get payments from this . . . Valter Qlondike? Benjamin Hill? K&K Enterprises?" Eric let that hang in the air. He knew where this was going, knew he wouldn't like it, but had to do it anyway.

Nobody appeared to be paying much attention to them, because they hadn't raised their voices. Yet. Eric heard someone order the "melonade special." Vilest drink in the house. He listened to the straw slurp.

Vail took a tiny sip, leaned back on their stool, and crossed their arms over their chest. "What if I did?" Vail's soft tones weren't menacing, but this game wasn't fun.

"Then I'd have to ask you why." Eric felt warmth leach from his body. A month ago, he would never have admitted to being terrified of losing his friend. That fear trumped his sense of betrayal, surprisingly.

"Eric, I could be angry that you sought help outside HarborSec, but you didn't do anything I wouldn't have. Seymour charged you with finding the culprit." Their fingers trembled a bit.

He wondered which one of them was more uneasy. Right

now, he wouldn't put creds on either of them. "It's a case. It's not that important."

Vail made a cat's cradle with their hands. "It's your career. Last I checked it was your top priority."

"Maybe my priorities have changed."

They blinked and uncrossed their arms. "That's ... interesting."

"Ah-yeah. Sure." He waited for them both to process that.

"Why?" they asked, brows furrowed.

"Could ask you the same." Eric didn't think his poker face was holding up. What was the point anyway? He held the better cards.

Silence stretched. Vail avoided the question again. "Would it by any chance have something to do with your lovely femme fatale?"

"Well, uh . . ." He couldn't deny it.

"I'm not blind, monsignor. When you're in love, or at least hard up and itching with your teeth aching, things you thought were true go out the window." Vail smiled and fluttered their fingers. "So, you nail her yet?"

How had this conversation taken a hard right turn? He would have normally appreciated Vail lightening the mood. But he couldn't let himself get sidetracked. "Why'd you lead me on a fucking goose chase?"

Vail's grin vanished. "I never meant to deceive you."

"Hard to believe."

"No, really. I didn't anticipate you coming back to the office or Seymour putting this on you."

"You still haven't told me why." It's not like he'd thought Vail incorruptible, but they'd never shown any signs of not being on the up-and-up before. Vail didn't have any expensive habits that he knew of, no close family to threaten.

"Why deceive you? Like you said, you weren't supposed to be there that evening," Vail said. "Maybe I should have made sure of that," they grumbled.

That would have let the perp get in, but ... "I would think the theft would have been noticed regardless, and I'd still be on the investigation."

"No. Nobody was supposed to notice."

The chair scraped. "You had some replacement footage for security?" Add curiosity to his cocktail of emotions.

"I was going to fuzz it and hope for the best."

Finally, something as good as an admission of guilt. Cold confirmation settled into his gut. "I guess that's easier."

Eric willed himself to stop clenching his jaw. Trez was depending on him, and he needed Vail's cooperation. "You know what they wanted from the lab?"

"The break-in artist was going to reprogram one of the prototypes before a demo for the Security brass," Vail said. They looked away. "To embarrass and discredit a decryption project."

And, of course, make a fool of its boss. "Seymour?"

A shadow flitted across Vail's face, then they bracketed their mouth. "Seymour."

A perverse sense of satisfaction rose. "You nailed her?" Old patterns of humor weren't completely gone.

"Fuck no. I'd rather hotsync with an ostrich."

"Sounds kinetic." He'd known the two didn't get along, hadn't since before he joined the division, but he'd never pressed the issue.

"Less dangerous than Seymour." Vail shuddered. "Ostrich can only break all my bones."

Eric usually tried not to attract the attention of R&D staff. He thought getting ahead was cutthroat in Security, but the scientists were always watching their backs for hidden shivs. "She been controlling your assignments?"

"She has Kline's ear. Biggest wig in the division." Vail stared into their highball glass.

"Have it out for you?" He got a grunt as his answer. Vail hadn't made a lot of enemies at work, but some of their coworkers avoided them. "Just makes me uncomfortable, that giggle," someone had told Eric once. "Like a monkey giving birth."

"More so since the Michaud breetva got us few years back. I fucked up, I know. I didn't keep close enough to her. Careless." They stirred their liquor slowly with an index finger.

"She file a complaint?"

"We both had to have some repair surgery done. She was so pissed. Ate into her timeline for her next pet project."

That sounded a little lopsided to Eric, Vail's mistake notwithstanding. "You only got a manufactured hip and oh, an entire leg."

"Yeah, but it's not like I had an important job to do, beyond guarding her ass." They rubbed their eye and winced at the sting of alcohol. "Fuck."

Seemed reason enough for mutual dislike. Eric hummed in acknowledgment.

"Always on my case since then, because she thinks I owe her. She said I could make it up to her. Didn't specify what, but I could guess. I didn't have the prosthesis fitted yet. Amputee sex isn't really my thing."

Eric didn't want to explore that mental image. That was borderline too much information. "I can order you another mixed drink." Best he could offer.

"Yeah, seems like I'll need it tonight," Vail said. "Though

maybe you're trying to take advantage of my insobriety." They shook their head. "Sacrament, you're the one paying."

He'd always taken it for granted that Vail had his back. He should have thought more about their feelings. Maybe he just wasn't a good partner. But he still didn't understand the break-in. "Okay, now I've got why you. But I don't know why them."

"Them?"

He had to stop asking such open-ended questions. "The perp. Whose idea was all this? How did you find them?" The idea of Vail cruising neighborhoods itching for a goon to hire seemed far-fetched, mostly because Vail would probably ask weird questions the goon wouldn't understand.

"I didn't." Vail scowled at their reflection in the glass.

Why did all the people in his life have to be so moose-headed? He'd have to stick with yes or no questions. "They found you?"

"Mmm-hmm." Long fingers gripped the highball glass, tendons tight. "Don't know how. Best guess is they have good data hounds and somehow caught wind of that. Or rumors. Seymour didn't keep it a mega-secret that she wanted to kill my career."

"Did you get their names? Any other idents?"

"They kept their dealings with me as anonymous as possible, so I couldn't rat them out. Untraceable calls, dead message drops, multiple factor encryption. So they didn't give one, no." Vail shrugged.

Eric wanted to get up from his seat and pace, but that would likely attract attention. "So ... what were you going to do next? Before we spoke today, that is?"

"Since you found the infiltrator at the scene, Plan B was to put the blame on someone else in the building and somehow convince you. Hadn't figured out that part though." Vail had somehow finished the second glass soundlessly.

"You've had a few weeks to do that."

"Like I said, I was tired."

"And now?"

"And now what?"

"I'd say you fucking tell me, but I don't think that's useful."

"You could write it up in the investigation."

"I could. But I don't have to."

Vail almost barked a laugh. "Telling me you're not?"

Marde. "Look, I'm not overjoyed my partner lied to me. But this ... I don't fucking know. It's not like you wanted to screw me over." He ran his hands through his hair. There wasn't a delicate way to put this. "I have bigger things on my mind. What I need is ... Can you get ahold of a Gauntlet for me?"

A raised eyebrow. How Vail did that with elegance, Eric had never figured out. "That's an unusual request."

"I also need you to wipe the feed from it."

The eyebrow lowered, and Vail waited. After a few seconds, they smiled ruefully. "I take it you won't tell me the details."

"Maybe after."

They stared at their almost empty glass for a while then swirled the dregs around. "I do this, it helps Trez?"

"This isn't ... Marde. Well, yes. She's in deep marde." He'd assured Trez that her secrets would be safe with Vail, but still ... Was he making a mistake? What would he do if Vail told him the same secrets?

"Thought so."

"Huh?"

"She hasn't looked well for a while. I mean sure, strikers always look pretty fucked up, but she was completely zoned out the past few months whenever I talked to her. Not great. I asked and she said she was okay."

"You knew and didn't say anything?" A lick of anger rose.

"I wasn't getting anything out of her, so I thought she might be in a bind. But what can you do with someone who refuses to confide in you?"

"Why didn't you tell me?"

"I wasn't sure you cared!" The smirk blossomed into a self-satisfied smile. "Plus if you wanted to jump into that minefield with her, well, that's part of the work you need to do in an adult relationship."

Why had he doubted Vail? Relief bubbled up in his throat. "You jackass."

"To start, figure out what we're going to fucking tell our boss about the break-in."

"If we want to pin it on Fairchild, does that affect anyone we care about?" It was all the same to the Corpfare employees, really. Trez and the other strikers would continue to get deployed for the satisfaction of executives' egos.

"Hah. Not really." Vail shook their head. "I guess I can do that much. You know that if you don't find someone to pin this on, Seymour's going to try to block your promotion indefinitely?"

"Ah-yeah." Eric downed the contents of his own glass. "Guess I have to hope she gets distracted by something else and forgets about this."

"Like that's possible."

"Worst case, I can find another department." That wasn't actually the worst case. He might be committing career suicide. But he would make his peace with that. Somehow.

"If you say so." Vail ordered another round. This time, just water. They spent another hour trading barbs. Not quite like old times, but it didn't need to be.

Eric looked up from his comm. "Anything from Jenna?" Planning feverishly in only one room got old, so they'd relocated to Trez's apartment.

Trez stretched her arms above her head. "Don't think she has any leads that could help us out with money or Makos. And she sure as anything isn't going to petition to let me return to work."

"Could she actually do that?"

Trez shrugged. "If we both petitioned, it might get me reinstated. But she says at least I won't work myself to death this way." She curled in a bit on herself.

He'd already made his feelings clear about Trez's risk assessment when it came to her life. No need to comment further, so he changed the subject. "I directly contacted your Runner friend, like you advised. Sent her the security logs I was looking into, and some questions about bank transfers. She said they masked the IPs they used to disable the building's security system. But she might be able to find some evidence that the Libertists were the masterminds behind the break-in. Or she might be able to get me some location data."

"Why are you paying for information you already know?" She seemed distracted by something flashing on her comm.

Eric shook his head. "I already said I'm not going to tell Seymour that you told me whodunit and how you know about the Libertists," he said. "What's that on your comm?"

"Oh. Nothing important. An alert about a hazmat situation near my apartment." She looked up. "Sorry for spacing out. Uh ... seems like we need to give Kayla Esperes a comm," Trez said. "You ready to see her?"

"As anyone can ever be to see her," he said. He input the newest key into his comm. After ten seconds, her image popped into Eric's comm's holo. "Hello!"

"Good to see you again. Do you have time?"

"Why yes. You're a special security man, so I have time for you. Are you special enough security that you got the new spiders?"

Eric shook his head. "Ah, no. Are these friendly or enemy spiders?"

"Spider weapons. You can deploy them from your dress if you like. They're designer, you know." She performed a slow pirouette.

"What?"

"Harbor specials from R&D 2. Not yet released to the public."

"Oh," Trez said. "I've heard about these before. A few strikers have taken them out on test missions."

Esperes perked up. "Ah! It's you! Cyborg ninja!" She focused on something above Trez. "Unless I miss my guess, that's a copy of Dinoroid Dana's *Liberty Bell Collage #2* series."

Trez's eyes went wide, and then she smiled. "I should have figured you would recognize it."

"What kind of gonzo journalist do you take me for?" Esperes turned to Eric. "Your cyborg ninja has wonderful taste. Dana's work is of great historical import. She took Hunter S. Thompson's approach and refined it into something that is both a gut punch and life-affirming. But that's not a thing any old mugwump would have. Especially not one as young as you."

"A friend of my ma's got me into the audiocasts and art when I was a kid." Trez's eyes looked soft and wistful, and she made a small smile.

"Are you secretly some kind of elite historiographer? Journalist? Would you like to be?" Esperes waggled her fingers.

"I never had the time to pursue it myself," Trez said. "But I always thought what you people do is important to society."

"Ah, if only importance to society paid for enough designer drugs. But! It's never too late to start your journalism career," Esperes said.

They weren't here for career counseling. "Ah," Eric interjected. "Back at the gala you told me you were interested in tips about some local anarchists?"

Esperes stopped smiling at Trez and stared at him. "Yes. You got something?"

"I think we do," he said. "What's your deal with them? You said you had some kind of vendetta?"

"Yep. Any information about their personnel would be especially helpful."

"We did some digging, haha. We've learned a bit about their operations. They're backed by no small sum of money."

"I suspected as much. Any idea who gave it to them?" Esperes took off her papier-mâché optics and squinted at them.

"Sadly, no. I wouldn't be surprised if they didn't know either," Trez said.

"Why do you say that?"

"Just a hunch. Anyone big enough to bankroll them is

probably a party they wouldn't be comfortable working with. What with their anti-corp sentiment and all. Anyway, that money let them hire some elite muscle, I didn't catch the name, and also a Runner named Yang," said Trez.

Esperes had never stopped being attentive, but now her body was almost quivering with curiosity. "You sure that's the name?"

"Yes, but it's not an uncommon name. What else do I know ... They used to work at a bank in New York."

The journalist jumped. "Yes! That has to be it!"

"Friend of yours? Rival? Sworn enemy?" Eric asked.

Esperes didn't respond directly. "They must have left a trail. Possibilities, possibilities. Since you were so useful, hmm, thanks for the tip. Is there something you want in return? In-for-ma-tion?"

"Turns out I am also interested in the anarchists," Trez said. "Do you have any intel on them?"

"Or, oddly enough, the Makos?" Eric asked.

"You're picking a fight with the Makos?" Esperes asked slowly.

"No. Possibly the opposite. We want to know what they might need. If we can send them some information they might find valuable ..."

"Play them all off each other? That's some moxie right there."

"The Makos might need some help fending off the Libertists. Perhaps you could help?"

"I see, I see. So both the Makos and I have an interest in causing these anarchists some trouble. Well, in that case, they might find this map useful."

She pulled up a photo map of an industrial area with

several buildings circled. Someone, probably Esperes, had scribbled stick figures and other inscrutable symbols all over the corners.

"What's that?" The buildings looked familiar to Eric, but he couldn't quite place them.

"I found a location seething with industrial-grade security. Guessing it's been made a bunker or something like that."

Trez scrutinized the map. Eric followed suit until he found some distinctive graffiti on one of the buildings. It clicked. "Funny. That's near the racetrack."

"You know the place?" She turned back toward him and stared at his face.

"Gone a few times. Squatter indigents live there, the ones who don't like the city. Someone set up some Bangor racing a while back."

"Wouldn't the Makos already know about this place?" Trez squinted at the screen.

Esperes frowned. "Maybe. But." Several pink glyphs appeared on the map. "I'm willing to bet they don't know what to do with these. Fancy schmancy security nodes, we're talking enterprise level. Not this consumer junk anyone with enough creds can smoke. Even their bagels have souped up lox."

Trez groaned. "Locks, lox, that's terrible."

Esperes pursed her lips in disgust. "Look, I would eat an entire toad if it meant I could get real bagels today. Not that Montreal wood-fired refuse. Is it such a Herculean task to make them? Boil and bake. Even I can do that with an old-style oven."

Trez, unfazed by the rant, bit her lip. "So you're telling me you've found an underground base with a top-notch security system."

"Yes! There must be important resources or people there. Why bother to set it up elsewise?"

"Tell us more."

"I don't understand most of it. But you, you're a special security man. You should know security systems! This one's two factor and there are locks you can only open remotely. Thankfully you're a team!"

"Are you suggesting we storm the base?" Trez's eyes narrowed. Her gaze shifted back and forth between them.

"No, but it seems like you did that yourself." Esperes leaned in toward them. "But! You shouldn't go alone!" She nodded rapidly. "I can tag along. Kick in your side for a day."

"Already got security." Was she high? Last thing he needed was to babysit a loose pulse rifle.

Her hands made small fists. "I can handle myself."

Eric closed his eyes and exhaled. "I can't guarantee your safety. We could encounter resistance."

"Though I don't know any kung fu."

"Do you think that would do anything against people with knives or guns?" His head ached.

"No! But I have a sawed-off with rubber ammo. And some armor." She waved her arms around in what he thought was a dance move.

"I don't want to be responsible for your possible injuries. If their top-of-the-line security system is any indication, they could have the resources for any number of security guards with any number of weapons."

She waved him off. "I'll be prepared. But there's something I need to check in there. My journalistic integrity senses are singing to me. Specifically, they are singing *My Darling Clementine*."

"I can't have you as a liability." And he really didn't want to get tangled up with the *Times* if Esperes got hurt.

Esperes huffed. "I have survived actual firefights! With live ammo!"

Eric sighed. "The two of us can handle this."

"The two of you? If one of you is needed at the remote tower, that leaves one other to open the basement door. What if you run into a goon squad?"

"We're pretty good at combat," Eric said. "Look, if we need additional muscle, we'll ask the Makos. Guarding you while storming the base would split my attention."

"If something happens to us, well, we're pros at taking our lumps," Trez said. "Your readers and listeners need you. Journalists like you are rare. Like I said earlier, you're important to society. Unlike us. If we're out of commission, someone else will step up to do our jobs. We're replaceable cogs."

"Well-paid cogs," Esperes said. She spent several moments bobbing her head, thoughtful. "Well, then I want you to grab any storage media at the location."

"That's a broad request. Can you narrow it down?" Eric asked Esperes.

"Terminal drives are probably the best bet. Yang's records could be anywhere."

Trez bent her head to one side. "So you're looking for data on Yang then? The Runner the Makos are working with?"

"It's personal."

"Fair enough."

"I miss my old videographer though. If she were still with me, I'd send her with you. She could kill you with her bare hands."

"No filming." He doubted Esperes's intent was to cause

him trouble, but there was not being paranoid, and there was not being a total moron.

"All right," said Trez. "We will look for the drives for you if we go. We'll get back to you in a week."

Esperes nodded. "Sounds like you have a plan, or at least, the beginnings of one. Keep me in the loop-de-loop, Cyborg Ninja and Special Security Man."

"For fuck's sake, I have a name." Then Eric realized the irony of what he'd said and shut his mouth. Seemed the two of them had the same habit of nicknaming people.

"Day, week, a matter of when we apply ourselves. Also if Q-Dave hits the right note with his viola."

"If you say so. Greis out." He cut the connection.

Trez stretched her neck then her shoulders. "I think I need a nap. Give me half an hour."

"Will do." Eric sat up again and got back to his notes. There were so many moving parts in their plans. He'd have to line his pieces up as precisely as he could. And hope he hadn't misjudged his friends and coworkers.

TWENTY-ONE

Trez walked arm in arm with Eric to the racetrack near Presumpscot. Withdrawal was hitting her hard today. She didn't relish meeting with the Makos when staying on her feet wasn't a given, but waiting was a luxury she couldn't afford. Her headache came and went. She'd put on leg braces and a lower back support to keep her steady.

As they approached the track, Eric's eyes widened. "They've spruced it up some since I was last here."

Odor of methane hit her nose, and a wave of nausea made her sway for a moment. "What are . . . those?" Colorful statues dominated the outside of the outdoor arena—tall figures of an abstract sort. Additional smaller ones were scattered around the inside of the arena, some on the tracks.

As she got a better look at one of them, she saw that it was almost oozing across the track, moving its own statue matter around. It picked up blocks of itself from the left, and a bulge would travel through the sculpture to the right until it touched the ground. The blocks seemed to be replicas of lizards. The intermittent rain made them gleam.

Eric let out a bark of laughter. "That must be the project Sam's working on for Yavis."

"Is that live already?"

"I don't think they've launched the installation, but she

said they'd be running some tests," Eric said. "Guess we'll find out if we watch the races. You see our guys here?"

"The pictures you showed me were the first I've seen of them. I've only talked to Withers and Withers's spokeswoman."

"I'm not sure if they report directly to Withers, but they've got to know her. They're not just meatheads. Surprisingly."

"Surprisingly?"

"My first impression of them involved pratfalls. I think it was one of Staplehead's more humiliating moments."

Trez scanned the crowd for Kalla's face: eyebrow tats, semi-fauxhawk, and chop shop cybernetic scars on his head. He wouldn't stand out here though. Many of the spectators here expressed their defiance of cultural norms through bod-mod and punk fashion. They wore customized rubber blazers with riotous patterns and metals and other materials grafted into them. What were any of them rebelling against though? Bad parenting? Societal expectations? Or simply everything she'd worked on behalf of in the past decade?

"Over there," Eric said. He gestured to the near side of the track.

The two men turned at the same time to face them. Dorgo was tall, with a severe slant to his brows. In contrast to Kalla, he wore no makeup or jewelry. He gave Eric a brief nod and then sized Trez up. Her pants and jacket felt tight over her braces.

"This the company you said you'd bring?" Kalla asked. He made a peace gesture to her.

"This is my lady, Trez," Eric said. "You've probably got her on the books for the Harris debt."

Dorgo stopped his appraisal. "Yes, I know who she is."

His lady? They'd have to discuss that later. They hadn't

done anything loverly since she'd tried to dump him over the comm. "Eric here tells me that you're interested in a bad crowd who's set up digs 'round here." Her rainshield deployed along with those of a few hundred other spectators, making a loud *whump* to punctuate her speech.

Kalla scratched at his scars. "Had a bad run-in with 'em?"

"She doesn't have a bike, so not quite." Eric smirked.

"They're not exactly new to town." She concentrated on keeping her posture straight. Why couldn't they have met somewhere with seating? "They're the same Libertists who trashed parts of the municipality and cleaned out the local gangs before your associates moved in here fifteen years ago."

Dorgo's eyes narrowed and he craned his head forward. "We knew that much. You've lived here your whole life, your records say. You knew them then?"

"Unfortunately." Her voice sounded scratchy. She regretted forgetting her canteen.

Eric smirked. "Maybe you should thank them. They left a nice clean place for you to move in and get some business done. Am I right?"

"I used to be close to one of them," Trez said. "Santorini. She's one of the directors, or at least she was last time the cell was in Portland." Pain spiked in her skull.

"I know who she is too." Dorgo drummed on his collarbone through his raincoat. "Hmm."

Trez's stomach tumbled. She couldn't lean on Eric too much, couldn't show weakness to the Makos.

"You weren't on good terms with those folks, I'm guessing," Kalla said.

She hoped her face didn't betray her feelings. "They're a gaggle of self-important geese."

Eric put his arm around her back, a firm pressure she could

lean into just a bit. He saved her from having to speak. "Sure. We've some intel you may be interested in." He inhaled slowly, and his hand on her back trembled. "About these anarchists, that is. Their safe houses. Know where they are?"

Kalla pointed across the river. "Ah-yeah. There's one underground down the road apiece. For fuckall that helps us."

"Because of the security system, am I right?" Eric's voice was light and genial. "What if you could bypass that?"

"Then we would." Dorgo said it slowly, as if to a toddler.

"So you'd be interested in making that happen."

Kalla's head jerked back. "You offering?"

Trez bent forward slightly. "We can take care of the security for you."

Dorgo looked to the side for a moment. "Maybe." He fiddled with something in his pocket.

"You've a way 'round that security system? It's iced like layer cake," Kalla said.

"She does." Eric smiled and squeezed one of Trez's hands.

"This you got to tell me." Kalla had leaned forward at Eric too. "The system's enterprise-level. You don't see security like this anywhere except on private Corp facilities."

"So use enterprise-level infiltration tools on it." Eric gave a small shrug. His hand on her back had tensed though. "This lady knows how to operate a Gauntlet."

"Sure," Dorgo said. He shifted his weight left to right and back again. "Not like she has one when she's not on the job though."

Eric smoothed his hands on his pants. "And if I made it so she did?"

"You think she could disable the system?" Dorgo said. He made it sound like an insulting question.

"It's what I've been paid to do for years." Trez's hands

tightened into fists. She wanted to cover them up in case her claws came out. But putting them in her pockets might draw attention to them.

Dorgo blew out a breath and narrowed his eyes. "What exactly is your suggestion?"

"Well, you know the security is controlled at a remote location. Deliver Trez there and let her exploit the system. Then you can move in on the target when as few people are there as possible. I assume you can figure out that part."

"To some degree," Dorgo said slowly. He blanched after a moment, an amazing feat with his complexion. Probably getting backchannel from Kalla.

"It's risky." Kalla smiled, showing all his teeth. "The details matter here. You know, we could go in on your say-so and get zapped. Now, if you had some literal skin in the game . . ."

"Meaning I go with you? Moonlight as Mako muscle?" Eric's hand had relaxed.

"Now, you lot." Kalla said. "You Corp samurai, you specialize in the meat."

"Put that way, we almost sound like chefs instead of warriors," Eric said.

Trez heard their voices as if through a fog. She would have said butchers.

"An apt parallel. Ever seen a chef dismember a lobster while it's still alive?" Kalla asked.

"Never had the real stuff," Eric said. The closest Trez had ever gotten was eating the cloned stuff once, on a night Linus had made out well. They couldn't spring for real butter, and the result ended up rich to the point of disgust.

Dorgo snorted. He'd gone without a rainshield, and his hair had taken on an iridescent sheen from either personal care products or rain pollution. "Takes skill. Boiling them alive shocks the flesh and it doesn't taste as good."

That sounded ghoulish. But then again, she'd cut off someone's arm once. She'd thrown up later. Hadn't eaten for days.

"Wouldn't be the first time we got some moonlighting Corp samurai looking to slum it for some cash," Kalla said. He nodded his head back and forth. "I have faith in your ability to filet anything we encounter."

"You think this is worth it, Agum?" Dorgo asked. His brows crept up, trying to make a break for his hairline.

Kalla was undeterred. "We'll run it by Withers. She's a smart croissant. She'll see the value in this."

Trez thought of a flat-gazed flaky warm pastry with a bored, icy effect. She failed to stop an inappropriate giggle from escaping.

"Would that make this our op or yours?" Dorgo craned his neck.

"I've laid the outline, but I'll defer to your ground team. I know how to take orders." Eric kept his expression neutral, but she could see tightness around his eyes.

"What's in all this for you?" Dorgo asked.

"Getting the Harris debt forgiven," Trez said. She willed her tight shoulders to relax, but they didn't obey.

"Fair enough." Dorgo turned to Kalla, then back to Eric. "Your proposal has merit. We'll consider it."

"Withers handles the debts, not us." Kalla scuffed a boot on the pavement.

Eric actually batted his eyes. "You not so much the kind who's good with money?" Trez's claws came out, cutting through his coat, but he didn't react.

"I'm not a fucking accountant," Kalla replied. "Like Dorgo said, we'll get back to you on what kind of remittance might be possible."

"I don't see the harm in keeping the lines of communication open," Eric said. She made a small sound at that. She hadn't expected that he'd want to drive his career into a wall. She looked up and her eyes went back to Dorgo, who raised one eyebrow and smiled on one side of his face. She'd have to learn how he did that.

"Bien sur," Kalla muttered, paying Dorgo little mind. "We'll make the pitch and get the details for you. Then it's off to the races, as they say. Join us?" He motioned with his chin to the racetrack.

"Nah," said Eric. "We can't match your passion for the game."

All she wanted was to go home and collapse.

"Ta then." Kalla shuffled off, and Dorgo followed.

Trez turned around to face Eric. Her head throbbed. He looked around for a while then rubbed the back of his neck. "Come on, let's go." He turned her around, put one arm about her shoulders, and input a message to her text channel with the other. *You can sleep on the train if you want*, it said.

She followed him numbly. They had done what they could. Now they just needed a reply from Withers.

———————

Trez woke up to a comm chime. Fuck. She hadn't intended to take another nap.

Eric was at her door. She told her comm to let him in. She wondered if she should give him access, but that presumed he'd be coming around all the time for the foreseeable future.

Best not to engage in wishful thinking. Eric had chosen a very strange time to get involved with her. Whatever they were involved in.

He was still in his work fatigues. As soon as he entered, he made himself at home in her kitchen, taking up almost all the space in front of the food prep. He dispensed himself a cup of purple liquid. "Anything for you?"

"Well, if I'm getting the service …" When she sat at her excuse for a dining table, her hips creaked. "The blue stuff. You know, with the algae."

"Coming right up." He downed the contents of his tumbler while getting her drink. "How're you holding up? I mean … I expect you're tired, but, ah, the recovery. That going okay?"

Would it change any of their plans if it wasn't? "I've been going a bit stir-crazy here."

"Forced medical leave is nobody's idea of a good time." He sat next to her, leaving plenty of distance between their bodies, and plunked down their mugs.

"I hate not knowing when I'll be reactivated." She rubbed her forehead.

"Ever had that happen before?"

"Once. After the capture. Surprised I didn't grow mold while they waited to determine me fit for strikes or even drills again." She'd spent three months out of work. "Thanks for checking in on me. Any news?"

"Of course. Heading to your place after work has become a welcome change to my routine," he said. "As for news … I secured the Gauntlet for this operation. Vail will pull some strings."Trez felt Eric's fingers on her temples, and he began to massage them. Her head dropped with relief. "Do they know what's going on?" she asked. "With the Makos. With me."

"I only told them that there's trouble involving you, and I'm going to help make it right."

"Awful nice of them." Pretty far for them to stick their neck out.

Eric's hands stopped momentarily. "Vail and I, we've worked something out between us."

"That so?"

He skated his hands down the sides of her skull and began kneading her shoulders. "You keep your secrets, they keep theirs. For now."

"You're calling in plenty of favors. Should I worry?" She had to trust that he knew what he was doing. He was taking on risks that she would never have asked him to.

"Not . . . I don't know. I can't think of any way it would affect you." He stopped his fruitless attempts to loosen the knots in her muscles and began to fidget with his mug. "But I've been thinking. If I throw Seymour a few crumbs about the break-in, she's going to learn about your ma and her friends. Seymour wants to keep attention away from that lab, so I doubt she would mobilize Harbor to go after the Libertists. But there's still a risk."

Trez took a deep breath and closed her eyes. "Maybe there is. But they're going to get caught soon anyway. And Santorini is good at disappearing when she needs to."

"Have you told them you're not joining them?"

"Not yet. There wasn't a time limit on the offer. I don't know if I'm doing the right thing, essentially betraying them to the Makos." She turned to him and leaned in close, as if to search his eyes. "What would you do if you were in my situation?"

"Honestly? Pray, mostly."

"Didn't know you were religious." She shifted.

"Gramma Rachna prayed a lot, whenever she visited us. Maybe the habit rubbed off on me." He put his hands back into his lap. "That and there's enough Catholic back there somewhere that it comes out when I'm nervous."

"You believe though?" Maybe that was pushy to ask.

He didn't seem to take offense. "Believe what?"

"In God. Or multiple gods?"

"Don't know. Not the Catholic one. Gramma's god was a universal soul thing, and the idea of that's nice."

"Huh." She looked out the window.

"Never seen you pray or take Christmas off." He sounded hesitant.

"Never had much occasion for religion," she said. "Guess I thought about it but it didn't stick. Didn't seem real or important to me or my life." Outside, the clouds were low. Made the sky seem finite.

Eric's voice became teasing. "Isn't the point that it's not real?"

"I don't think so, unless you're joking."

"Sort of. Something ineffable can give people something to cling to."

"Huh." It wasn't like she had a better answer.

"All the same, this isn't real praying. More like reflex." His voice sounded tight.

Trez turned around to see grooves between his brows. She could try to be strong for him, even though her fatigue and aches made it hard to concentrate. She took his hands in hers. "You don't have to spend too many days praying. This will be over soon."

He stared at their hands for a few long moments, as if those held the answer. "Not sure if that makes me feel better."

She smiled, hoping to ease him a bit. "You're doing everything you can. I can see that much."

Eric stroked the edge of her palm. She'd never thought that would be more stimulating than soothing, or someone would focus a caress there. "What happened last time anyway? After you engaged with the guards," he asked. His question was soft, almost as if he were a psych.

Trez didn't bother dissembling. "I don't know where to start. I think I told you about the problems I was having after I killed the civilian woman."

He closed his eyes. "Guess it doesn't do any good to go back and rethink that."

"Like I said, I started seeing that woman everywhere. One of the guards looked too much like her this last time, and without the anesthesia, I lost my marbles. I kept seeing both of them fall, and they became the same. And then . . ." Trez exhaled hard. "This is . . . man, this sounds so fucked up." She dragged her eyes up to his, direct. "I thought the woman was my ma. I thought she was the one screaming, and I had to make her stop."

He didn't respond for a few moments, schooling his expression into thoughtfulness. "Why did you think that?"

"I don't know. Ask a psych." Maybe not the whole truth there, but she couldn't analyze it now. She had to keep it together a few more days. Then . . . then she could fall apart on her own. Unless Eric wanted to stay.

"You'll get help for this problem after?"

Trez tamped down the urge to be defensive. He was trying to be kind. "Maybe. I guess . . . I'll worry about it later. After."

He didn't poke too hard at that sore spot, but continued to talk around the issue. "You sure you'll be okay suited up and maybe fighting? You don't think you'll have a flashback?"

She couldn't assure him of that, but she could try to play it down. "There could be civvies, but if it's really a Libertarian base, people there know what they're doing. Probably no one's hanging out at the remote terminal by accident."

His comm pinged. He checked it and slouched in the sofabed. "Esperes has new info for us."

"What is it?" She was afraid to get too excited.

"An updated map, with access to the raid location." He squinted at his HUD. "With scribbling on it. This is the place where they keep the ... I can't make that out. Why doesn't she just input text?"

"Is it art?"

"I'd have to ask Sam." He scowled. "Wait, seriously?!"

"Hmm?"

"I'll share it with you. She didn't protect the file." He waited for her to check her comm for the data.

She squinted. "Those are terribly drawn ... lizards?"

"Speaking of Sam, those must be the ridiculous sculptures she's working on. I guess Esperes did some recon."

"Should we send them over to your Mako buddies?"

"They already have their own maps. And they're not my Mako buddies."

"I think Kalla likes you." She yawned.

"Well, he can't have me."

"No, I mean ..." She cast around for the words. "I admire that. You have important people taking a shine to you."

He sat up straighter. "Eh, I took a shine to you, as it were."

"That's ... good. You're resourceful." Trez let herself lie back down. She struggled to keep her eyes open. "Help yourself to dinner. You can stay, but I'm not very entertaining company today."

"You don't have to be." He smiled. "We have everything

in place now, and we all want to run this operation as soon as possible. You should prioritize your own rest. Don't focus on me."

Difficult, that. He was the best anchor her mind had, and the most pleasant one. If she had a future where she could keep him, she would fight for that.

TWENTY-TWO

Kalla let Trez off his beater bike a short walk from the racetrack, within view of some of the warehouse towers. His off-road capabilities had her ass feeling somewhat numb from gravel impact, but he'd gotten her there faster than the metro would have.

At the site, she checked her condition and equipment. She stretched her shoulders and back by hugging herself, wincing at the discomfort. She'd gotten a scrip for some restoratives and boosters from Ten a while back, and she'd have to depend on those. Vail may have authorized her suit and Gauntlet for her, but she wouldn't have access to her regular complement of performance enhancers.

She activated her suit's HUD and pulled up the remote monitoring interface. Eric, Esperes, and Dorgo's team appeared as blinking lights in the bottom corner of view. She commed Eric to let him know she was almost ready.

"Got your position," Eric said. Hearing his voice let her release a breath she didn't know she'd been holding. You could see any number of metrics on your screen, but that didn't have the same visceral lizard brain calming effect audio did.

"Just running final diagnostics." Her suit didn't pop up any warning lights or exception messages. With her current fitness level, she estimated she was at about eighty percent.

"I'm not in tip-top shape, but I've worked with this handicap on sims before."

"You'll be fine. You're a professional." He didn't say this op wasn't a sim, but she knew they were both clenching their jaws. He signed off.

Trez flexed her fingers, tapped some of her ports, adjusted her helmet askew and back. Bit of a nervous tic. Didn't matter that she'd already checked everything. She put on her Gauntlet but didn't activate it. She glanced at Esperes's maps again.

Eric and the others would be breaking into a safe house underground. A network of tunnels connected all the warehouses in the area. The remote terminal she was going to crack was in one of said warehouses, not far from the racetrack.

A shame Kalla couldn't get her across the river to her objective, but there was some security checkpoint he'd have to get around. How many hundred years as a city with urban planners, and you still couldn't get there from here? She'd have to cross the river to access the warehouse. Climbing and using the track would be her best bet. It extended most of the distance over the river. From there, she could leap across.

She inhaled through her nose then exhaled sharply through her mouth before she started walking. The sound echoed in her helmet. The buildings around her reduced to two-dimensional blocks in her visual rendering, asphalt gray and featureless. Two drunken louts came into vision as she approached. Shouldn't give her much difficulty, but she'd avoid them if possible.

Reflectors glinted on the figure-eight track. The lights appeared to move. Must be activity on the track. Her binocs resolved some of them into small mechanical quadrupeds. Trace heat signatures. Of fucking course. Sam's robot lizard art.

Trez found a place to lever herself up on the track, checking again for any interlopers. Nobody nearby enough for her to care.

Her claws found enough purchase on the cement walls to let her scrabble up onto the racetrack. Trez saw the iguana robots better now. The critters wandered around the track, and some of them assembled together to form obstacles. For her? No, for the Bangor karts more likely. Ceramic shards from casualties of the last race littered parts of the asphalt.

She was plotting the best way around the metal critters, accounting for the debris, when a heat signature popped up across the river, near the far end of the track. It sped toward her as she started walking across the track. Her display showed a person in light blue armor rappelling onto the railing. As Trez made progress toward the center of the figure eight, the goon detached their climbing gear and turned toward her.

"Ey." The figure was taller than her, lean and warrior like. Trez didn't know what to say in response, so she kept walking. "Fink. Punk. You's trespassing."

Technically true, she supposed, but she didn't know who actually owned the property. "Who're you?"

"Not your business," the armored guard answered. "Now you can just turn back nice and steady, but I don't think you need to go any farther." The guard's helmet muffled their voice, but it sounded feminine, with something of a Philadelphia accent.

"No need for you to go into the water." Her adversary

indicated the river under the track with a wave. "But I'll put you there if I have to."

Trez couldn't suppress an incredulous laugh-snort. "Well, don't you have moxie."

"You's wearing a nice and hardy suit," the guard said. She cracked her knuckles and adjusted her head side to side. Trez resumed walking. Any ground gained could be important. Several robot lizards, garishly green and metallic, lay across her intended path.

Her opponent sighed loudly. "Fine. Next intimidation tactic. Last chance to back the fuck off, little ninja. You think you're good with a fancy suit and the silent treatment." The woman put her hands to her shoulder, unholstering the hilt of a weapon. She drew it to eye level and extended a vibroblade almost a meter long, snapping the flexi wire in place so that the sword pointed down.

Okay then. Serious business. Those weapons took training to use properly. Trez wouldn't need to worry about the electricity in it—her suit was shockproof—but those blades had enough power to slice through her suit and muscle weaves. She had to take down the guard, big fucking sword and all.

Trez hadn't sparred with somebody new in months. Her own adrenaline—not the hits she'd need to stay flying high—ramped up. Foolish to get excited about an interesting opponent.

She tightened her abdominal muscles, ready to rush her opponent. She would need to close within that range. A tingle, sweet pain as her elbow and fingertip ports opened and blades burst forth. Almost knocking her back on her heels though she pitched her weight forward. She bit her tongue, tasted liquid copper.

"Going somewhere?" the woman taunted. She waited for Trez to make the first move. "Though I don't know where the fuck you think you're going with those swords. Fancy dinner party?" She moved her blade to threaten.

Trez charged, but the guard was fast and caught her with a glancing blow. Another foray to test her opponent's skill got the huge sword out of the way with one elbow blade before she landed a swipe with the other. The goon twisted and body checked her, knocking Trez back a little.

Trez continued to try to dart into the swordswoman's guard and push her back as far as she could before her enemy could retaliate. She made some progress, forcing the lady back on the track. Then she stumbled over an iguana. Her boot brushed the metal and she heard a *ping*: the sound of machinery starting up. She must have triggered the art.

Dozens of iguanabots activated along with the one she'd touched, scampering between the two women. Fast little robot bastards. Trez's opponent recovered first. She pressed Trez back, making downward cuts with her blade.

No time to counter or parry. The vibroblade slashed Trez's left arm. She rolled to the side. Her suit administered more painkillers, more adrenaline, and a sealant over her new wound. Her suit wicked away some moisture, but she still smelled her own sweat. Her left arm was heavy and throbbed. She had a moment to catch her breath before they swung at each other again, and she couldn't put any strength into parrying with her left blade. Fuck. Once the adrenaline ran out, she'd be almost unable to fight.

Trez retreated and tried to run around the other woman, hoping she had a slight speed advantage. She leapt away from the next blade coming at her legs, and her back hit a large metal structure. When she looked behind her, she saw an enormous wheel made of robot iguanas. Off-balance, she put her hand on it to steady herself. She nearly pierced the structure with her finger-blades, but an awareness that would be a bad idea itched at her.

Sam had complained about the critters reacting to the metal in her tools. Lots of the racers were made of the same anodized titanium, and so were most edged weapons, like her razors and the vibroblade. It wasn't like Trez had a better idea than dodging right now; she was at too much of a reach disadvantage to continue.

Her goal was to get her opponent to strike the iguanas. She retracted her left arm-sword and took a deep breath, watching the blade and the guard's slick navy boots. The surface of the wheel was a smooth weight pressing up against her back.

The tang of the booster, herb-flavored, flooded her mouth. Trez had to wait until the last possible millisecond to jerk herself away from the blow. She tensed, waiting as the edge descended toward her then forced herself off the wheel sideways as fast as she could.

She caught herself on the ground. The track was slick beneath her hands. She kicked out and spun to regain her feet. The wheel came apart. A stream of green metal figures launched at the guard.

"Fuck! What the— Motherfucker!" Her opponent wasn't so articulate now, it seemed. Dozens of the robot creatures swarmed her and her sword, wrapping around them. Their eyes flashed, glinting off each other's emerald exteriors. Trez had to blink a few times to get a good look at them. Her opponent was somewhat disabled, but Trez couldn't use her own blades now without getting the same treatment from the lizards.

She retracted her right sword and ran at her opponent again. Trez seized her by the shoulders and tried to wrestle her over to the edge of the track. She was lucky that the guard was grabbing at the iguanas, a giant sword trapped against her body. Trez got one arm around her midsection as she neared the track wall. Fuck, those robots were an added weight.

It was one of the least glamorous throws she'd managed. The guard landed on the wall of the track itself, still struggling with the lizards. Trez had to push her over the rails into the inky river.

Chemicals sang through her veins. Fighting someone skilled who could actually injure her was a thrill she almost couldn't remember. She screamed in triumph.

Trez's vision swam a bit, an aftereffect of the boosters. When it cleared, she made out a glittering vessel in the water. The iguanas had assembled into a boat, ferrying their captive away, their jeweled eyes flashing merrily.

Trez blinked in stupefaction. Her left tricep throbbed. The blade had almost sliced through her muscle weave to the bone. She took a few more deep breaths, closed her eyes, took a moment to feel the press of her feet into the asphalt. When she felt a little more centered, she ran to the other end of the figure eight to cross the river.

———————

Trez unmuted the comm to let Eric speak. "The fuck just happened?" His voice sounded somewhere between shocked and angry.

"Art, I think." She gauged the distance between the track and the water. The current swiftly pushed debris downstream, off in the direction the iguanas carried the swordswoman.

"Are you trying to be funny?"

"No. It was Sam's installation. She's an artist, right?" The river was narrow enough that she wouldn't have to swim far to get across.

"Sacrament. I know that." She pictured him shaking his head. "But who were you fighting? And what's with the light show and iguandola?"

"My best guess is that she's the Libertists' hired muscle. The rest, I don't have the headspace to figure out right now." Trez tested her grappling hook on the railing. She'd need it to climb up to the opposite side of the river to get to the warehouse.

Eric tried to give her a status update. "Your vitals are okay. Your arm—"

She muted him for the moment, steadied herself, and tried to ignore the pain signals from her arm. Her jump into the river was about as graceful as Philly guard's earlier tumble had been.

The water hit her, cold enough to feel through her suit. She surfaced and tried to tread water while she got her hook out. It was only a few meters up, but with one arm she couldn't push herself out of the water unassisted.

The hook deployed with a snick. She gave the cord a tug once she saw it adhere to a lamppost. She supported herself by trapping the cord between the soles of her boots. Satisfied, she shimmied up with the grips on her right glove as quickly as she could.

When Trez finished pulling herself up, she tumbled over the railing and rolled onto the concrete next to the river. She took a few deep breaths again and unmuted Eric.

"At least next time please fucking tell me that you're going to just mute me." Now he sounded exasperated.

"Look, I had to concentrate. I was, you know, fighting."

"Ugh." She imagined him pacing back and forth, his face set. "During that I know not to bother you. But if you couldn't hear me and I had new intel, I don't know that you're paying attention to your text channel—"

He was making her more nervous. "Stop that. You're worrying me."

"It's because I'm the one worried about you. I can't just turn that off," he said.

He was right. Anxiety didn't work like that. She felt her chest tighten. "Look, I'm sorry. This is what I'm trained to do. This is what my career is like." A warning for the future. If she could get her job back. "Now I smell like river grease, by which I mean fryolator. What about you? Are you okay?"

Eric made a disgruntled noise. "Ah-yeah. Nothing's going on here. Dorgo says the perimeter's clear."

Trez paced around several buildings, gray warehouses on the darker gray concrete. A few vagrants gawked at her and shuffled away. The dripping encounter suit must have activated what self-preservation instincts they still had.

"Hey, you with me?" Eric asked.

"Trying to find the best way in."

"I suggest the front door. Break the lock there and stroll in like you own the place," he said. "How bad is your arm?"

"It's sealed, but she cut some muscles. If I don't use it anymore it'll be fine for some basic use in a week." There was always the potential for further injury; the op wasn't over yet. But she couldn't think beyond now anyway.

"You sure you're okay? We can still abort."

The concern in his words made her feel soft, but she needed to focus on her task. "Let's try not to make each other nervous? Just for a bit?" Her voice sounded whiny.

He didn't reply. She concentrated on the Gauntlet's decryption protocols. The warehouse door slid open with a screech. "I'm in. Just need to find the terminal."

TWENTY-THREE

Eric coughed. The air in this subterranean hallway was heavy and dank. It smelled of mildew and flaked-off whitewash. Presumably the Libertists weren't interested in keeping old infrastructure squeaky clean. He leaned back against a wall and regretted it when he heard a squelching sound.

He wasn't successful at stopping his fears racing through his head. He'd never worried so much for someone's physical safety before. Loving Trez meant fearing for her health all the time. But the same was true in the other case, he supposed. He got paid to stop bullets and blades with his body. Maybe he'd gotten complacent. It's not like he knew what to expect with this part of the raid. The security system jammed his 'dar and he didn't know what the layout or inhabitants of the site would be.

Dorgo had introduced Eric to a Mako who would provide additional muscle if necessary. Betty, as she called herself, didn't look professional with her voluminous teased hair, chunky fashion optics, and cartoon character buckles. Eric guessed it was a check on himself should something go south.

Trez's status update flashed across Eric's HUD. Security down. Dorgo gestured to all of them, and counted to three on his hand. He pushed the door open and darted into the room. Betty watched their rears and placed an alarm of her own at the doorway. One fancy security system, down. His scanning for the area came online.

A few heat signatures in the next room of the safe house. Not great. With the alarm going off, Eric didn't think he could get the drop on anybody. None of the inhabitants made a move to the door. Eric could hear some conversational sounds through the wall, but nothing distinct.

"I'd hoped it'd be empty," said Betty. "Grab what you can anyway." Dorgo grunted in agreement.

The entry room was a bare prefab with worn furniture in shades of brown and gray. Credits and other data chips were strewn all over couches and a table. More chips and hardware littered the shelves. A handgun lay on the edge of the table. Dorgo strode over, ran his glove a bit over the firearm to scan, and picked it up. "Unregistered," he commed the group. That would be valuable in itself. Dorgo put the table on its side. "Some help," he commed Eric. "Push the table along the floor and I'll direct it in front of the couch."

Eric swiped up several data chips. Any of them might be useful for Esperes, but these were more likely money. He looked around for any terminals that might be plugged in. Maybe there were data chips in there?

Betty alerted everyone to a chest she'd just opened. Half a dozen unregistered subassault firearms were jumbled together with ammunition clips and a pair of metal knuckles. She sorted through them at a measured pace while Eric and Dorgo moved the metal table in front of the sofa and angled it toward the door. Eric didn't need the knuckles to be dangerous with his fists, but he picked them up along with the guns when Betty dropped them at his feet. He adjusted the couch to line up with the table while Dorgo resumed casing the room.

Heat signatures—six of them—converged on the opposite

side of the door to the adjoining room. Everybody scrambled for cover behind the sofa, although Kayla was still concentrating on one of the data cards while she curled up and unholstered her ridiculous shotgun.

The door opened, and the anarchists shoved a bodged-together barricade through it. Somebody yelled. Ammunition sprayed all over the room.

The sofa was sturdy enough to slow down the shot. Bullets pinged off Eric's armor. When the shots stopped, Eric's team returned fire. The two sides traded fire in several volleys.

The safe house's inhabitants weren't heavily armored, but they'd thrown on some gear and the barricade provided them with decent cover. Their helmets had standard face shields.

One of them had to be Trez's mother. She looked very much like the old photos Trez had shared with him. Marde. He didn't want to shoot Trez's mother. And he couldn't really tell Betty and Dorgo to avoid her. They weren't going to be merciful to the Libertist leader just on his say-so.

Santorini barked orders, timing when the Libertists fired. It gave Eric's team enough warning to know when to take cover.

He was going to run out of ammo soon though. The anarchists had enough time to bring extra clips, so they would win this firefight if they could make it last long enough. He chewed on his lip and slid the guns over to Dorgo.

"The fuck?" Dorgo didn't seem to find the prospect of being outgunned humorous. Eric fitted the knuckles over his own. He shook his shoulders and squatted then sprinted across the room to the anarchists' barricade.

"Focus fire!" Santorini yelled. Bullets whizzed by him. Some slammed into his armor, and he shook a bit from the impact. Getting shot in armor still hurt most everyone enough to disable them for minutes. But eating bullets was one of Eric's jobs. He crushed his teeth together, almost biting through his mouthguard, and popped some Spice to distract himself from the pain. Worse would come shortly.

Eric stopped running to grab the nearest person to him that he could—a middle-aged man. With surprise on his side, he was able to get the man in a chokehold.

"Fuck! Back up! Back away and shoot the man!" Santorini's voice shook. "If you have a clear shot!" Closer, he saw a face he'd previously only seen in pictures.

His prisoner struggled in his arms, and Eric punched him repeatedly with his right fist. More bullets hit Eric. He probably had a few cracked ribs by now. The Libertist's armor was weakest at the joints, so Eric went for those even as he registered additional hurts.

"Shit!" One of the Libertists hadn't been careful enough backing away from Eric, and Betty took advantage of that and shot him. One down. The man Eric held finally slumped in his arms, unconscious. One less.

Eric turned to tackle another Libertist, but nobody was within arm's length. He heaved himself over to another shooter, and got shot in the chest by his intended victim. Eric's vision swam, but he lurched far enough forward to take his opponent down with him. More shots hit him in the back as they fell.

He was used to hitting the floor, and the other body absorbed most of the impact. That said, he was amazed he didn't black out. His shoulder burned when he tried to lift a fist. The anarchist had a giant strength disadvantage, but Eric was out of it enough that the woman managed to roll him onto his back.

Another bang assaulted his ears. This time, not gunfire.

He tried to account for the door opening again and the new heat signature on his readout.

The leader jumped to her feet. "Beatrez?" Her chin came up. She froze. Ammo pelted her. Some of the buckshot got past her armor. She fell back in a heap, gurgling.

One of the gunmen screamed. Another started to chant "mondieu mondieu mondieu." The woman wrestling him got distracted enough that he could pin her. He'd have to sit on her to keep her down.

He looked to the doorway. Trez, all blades extended, stood still, eyes wide and jaw slack. Then she screamed too, and launched herself across the room.

Gunmen fired at her, but missed. Trez landed next to the wounded woman and shoved an anarchist aside. Trez immediately pressed her hands on the lady's shoulder to slow the bleeding. "You," she said.

Santorini tried to raise a trembling hand. Tears filled her eyes, and her mouth moved to form words.

Trez's face twisted up. "Someone get me an aid kit!" The Libertists scrambled to obey. Eric savored the first silent moments since the raid began.

"Surrender and we won't kill you," Dorgo said. He and Betty had gotten into position and pointed their guns at the remaining anarchists. They looked around briefly, gazes darting to their unconscious compatriots. "That includes your leader. We would prefer her alive for questioning."

"Ah, yeah," the woman he was sitting on said. "Get off me." He obeyed involuntarily when she jolted his body with her hip. Sacrament. Santorini's other compatriots murmured their assent, and Betty and Dorgo began the process of restraining them for capture.

The worst of his pain had receded, potent inhibitor

cocktails swimming in his body chemistry, so he made it over to Trez's side. She had an aid kit open while she worked on her mother, so he applied more painkiller patches to himself. He didn't say anything.

Trez held Santorini's hand, her finger-knives glinting. A bullet had gone through Santorini's shoulder. She was unconscious, but the aid kit said her vitals were stable for right now. Eric put his left arm around Trez's shaking shoulders. They knelt in silence. He scanned the room for hardware. Two terminals were set up, lights blinking. An assortment of peripherals, most of which Eric didn't recognize, were plugged into tangles of cables.

Dorgo walked over to Eric, leaving Betty to watch the prisoners. They seemed to have trouble sitting still, but didn't give her any lip. "You holding up?" he said.

Eric shrugged. His thoughts felt kilometers away, and he couldn't speak for Trez.

"We have personnel en route to help us with the prisoners and give any necessary medical treatment. You don't need to do anything else. We can take them in ourselves." Dorgo counted out most of the credit chips they'd grabbed. "Hazard pay. You took a lot of risks." Trez had one arm entwined with Eric's and was holding him tightly enough that he didn't move to take the creds. Dorgo crouched. "Every so often I forget that Corp troops are paid well for a reason," he mused. "Consider me reminded. Those were two amazing distractions." He put the chips down in front of Trez and Eric.

Eric made a wide gesture at the entire room. "Could I take some of this tech instead of a few of the credits?" The Makos had agreed to forgive the vast majority of Trez's debts already. He doubted they currently had the technical capabilities to make much use of the data drives and peripherals.

Dorgo pursed his lips. "I think so. I'll double-check with Boss."

Trez sniffed. Eric would decipher that later, when he could think about boring things again.

Dorgo's eyes darted to Santorini. "This person. Friend of yours?"

"Used to be." Trez stared at Dorgo, her face set. Eric would pay a month's salary to know her thoughts.

Dorgo's head tilted in speculation, but he didn't ask any further questions. "I can arrange for a van to pick you up."

"That okay with you?" Eric asked Trez. She nodded. Walking and getting on the train would draw a lot of attention to their wounds.

"I'll leave you alone then." Dorgo gave a small smile and turned away, going back to watching the prisoners.

"Hey, Eric?" Trez whispered. She put Felicity's hand down.

"Ah-yeah?" He kept his voice low too.

"Hold me?"

"Mais oui." He scooted around and enfolded her in the closest embrace he could.

Trez muttered inarticulate things into his shoulder for a few minutes. When she finished, she lifted her head and rested her forehead against his. They helped each other up, and he let her lean on him despite his injuries. He didn't know what to say to her. Dorgo seemed satisfied. Her debt troubles were over. But there wasn't total relief. The Makos had her mother. Trez and Santorini may have a fraught relationship, but maybe Trez still felt guilty.

"I'm exhausted but I don't think I'll be able to sleep tonight," she confessed.

"I'm not sure sleep will come easily to me either. Come over to my place. We can talk more if we want." Maybe he should take a heavier dose of painkillers. That might help him get some rest.

"Sure, but ... I don't know what to say yet." She shook her head. "The past few hours don't feel real to me."

"I didn't say we had to talk," he said. "Take your time. You actually have some now."

She raised her chin. "Yes. I don't know what to do with it though."

"Worry about that later," he said. "Let's focus on getting home now."

"Home ... that sounds good," she said. Her voice drifted off, and she stayed silent until the van picked them up.

Trez took her eyes off the tenement across the street. Somebody had graffitied "FUXC ALIEV SUCKS" and the logo of the Sea Dogs in blue and yellow on the third floor outside wall. She still didn't have any idea what the artist was trying to express. But enough procrastinating. She'd dawdled an hour.

She opened her comm and dialed the Mako contact number. As soon as Kalla's image popped up, she said, "I'd like to talk to Santorini." She sat on her sofabed, keeping her back as straight as she could.

"Ah-yeah," said Kalla. "Dorgo told me you would. Told me you used to work together?"

"Something like that." If Dorgo knew the familial relationship, he hadn't clued Kalla in.

"From before you were Corp?"

"We all have parts of our pasts we'd like to forget," she said.

"Not really. My life's an open book." He made a tiny smirk. "What do you want to talk about?"

She pressed a hand into her thigh so she wouldn't make a fist. "Just personal shit," she said.

Dorgo walked into the field of view of the holo. "We've got Santorini at a secure location," Dorgo said. "You can comm, but I can't give you much privacy."

"Won't be an issue," said Trez. The Makos watching would actually be convenient. Remembering that would help her keep the conversation from getting too heavy.

"You can keep it short then?"

"Sure." If only because she'd no idea how long she could keep her composure.

The screen switched over to a cell with two bare lights. A shiny length of chain bound Felicity's wrists to a dinged-up, rusty chair. The walls behind her were the gray of every public works project in the past twenty years. No decoration to identify them. Felicity's clothing was wrinkled. She had a black eye, and a dressing covered her neck.

Trez touched her sling and smoothed out her sweater. Words stuck in her throat.

Felicity saved Trez from having to break the ice. "Beatrez?" she asked. She put a hand up, as if to touch Trez through the screen.

"That's me."

"You look . . ." Her voice cracked a bit. Felicity had lines under her eyes and between her brows. Her gaze darted to Trez's sling.

"Not great. We're both mugshot worthy right now." Trez stopped herself from smoothing her forehead. Maybe she'd look less drawn and washed out with several months of rest.

Felicity shifted in her chair. "Betty said they would let you talk to me?"

"For a little bit. Supervised. Welcome back to the neighborhood." She was terrible at sounding dry, she thought. She should leave the sarcasm to Eric.

"I must admit, I didn't expect to see you. I had no idea you'd be involved with these ... people." Which word had she originally intended to use for the Makos? Couldn't be anything flattering.

"Sorry." Trez scowled.

Felicity shivered. Trez would bet a few creds that the Makos weren't interested in keeping their holding cells warm. "Not sure how you got involved with this crowd."

Trez's scowl intensified. "You of all people giving me social advice? Seems several decades too late for that."

Felicity closed her eyes for a moment. "No. I don't have that right."

Trez inspected Santorini's face for a slight pinch in her lips or signs of tension in her jaw. But if anything, her mother seemed pensive instead of hurt or betrayed.

"You don't seem upset about it. Me showing up at the warehouse, that is," she mumbled.

"What's done is done, I'm sure you had your reasons." There she went being all generous and magnanimous and all that crap.

Trez didn't know if the woman bought her own bullshit. Her daughter had gotten her captured and wounded. Was she trying to play it down? Had she accepted the possibility beforehand? "Aw, that's sweet." She tried to smile, but ended up baring her teeth instead. Sarcasm bled from her words.

"I was surprised though. I thought you wanted to help us out. You seemed to believe in the cause." Felicity made a face Trez didn't like. Mostly because she had seen it on her own face too many times. Well, that was where the brow lines came from.

"Seems like you were projecting." A lump of resentment in her throat twisted everything into an accusation.

"That's what you thought?" Felicity brushed her braids to the side. "Seems I really fucked that up."

When had Felicity finally figured that out? Well, it didn't make any difference now. "You running off didn't inspire further loyalty." Trez brought up her nails for inspection. The metal needed some maintenance.

Her mother gave a small shrug. "I kept telling myself you were safe. But then Morrison died. He was carrying a message. Just like I had you doing. Where he died ... You'd crossed that street many times on your regular routes."

Trez hadn't known that. "You got scared then."

Felicity shifted in her seat. "Yes. I may not have been the greatest parent for you, but I didn't want you getting killed on my account."

Trez tried to throw her hands up, but her sling got in the way. Her shoulder throbbed. She tried to suppress a hiss of pain. "You made a decision unilaterally and ran off."

"I didn't want you to have to deal with my bullshit." Felicity's voice was toneless.

That sounded far too familiar. "Nice try, but I made my own instead." If Eric could hear this conversation, he would be laughing hard enough to fall out of his chair.

Felicity flinched. "Fair enough. But I am curious. I don't know what Linus's problems have to do with the Makos. But did you know I'd be in the warehouse?"

"I knew it was possible. But I didn't expect anyone at the site."

Felicity's fists clenched at her sides, and she took a deep breath, probably to steady herself. "Is that all?"

No, but with the Makos listening in, she didn't want to

get any more worked up. Picking further at their emotional wounds wouldn't lead anywhere she wanted to go. "For now. Maybe we'll talk again."

"You think these Makos will let us?" Felicity schooled her expression into blankness.

Trez raised her shoulders a bit. "Hard telling not knowing. So that's why I'm saying hi now. And perhaps goodbye." She immediately thought that sounded too melodramatic, but it was too late to take back.

"Thank you, Beatrez, for saying hello. Even if it was just to curse me out." Felicity smiled. "You're a fascinating person."

So she chose now to take an interest in Trez? "I guess it's cool you think so. Even if fascinating doesn't help me with my problems."

"I hadn't intended . . . No, I mean—" Felicity's eyes were misty. "Trez . . . stay out of trouble. Unless there's really something you believe in."

Well, sounded like Felicity's idealism hadn't changed. "Like you do? It's not like I've swallowed your whackadoodle anarchist crap."

Felicity hunched over in her chair and put her hands in her armpits. "I didn't think so. But you might believe in something else. Make the most of it."

Fucking platitudes. "You sound like a motivational speaker." She couldn't keep still anymore. She began to pace, just as she'd seen Eric do.

"You did ask."

"You're terrible at goodbyes." Bands of tension squeezed her head. "But good luck. Take care of yourself."

"You mean . . . ?" Felicity's eyes were bright. Fuck. If she started crying, Trez would have to disconnect. Even if the Makos would laugh at her weakness.

"I mean I don't know what else to say now, except I'd prefer you don't get yourself killed. I'm sentimental enough for that." The edge hadn't left her voice.

Felicity blinked, keeping back her tears. Probably knew Trez cared more than she let on. "You're safe now though?"

"No, my life's a complete mess and I have too many decisions to make. But thanks for asking."

"Ah ..." Felicity sat back.

Trez shook her shoulders out. "But that's all. For now." She switched the channel. Seemed she was equally shitty at goodbyes.

Kalla looked up abruptly from the media he'd been consuming. His hair didn't move a millimeter. "Well, that was, as the lady said, fascinating," he said.

She grunted. It was that or tell him to fuck off.

"Like sharks circling each other." His hair maintenance budget must be a double-digit percentage of his take-home pay.

Trez gave him silence. She didn't need to discuss this with him.

"In any case," Dorgo interjected, "I know your debt is paid, but I was thinking you could help us with something. Maybe consult for us."

She shook her head. "If you're asking about the Libertists, chances I have any useful knowledge are nil."

Dorgo opened a hand out toward her. "You can identify some of them for us."

"I recognize Levin. I recognize her. Everyone else I've heard of or seen is new to me."

"You know their methods and what they do."

"They're not exactly secretive with their beliefs. And it was a long time ago."

He didn't push. "I don't need an answer right away. We'll keep in touch."

"Sure." Ideally, she didn't need to talk to him anytime in the near future. Trez hung up and walked over to her dining table. How long would it take to destroy all her chairs with one arm?

She pulled herself back. She should go for a run instead. Pound out the turbulence inside her. No, she'd jostle the sling that way. She could cycle at the HarborSec fitness center, but Mihai or another coworker she knew might be there, and she didn't feel like answering more questions about herself.

Maybe Eric would understand. He was at home, so she asked if he'd like company. When he replied with a happy smiley icon, she let him know she was on her way over.

Trez tried to empty her mind as she struggled to put on one arm of her coat. After several unsuccessful attempts, she cursed and threw it over her shoulder. It wasn't raining. She'd keep warm enough if she walked fast.

TWENTY-FOUR

Eric checked the memo he was working on for what felt like the fortieth time.

Attn. Director Seymour: My investigation led me to seek outside help (with the data anonymized, of course). We were able to geolocate the masked IPs to a mostly-uninhabited area near Presumpscot. I investigated the area personally. There are several abandoned warehouses. One of them had some furniture and electronics, but nothing else. From the age of the footprints I analyzed, I'd say the place was inhabited until recently. I found some hair samples for DNA, but those don't match anyone in Harbor or municipal databases. —Eric Greis

Would Seymour accept that? It wasn't anything concrete for her to pursue, but it looked like he'd made a good effort to solve the case. He'd spent hours editing the memo in the hopes that different words might keep Seymour off his back. By now, every change he could think of made it look worse in one way or another.

When his doorbell rang, he pressed send on the memo before he let Trez in. When he greeted her at the door, Trez was frowning slightly. She shuffled in, one arm in a sling, the other holding the sling.

"So how'd it go?" he asked. Obviously not ideally, but he

had to ask in case she wanted to talk. He would have liked to be on that call, but she'd said she had to do it alone.

Trez shook her head. "Not great."

"Want to talk about it?"

"Not right now. I need to figure out my thoughts."

"Fair enough." Relationships with mothers were tangled to begin with, and Trez's was knottier than most.

She collapsed onto his sofabed with a big exhale. "Just ... well ... reminds me how stove-up in the head I am." She curled up, tucking her knees below her chin.

He didn't comment there, because nothing he could think of would lead the conversation anywhere good. "Makos behave themselves? No Staplehead antics?"

"I'm not sure what you mean. He's never given me any trouble." She slumped deeper into the futon.

"Well, guess we've proven ourselves to them. Not that I would suggest going and running up a bunch of gambling debts."

She scowled at him, but the effect was minimal with her in hedgehog pose. It was adorable, actually. "You're asking for a beating."

"I can take it," he said. He walked over to the counter. "You need a drink. One with a bit of alcohol in it."

"Probably."

While he got her a beer, Trez ruminated on the sofa. Worry lines creased her forehead. But as usual, she didn't fidget. Made her seem more dangerous somehow, like she'd spring to life and there'd be pink spray all over any second. Usually he found that hot, but right now he doubted flirting would go over well with her.

At least they were out of danger for now. He could be

patient. She'd talk when she was ready. He placed the cup on the coffee table next to the futon.

"Thanks," she said. She didn't make any motion to pick up her drink though.

"I haven't tried this brewery before, but they seem a decent midrange shop. Run by this card who wanted to talk to me about esters." Eric had picked up the pale ale as a safe bet. Trez liked the bitter brews; she drank her caff black instead of regular.

"Oh." She regarded her tankard, her nose and forehead scrunched together, for what he considered an inappropriately long time. He'd have to start for her before she stared her drink to death. He picked up the tankard and sipped. Decent. Almost lemony.

"I meant, not only for the beer," she said.

He put the tankard down. "You're welcome?"

"Do you want me to make a list?" Her voice was low and soft.

"Haven't we been over this before? You don't owe me anything. I'm just glad you're safe now."

"I can say thanks anyway. Because you had my back, and I never doubted that. And you got hurt for me." She took a sip and made an approving sound.

Getting shot wasn't high on his list of preferred activities, but ... "It's nothing I haven't done before. I thought the situation called for it."

"Yes, but ..."

He put an arm around her shoulders. "I'll heal. I had some medical time saved, so I'm just doing paperwork now. With luck, nothing will happen on my regular rotations."

Trez's mouth quirked. "You mean like anarchists breaking

into a lab they shouldn't have access to in a million years?"

"Yeah, like that."

"Well, I'll hope for that, I guess. Anyway. I've been thinking."

Eric tried to keep himself from tensing. Those words rarely ended up being anything good. "Ah-yeah?"

"I've scheduled an appointment with someone Doc Ten recommended me." She sat up straight and knocked over her drink with a flailing wrist. "Agh! I'm sorry."

"It's okay." He stood up and took her cup back to the dispenser. He sanitized it, refilled it with water, and found a towel and detergent to clean up the spill. "You were saying?"

"A headmed."

"That's good." He brought back her tankard and placed it at the center of the table. The beer didn't show up much on the green carpet, but it wouldn't smell great if he didn't do some cleaning. He sprayed the stain.

"I don't know if I would have done it without you," she confessed.

"Therapy's difficult to do. But it's good you're starting, yeah?" Eric scrubbed at the carpet with the towel.

"Yeah." Her expression became pensive. "Seems necessary. Especially if we're staying together. Unless you don't want to."

"No." He dabbed at the detergent foam. Not a professional job, but this was his apartment. It would do.

"No what?"

He dropped the towel on the floor, then sat up straight and caught her eyes. "I mean no, I don't want—"

Her eyebrows went up. "Then I won't bother you. You've given me more than I deserve—"

"Let me finish! Câlice!" He wasn't sure if he was more exasperated or amused.

"Okay." Her face was grave. "I'm listening."

"I mean no to I don't want. I do want." A smile crept across his mouth. "I want us to be together too. If you're sure."

"I'm sure." Still that intent gaze.

"Well, then, all we can do is try our best. Like any other relationship." Trez would probably forgive him later for sounding so corny. If she even noticed.

She nodded. Her sincerity might aggravate him some-times, but right now it was delightful. The seriousness on her face had to go though. He scooted over and knelt across from her, leaning in so they could touch foreheads. "I know it won't be easy. You still have shit to work through. And me, well, who knows. I have a few things I could change in life. Priorities. I could get hurt on the job." He kissed her in the space between her eyebrows, but she didn't relax.

He hadn't considered how she'd feel about him being in danger before. He hadn't liked her facing off against a highly armed, highly trained combatant. And that was part of his job description. He'd had a lot of broken bones and torn muscles. Some head trauma. Vail wasn't the only guard in CorpSec with artificial limbs. Eric had only gotten his job when another guard had died, giving the department an open head. Another guard had slipped the wind four years ago.

"I know," Trez said. "We're people who have jobs where we fuck other people up and get fucked up in return. That's what we're good at and that's why they pay us." She gave him a bitter smile. "Like you said, it won't be easy. But we've been through so much already . . ."

"It's difficult to imagine things getting tougher, isn't it? But I shouldn't tempt fate."

He got a smile for that, this one genuine, and he held her

for a few minutes. Envisioning the future ... he'd no idea where it could go. They both had decisions to make. They could make them together.

When he pulled her in tighter, he accidentally jostled her sling. She winced.

"Sorry." They were both clumsy today.

"I've had worse." She shrugged her unencumbered shoulder.

"You're pulling the macho marde with me again," he said. "What did your back-alley doc say?" It wasn't as if she could have gone to Menendez with sword wounds when she was supposedly off duty.

"It should heal without complications. The suit kept me clean of infection. I can remove the sling in a week."

"I assume you won't be going swimming straightaway though."

"Not so much. Ten told me I'd need to wait a few months before I did contact sports. I laughed at one of his jokes for a change, and he didn't know why." She paused. "Speaking of medics, I got a comm from Harbor Medical while we were talking. Can I open it now?"

"Be my guest." He made an expansive gesture with one hand.

She brought up a holo screen. Charts came up with numbers, some of them in red.

Trez frowned, and slowly scrolled through to the end of the document. Eric watched her as she perused the summary. She closed her eyes, and her shoulders slumped.

"Anything interesting?" He kept his tone as light as possible.

"You can see it right there." She indicated the screen with her chin.

"But I was watching you instead."

"I think you can tell that it's not good news." She looked away, staring at a painting of waterfowl that Sam had given him a few years back.

"Sure, but ..." He gently rubbed her neck. "Anything unexpected is a better question, really."

Trez let her head drop forward. "I expected nephritis and liver damage. Or at least I told myself I did. But it's still depressing."

Of course. Her pharma blend hadn't killed her, but he hadn't heard of anyone who took the magnitude of chemical load that she had without sustaining organ damage. "It's normal to hope for the best," he said.

"The liver damage might be reversible. If I don't take any painkillers or drink heavily for at least six months, that is. The kidney problems ... well. Those aren't, really." Her voice climbed in pitch. "And they'll only progress once I return to work. If I can go on strikes again."

"Could you get a cloned kidney transplant?" He reached under the bed for one of his squishy flannel pillows.

"Only if I convince HarborSec I'm worth the investment." She exhaled sharply.

It wouldn't be an easy sell. Her cybernetics and training may have been expensive, but Harbor probably considered that sunk cost. Her recent track record wasn't stellar. And she was past peak fitness. "Do you want to?" Gentleness seemed called for here.

Her muscles tensed under his hand. "I feel very old."

"You're not even thirty-five," he said.

"How many strikers do you know past thirty-five?" she asked.

She had a point. The few who kept striking that long were

exceptions. He didn't know of any currently active. "It does happen."

Trez shook her head. "I'd only have a few years left. And that's if I got the new kidneys." She was quiet for a moment, and he handed her his pillow. A nonplussed look crossed her face, but then she embraced the pillow with one arm. She squeezed hard enough that he could see a tricep flex.

"You're good at it though." Encouraging Trez to pursue that avenue wouldn't be good for his sanity, but he had to let her make her own choices.

"Getting back into shape after that long a leave though . . ." Her eyes widened as she entertained that thought.

"Brutal training? Like all the muscle rehab?"

"My body needs a long time to heal, and that's just going to render me out of shape. And there's no guarantee I'd be able to do the job after all the rehab."

Something didn't add up. "You've never complained about physical effort before," Eric said. "There's got to be something else."

Trez took his hand in her free one, lacing her cold fingers with his. "Can I even do this anymore? What if I have a flashback?"

"You handled yourself well back at Presumpscot."

"Well, you were the one who told me it wouldn't be like a strike." She squeezed his hand hard. Luckily he'd had his phalanges reinforced—otherwise he'd likely have some broken fingers now.

He refrained from grunting. "You can use the time off to deal with the . . . psych stuff. Since you're seeing a psych anyway."

"It's not just the trauma. It's . . . I don't think I have it anymore." She released her grip on him and looked at her lap.

"It?"

"The spark. Motivation. You know, what keeps strikers not washed up," she mumbled.

He had no answer for her there. "Well, you don't have to go back to it if you don't want to do it."

"There is the matter of money."

He wasn't completely sure of her situation, but— "You'll be fine even if you never go back to Harbor though, right?"

"I can scrape by. A few odd jobs would pay the rent and for dessert every so often." She exhaled hard. "Not enough to pay any more blackmail though. Especially if Linus runs up that kind of debt again."

"You got that handled?" Her pa was a walking disaster.

"The Makos don't need him around anymore, so we agreed that he should move out to DC. Smaller chance of someone finding out his secrets there. If he gets into trouble, he can face the consequences himself." Her mouth flattened to a line. "I'm two for two with parents leaving me. New fodder for my nightmares."

"Why DC?"

"It's warmer there. Better for his arthritis."

"Well then," he said, "I think you should feel free to make your own decision without worrying about him."

Eric's comm rang. Seymour. He had no acting training, so he could only pray that he came across convincingly. He took a deep breath to brace himself.

Seymour's desk was a mess of electronics and office supplies, and her face was tight. "Greis."

"Director Seymour." He wasn't sure who seemed less pleased to see who.

"Your report. Is that all you have? A dead end?"

"Unfortunately, yes." He hoped that he projected chagrin instead of caginess.

She picked up an adapter from the pile of electronics and began fidgeting with it. "It sounds far-fetched. An abandoned warehouse? And you couldn't find anyone connected?"

"Director, I did contract outside help. But if we're going with just my resources and connections, I don't know if there's anything I can do further in that avenue."

"We still have no useful information about the intruder either," Seymour muttered. "The culprits must all be from away, or be elite enough to remove the records from our local databases. Unlikely. I'll look at those logs you found again."

"I wasn't able to find any links to Fairchild or Michaud, which would make sense with your theory. The technique they used to cover their tracks isn't copyrighted by any corporation, including Harbor. That's what the Runner said anyway."

"I'm disappointed, Greis. Are you sure there's nothing further you can do?" She bared her teeth at him.

It was an effort not to blanch at that. He tried to dial in the correct amount of shame. "I'm sorry, Director."

"Don't consider this matter closed just yet. I may send you instructions." She disconnected before he could say goodbye.

Trez kept her expression blank. "Did that go as you expected?"

He half shrugged. "Well, she could get me fired, but I could damage her on the way out by leaking information. Until this secret project of hers comes to fruition, I'm relatively safe. I can try to transfer to a different department, but I think she'll block that. But if she fires me, I can always interview with a department far away in the org chart that she can't get me fired there. It will invariably be lower prestige and pay, but

I'll survive. If the worst comes to worst and I get hounded out of Harbor, I'll end up a small business rent-a-cop." The thought didn't evoke the same disgust it would have a month ago. It would mean he couldn't help Sam try to break out as an independent artist any longer. She'd have to move back in with him and take gig work to fund her lifestyle. But he accepted that as the possible price of Trez's continued safety.

"I thought your career meant a lot to you though."

"It did. Approval from the higher-ups feels good. But once people I cared about were in danger, I realized that they were more important. You, especially."

"What about Vail? Why are you staying silent about their involvement? Aren't you angry at them?"

"For possibly stoving-up my career? I mean, I wish they hadn't. But if I were in the same situation ... chronic pain plus an abusive boss ... would I have done the same? The bribe money would shave several years off my retirement age.

"I'm not pleased with them. But I don't want to throw them under a train." He might be playing his feelings down, but he wanted more distance from the past few weeks' events before he got inspired to do anything stupid. "But I'll think about that more later. What about you? Do you want to retire from striking now?"

She went back to looking at—or past, he wasn't sure which—the gull painting. "Retiring? I don't know what I'd do with myself with all that free time." Strikers didn't tend to enjoy retirement. Without the state-of-the-art security toys, the rush from sanctioned violence, and the status they had within society, they got wicked bored and depressed. Many turned to pharma to deal with their chronic pain.

"There are other Security jobs," he said. "Harbor considers your expertise valuable."

"A desk job?" Her eyebrows attempted to climb off her forehead.

Eric collected her in his arms and put her chin on his shoulder. "Well, you said you'd thought about training the rookies."

"Don't know if I'd be any good at it. I can follow directions and a regimen, but can I give direction? Plus, I'd have to work with the other trainers. I don't know how to work in a team." She squirmed a little on his lap and stroked the inside of his forearm.

"You did fine a few days ago." Was she trying to distract him? He'd be down with that.

"All I did was tell you my status and give a signal. And ended up snapping at you because I didn't know how to deal with someone being worried about me." She kissed his neck then bit it lightly.

He shivered a bit. "You could learn. May be worth a try."

"I'll think about it." She took his hand and lifted it to her mouth. She looked up at his eyes and licked her lips. "What about you?"

"About me?"

———————

Trez had too many hormones swimming in her body. She'd been crying, she felt like a slug, and she couldn't think of a muscle that didn't feel tense. Sex would at least be a release. Eric felt real and strong against her. Like he could weather any emotional Nor'easter that she threw at him.

Trez nibbled the bump of flesh under his thumb. She'd say heat rose in her, but she wasn't in control of her body temperature these days. She just got hot flashes and random chills. She sucked his thumb into her mouth and flicked her tongue against the digit.

"Thought you had dinner. Still hungry? Want dessert?" he joked.

"Not the kind that has calories," she replied. She gave him a look out the sides of her eyes.

"Some kind of foam then? Diet foam? With lime green flavor?" He waggled his eyebrows.

"That's disgusting." She dropped his hand.

"It's a palate cleanser."

"I'll take your word for it." Trez raised her mouth to his and placed it lightly. She took a few moments to feel the pressure their mouths barely exerted on each other. Tenuous. Her focus narrowed with her eyes closed.

His breath grew deeper too, and he put a hand to her breast. She felt a bit of stubble where his jaw met her chin. A feeling she couldn't name suffused her. As if she could burst out of her skin, some sort of raw sorrow monster.

When Eric tweaked her nipple, she breathed, "No."

He sat back, blue eyes clear and meeting hers. "I thought you were hungry."

She shook her head. "I am. Just . . . don't do anything with your hands."

"Fine. I'll let you do the work. I adore being lazy." He made a show of putting his hands behind his back, against the sofa cushion. "Hunger all you like. It's hot."

"What?"

"Your eyes, they almost glint. It's like one of those nature documentaries."

"What?"

"Predation is hot. I can handle myself." He cocked his head and challenge set in his jaw. "Do your worst."

"It's not quite like that. It's like ... Oh, sacrament." At this rate she'd end up using sacres like him. "I'm afraid I'll explode."

Eric smiled. "I think that's the point. At least if we're doing it right."

"I can't explain it. I'm sorry." She looked away from him.

The tension left his shoulders. "Hey, it's all right, you know. No, I mean it's not all right. Fuck. I mean ..."

"Just be with me now? Please?" She'd spent days wanting to destroy something. With Eric, at least, she felt he could handle her savagery.

"You wanting to take it out on my body again?" He sounded far more hopeful than she would have thought.

"If it's okay." He'd been through a lot too, she realized.

"Yes. Please," he added.

It was like their first hotsync in the sparring room, the transmutation of every ounce of tension into animal desire. She leaned back on him and took his mouth with more vigor this time.

He opened under her assault and pressed into her, lips firm. "You know," he said, between kisses, "we could go hard and fast once to take the edge off then again to get it out of our systems—"

"Keep your hands where they are."

"I'm still sitting on them," he protested.

Trez placed her free hand on his shoulder and leaned into him as she gave him more kisses, varying the angles at which their mouths met.

He pulled back slightly. "You feel like you don't have control over anything? You need this?"

"I need something to go how I say it does. Just for right

now." She maneuvered herself onto his lap, putting her thighs on either side of his.

"I'm kind of confused, but I'm also horny." His hips lifted a little under hers, exerting pressure. She squeezed in response. "So you call the shots."

Maybe later she could explain. But for now she moved her mouth to his neck, giving little bites until she reached the hollow of his throat. His pulse thudded under her lips. "This comes off," she said, sliding a hand up underneath his gray tank top.

"Yes please." He didn't make any move to help her though.

Her talons came out and she sliced cleanly up the sides of his shirt. He inhaled sharply. She scratched his sides to remind him to stay still.

She walked her hand up his sternum, the points of her blades digging in only enough to tease. She peeled Eric's tank off then returned to kissing his bare skin. His breath grew uneven when she flicked one of his nipples. With her mouth she explored the contours of his collarbone, his chest, and his abdominal muscles. Faint scarring marked him haphazardly. She ran her tongue along those shiny lines.

He shifted his legs a bit wider apart under her. "My legs only go so wide," she warned.

Eric gave her a lazy smile. "I know how flexible you are."

"Don't push it." His ease made her a little angrier somehow. She squeezed his thighs with hers to assert her strength again, and his smile got wider. "You're getting off on this?"

"I said I'm confused, not that I'm worried or scared. Still horny." He looked down pointedly at the bulge in his pants and shimmied his shoulders. "Maybe less confused now."

She leaned over again and met his mouth with hers while

she unsnapped the front of his pants. His erection fell into her hand, and she gave it a quick squeeze before pushing herself up to shove his pants down.

"Guh." Well, at least he didn't have words for everything. He lifted himself on his elbows, almost bridging himself up to provide her access to him. He'd taken his shoes off earlier, so shucking his pants was trivial. She kissed one of his calves.

"Trez, take your clothes off." His words might be an order, but she chose to hear them as a plea. He still had his hands at his side and he looked a little lost.

"Hmm?" She'd been so wrapped up in exploring him, she hadn't shed any clothing. Well, if he liked her predatory, he'd get his wish. She stepped back to the edge of the sofabed, within easy reach if he wanted to grab her. "Just sit there and watch."

Trez took an exaggerated breath, watched his eyes follow the movement of her chest, and smiled. She wasn't wearing anything provocative in itself—a simple tank and stretch shorts—but she could tease a little. She put her fingers at her sides, took hold of the fabric, and eased it up inch by inch. She struggled when the sling got in her way.

Eric's eyes went wide. The better to see her with, she supposed. His mouth was parted slightly when she dropped the top into a puddle of cloth on the cold floor. Her thighs quivered a bit, feeling the air and empty space between them.

She was in a bit more of a hurry with her shorts, so she pushed those down. She climbed on top of him and he leaned forward and kissed her high on the chest.

Trez frowned. "I didn't say you could—"

"I'm keeping my hands right where they are," he replied. "If you don't want something, just say no."

She couldn't, truth be told. She even helped him a little,

arching her back so he could attend to a breast. He laved her with his tongue, nibbled on the nipple, then sucked her into his mouth. He didn't make any wisecracks about her eagerness.

Lust twined with aggression in her blood. Later they could have sex however he wanted, once she burned this anger out of her blood. But she shouldn't just focus on herself.

Eric nuzzled between her breasts and she stilled. He looked up at her, expression serious. "What's up?" he asked. His eyes were clear. But the past few weeks couldn't have been easy for him.

"Just thinking about you. You okay?" Strange timing on her part, but she should consider his pleasure.

"You're naked. That makes things great." He kissed the inside of each breast.

"No, I mean . . . Is there something you need? Somewhere I should touch you?"

"Ah." At that his hands did come up, and he put them on her hips. He squeezed them. "For this? For right now, I'm having a lot of fun. Another time," he promised, "we can mix it up. I have a few ideas. But just now, I liked the way you were going with this." He slid his hands down to cup her ass, but didn't pull her forward. Her breath caught.

Trez took a slow breath then licked her lips deliberately. She made a show of looking down at his lap, following the arrow of hair down to the goods. His abdominal muscles flexed in response. She looked back up at him and held his gaze. His nostrils flared.

"You want it?" she asked.

"Yes please." His voice had dropped to a growl.

Ideally, she'd sink to her knees and take him in her mouth in one fluid motion, but her muscles were already cranky.

They wouldn't last an extended squat and a ride later. So she sat beside him.

Now to make it worth his while. She rolled onto her stomach, propping herself up on her elbows and eyeing his erection. "How long do you think you can last?"

"Is that a rhetorical question?" His words were a little strained. Probably because his neck was corded with tension.

"You can come up with big words when I'm about to suck your cock. Guess I shouldn't be surprised." She leaned over and brushed her lips across the inside of one powerful thigh, inhaling him: spice and vanilla musk and earth.

"Fuck," he said. So his big words were limited. She bit him lightly then licked her way to the apex of his thighs.

Her aggression had subsided when she worried about his pleasure, but his reactions to her touch brought it back. She swallowed him as far as she could. He muttered more expletives as she worked him. Her focus narrowed to the way his muscles tensed against her, the frequency and harshness of his breaths, the textures and taste against her tongue. Trez sat back on her haunches and drifted her hand down to his perineum. When she applied pressure with her fingertips, she felt him jerk in her mouth.

Eric groaned. "If you don't stop now, I'm done."

She relinquished him with reluctance. "Lie back," she instructed. She put a hand on his chest, following him down, but not pushing him.

Eric opened his eyes. They crinkled at the edge. "You want a ride?" He shifted his hips slightly, and she felt the suggestion in her core. She bared her teeth at him. He was smiling, but she could see his body straining against his self-discipline. Good. Let neither of them be quite themselves right now.

They could simply exist as a tangle of sensations, free from thoughts about the future and its uncertainties.

Trez crawled over him and put her face in his neck, breathing him in again. She lowered her hips to his and teased by sliding the seam of her lips against his arousal, getting him wet. He couldn't stop himself from bucking his hips.

She was done playing, so she levered herself up, adjusting her knees until she could get to a position of strength then impaled herself on him.

It took a moment to get their rhythms in sync. She powered herself onto him, almost into him. She felt the impact of each thrust at every place their skin met. Her hand pressed against his ribcage to help her keep her balance, and she felt his exhalations as percussive shots. Her thighs rasped against the hair on his legs.

He grew harder in her, and his hands fisted the sofabed. He met her downward thrusts with more force.

There was a curious blankness in her mind. All she could see was absolute brightness. Eric's hand came up to where their bodies joined, and he pressed against her clit. She screamed and ground against his hand.

Maybe she'd wanted to call the shots, but she'd gotten so wrapped up in what she was doing she'd forgotten to ask for her pleasure. When she detonated, her world went white. For a moment, nothing hurt—and nothing could hurt her. Keening wails erupted from her chest as she shuddered against him.

They both slowed down as she rode out her orgasm. As she came down from that high, Eric put a sway in his thrusts and she was climbing again, climax imminent and inexorable. He kept his hand where she needed it, and she came again. She heard him swear, some long list of Quebecois words.

Trez continued to work herself on him as she recovered. Her consciousness felt blurred at the edges. She bent her lips to Eric's ear and blew. "Go ahead," she whispered. "It's your turn. Take what you need."

Eric sat up under her, which did wonderful things inside her as they changed angles. He shifted them over until his back was again against the back of the sofabed. "Let me," he said.

She wasn't sure what he meant until he put his hands to her hips and held her up while he hammered into her. Trez ran a hand down his chest. When he groaned, she took his mouth with hers gently. Then she repeated the caress, this time with her claws extended. For several moments he twisted against her, then he jerked his head back to shout his release.

Everything in them went lax, and she slumped atop him, skin slicked with sweat. She might be flattening him, but she didn't care.

TWENTY-FIVE

Trez removed her head from where it was buried in Eric's shoulder and looked up at his face. His eyes were closed, but he didn't appear to be asleep though. She dimmed the light, then snuggled up, her front to his side. She took a moment to feel his strength, pressing a hand into his chest. His skin had tiny freckles. She hadn't noticed before.

The scratches on his side had already healed. Good thing she hadn't broken any skin; he had plenty to recover from already. No need to add to his wound tally. She drank in the sight of him: his relaxed-for-once brow, the curve of his lips in repose . . . She could get used to this.

"You better," he mumbled.

Shit, she'd said that out loud. He was pretty warm, but his apartment wasn't. Her skin had cooled in the air, and she shivered. She sat up and began to put on her clothes.

"There's a spare blanket in the closet somewhere." He opened his eyes, his gaze the softest she could remember seeing it.

"I'll use that too," she replied. "But right now, I need water." She finished dressing and took her cup to the sanitizer. "Anything for you?"

Eric sat up from reclining on the sofabed. "Ah-yeah, why not? I'll have more beer." Trez filled a cup for him and set it down on the coffee table. "Maybe not the medic's first advice for either of our injuries, but it won't hurt."

"How bad is it tonight? The pain, I mean."

"Few more days, I'll be fine." He took a swig. "I'm holding off on painkillers until I really need them."

"I'd massage you, but . . ."

"But your arm's in a sling. It's okay, I'll think of a reason for you to do it later." He grinned. "You can rub me any way you like."

"Come on now." She gestured to where he was sitting. "Get over."

"What? Oh." He scooted over to his right so she could lean on him without putting pressure on her arm.

Trez would get stir-crazy in a few weeks, but for now she just wanted to float away.

"Heard back yet? From Withers, I mean."

She inhaled his scent while leaning on his shoulder. "Yeah." She didn't feel like saying anything else for now. Silence settled over them for several minutes.

His shoulders tensed a bit, and he put down his beer. "Hey, everything okay? I mean, as it can be."

"You mean . . ." she sighed. "Are you asking if the cluster-fuck that ate my life's no longer radioactive?"

"I mean," he said, cupping her jaw, "that everything's fucked up, and I can't quite comprehend what you're going through emotionally, but the Makos aren't sharking you anymore, right?"

"There's a new payment plan," Trez said. "Got forgiveness for some of what was left. Those chips paid off almost all of the rest. My—Santorini's capture was worth a lot to the Makos. I think I could only pay the debts off because she was at the warehouse. I had hoped she wouldn't be." Her voice was rising in pitch, and her chest tightened another increment. "I don't know what the Makos will do with her. She's caused so much trouble for them. I doubt they're in the mood to be nice." Envisioning the Makos torturing her mother opened the floodgates. She screamed into his chest, inarticulate wails of futility and confusion.

He patted her on the back, letting her cry. Once she'd spent her tears, he gave her a quick hug. "Hey, let me get dressed. Then I'll get a towel for you from the bathroom."

Good thinking. Her face was salty, and her eyes puffy. While she waited, her comm rang.

The caller ID was for Kayla Esperes. Odd. Trez connected and Esperes blipped in, this time wearing a faded pink-and-white houndstooth trench coat. "Ah, yes! You! Cyborg Ninja Digger!"

"That's me," Trez said. Why hadn't the journalist called Eric? He'd been her main point of contact.

"You and your special security man got me those drives, thank you thank you, this shall advance the cause."

They'd handed off the drives to Esperes's assistant the day after they'd broken into the warehouse. Esperes had been "in a sufficiently altered state" and unable to meet them.

"He's here if you want to thank him. I mean, I'm at his apartment. But he's in the restroom right now."

"When he's done, I can tell both of you my findings! But first, how did storming the castle go?"

Trez swallowed. She doubted that Esperes meant to pick at her family problems, but the question still made her want to cry. "Well enough that we could get you the drives."

"Were there daring escapades of a ninja nature?"

She winced at the thought of giving a blow-by-blow account of the whole mess. "You're the creative person, use your imagination. Anything you can come up with is probably more interesting than what really happened, I'm sure."

Esperes's posture relaxed, and she cocked her head to the side. "What really happened? Are we talking truth equivalence, as Dinoroid Dana once posited? Would my story be as true as yours if you never told it?"

"For the benefit of others, yes. Let's leave it that way." Dana had said that stories, not facts, were what people remembered.

"You don't want to tell your story yourself? Do you want me to tell it?"

"My life doesn't have a single story. People might get the wrong idea if you only tell this one."

"Excellent! You pass!" Esperes attempted to wiggle dance.

"Pass what?"

Eric walked back into the main room. "Oh. Hello, Esperes." He smiled faintly, bemused.

"Special Security Man! I was just about to give your cyborg ninja a business opportunity!"

"Business? This I have to hear." His eyes twinkled.

"I need a new videography assistant who can kill someone with their bare hands!" Esperes announced.

Trez's mouth fell open. "That's not a normal qualification for a videographer."

"Yes, well. Since when do I care about 'normal' qualifications? My thinking transcends boxes. Even hypercubes sometimes."

Wait. "You're asking me to be your assistant?"

"Your commitment to journalistic integrity is not something I see often in cyborg ninjas. Haven't seen it before you, come to think of it."

"Oh." She had to sit. How many cyborg ninjas did Esperes even know? Never mind.

"I know you have Corp work to do, but if you can spare the time, we would work together on a trial basis. At least while I'm in Portland. How would you like to do something that you believe matters to society?"

Completely changing careers? She'd thought of it plenty over the past few weeks, but her head had been too far up her own ass to consider alternatives for herself. "You said this is business? What's the pay?"

"Bupkis, I'm afraid. Minimum wage."

"So what would I do?" The chance to do something she cared about with her life seemed a foreign concept.

"Accompany me to sites and events. Especially ones in danger zones. The story pulses with more adrenaline when the teller's life is at risk."

Eric frowned. "How risky are we talking?"

Esperes pumped a fist. "As much as we can stand. Maybe a firefight or two. We could go explore some crumbling infrastructure! No sweat for a corporate cyborg ninja."

"What are you planning next?" Eric gave Esperes a sidelong glance.

"Well, thanks to the data you got for me, I have a few leads. I'm ready to find the truth about my nemesis. Their crimes must be exposed to the world!"

Nemesis? Trez racked her brain to remember what Esperes was referencing. "The hacker you mentioned?"

"Yes indeed. We'll follow their trail and, well—I won't go into the details until you sign on."

The damp towel was cool against her eyes. "I will think about it," Trez said slowly.

"Here's your key for a reply. I await with bated breath! So don't let me suffocate!"

"Right," Trez said.

When Esperes disconnected, Eric burst into a fit of snorts and chuckles. "When's the last time anyone you know got a job offer like that?"

"It's . . . Did that really happen?" She slouched back into the sofabed, eyes wide. A smile grew on her face.

He sat next to her and put an arm around her shoulder. "Do you want to start a new career as a journalist's assistant? It sounds up your alley. You look more at peace just thinking about it. And peace is not a word I thought I'd ever associate with Esperes."

"It's tempting. Definitely sounds less physically intense than trying to return to striking." There were her current injuries, the mess inside her head, and withdrawal to fight through. And after that, rehab. Maintaining shape was easier than training back to it.

Eric kissed her forehead. "Do you want to go back?"

With Esperes's words fresh in her mind, she didn't need to be afraid anymore. "I don't." She hadn't admitted that out loud before. Something twisted in her stomach. She didn't even know if she'd ever be cleared to return anyway. "But what if I need emergency funds?"

"Are you worried the Makos will blackmail you again?"

"A little." She wasn't sure she was out of the woods there. "Sometimes I think of running away and starting somewhere else. But I've lived here all my life. I haven't any idea where I'd go or what I'd do."

"Think you'll need to in the future?"

She'd have to start from scratch and in debt. "It's hard to

say. The Makos still have their dirt on me. I've only got their word that they won't try to use it against me in the future."

"It is business," he speculated. "I guess they could try to extort you in the future. But they're predictable, and they have rules. The Corps understand that, and I think they prefer a known quantity like the Makos to, let's say, an anarchist cell."

Funny. She never thought she'd laugh at those words. "Also, they have bigger problems. Namely, each other."

"There's a game to play no matter who you are," Eric hypothesized. "At the exec level it looks pretty ... well, sharky. Even with Seymour breathing down the back of my neck, I have much better job security than most vice presidents. Now if only I could get the severance packages they do."

"It feels like their worlds are different. All this complicated intrigue with information and politics and then all of a sudden they call us in and there's blood everywhere," Trez said. "I guess it keeps us in the grade B cloned beef."

Eric began fussing with his hair instead of immediately replying. She watched him for a while, and waited for him to fill in the silence. "Well, if you think you need to start over, anytime in the future ... you let me know. We'll figure it out."

"You'd just up and leave Portland? Leave Harbor?" She couldn't imagine him doing that easily.

"My job might go belly-up any moment," he said. "I thought I had to prove something to my coworkers, but I never knew what." He grimaced. "My main worry is Sam though."

Trez put her hands on his shoulders and stroked them, trying to be reassuring. She didn't know what to say. He'd been a middling fish in a middling pond. Most corporate employees fought over what they had, over little things that grew in importance. People tried to carve out their spaces and assert dominance however they could. "Do you think she'll be okay?"

"Sacrament. She's worked so hard to get to this point."

Sam's job as assistant to Yavis couldn't pay much. Some artists found patrons, but far more labored in obscurity. Trez didn't understand the glitterati well, but she figured that most artists and entertainers never managed to make the art they wanted to. Maybe she could scrape together some creds from working with Esperes.

Eric grabbed one of her hands with his own and took it to gesture with as he spoke. "She can barely make ends meet right now. Maybe if she broke out on her own she might find some other supporters or patrons and be able to work herself, but ..."

"Speaking of her work, uh, did she ever tell you what happened to the iguanas?" She'd wondered how much damage her altercation with Philly guard had caused.

"Yavis, she says, wasn't particularly amused."

"I'd imagine not."

"They have to repair a bunch of the lizards. Some didn't fare so well from their iguandola adventure. So the installation is a bit on hold. They have to repair and reconstruct the iguanabots, and the sponsor is antsy. That makes Yavis anxious, and that filters down to Sam."

"Great. Just great." She didn't relish the prospect of explaining that. Earning Sam's enmity was not an accomplishment she aspired to.

"She told me they also have security footage of a sword fight on the racetrack. I've been meaning to ask," he said, "did you ever figure out who you were fighting?"

"Forgot to ask Santorini. Probably someone she hired to

patrol the area. But I don't think it matters anymore." She fumbled with the pillow Eric had given her. That sucker had just the right amount of give for hugging.

"Well, I'm glad there was only one of her, and that she wasn't in the warehouse," Eric said. "That fight could have gotten tricky. Those jokers could fire guns, but weren't especially trained at fighting."

"Fighters of her caliber don't come cheap."

"Yeah ... about that. Still have no idea as to who's bankrolling them?"

"Hard telling not knowing. I assume the Makos will question Santorini and get some information there." Trez rolled her shoulders. They made a crunching noise.

"I admit I'm curious."

"Professional curiosity or something else?"

"Might be the same. I'm not sure. Not that it matters to Sam or Yavis anyway."

Trez's mouth tasted bitter. Sam's career could be more collateral damage from Linus's debts. "Do you think he would fire her?"

"Probably not. She's been his assistant for two years and finding a compatible apprentice is more work than he might want to do. Though she says she'll strike out on her own, with her own work. But she needs to attract enough patronage."

"You think it'll happen?"

"I have no idea. It could happen anytime. Next month, next year, maybe next decade. The longer she can keep producing art and marketing herself, the better her chances. But I don't know. Her works may never catch on. All I can do is give her more time to get lucky."

"I can help," Trez said. "If I take a few odd jobs in addition to Esperes's offer. I don't spend much."

"No." He thumped their clasped hands on his chest. "Sam isn't your responsibility."

A laugh bloomed out of her, unfurling and bursting from her lungs. It held her captive until she coughed to catch her breath, then started laughing again. Eric peered at her, his head tilted and eyebrows raised.

"We've had this conversation before," she said, once she'd calmed.

"What the hell are you talking about?" His eyes narrowed. He sounded cranky. That only sent her off into more paroxysms of laughter.

When she caught her breath, she hiccuped. "Linus wasn't your responsibility either."

"But you thought he was yours, and I wanted to make things easier for you."

"Yeah. Why can't I do the same for you?"

His lips compressed. "God *damn* it. Ciboire de osti de tabarnak de calisse."

"Pretty much."

"Look, if you want to repay me, there's no need to—"

"Eric, friends can help each other out if they want." A smile stretched mouth muscles she hadn't used much recently.

"Friends, eh?" He snorted, but didn't seem to take offense.

"Canadianing it up, Greis?"

"Shut up." His face took on a petulant cast.

"I love you, you know," she said, and his expression melted away. "Boot's on the other foot. I wasn't invincible, and I needed help. Let me offer it for once."

"I'll think about it." He frowned.

"You'll take it and you'll like it," she asserted.

He pulled her over him and she yelped. "That sounds like

my line." He rolled over so he was on top and pinning her with his weight.

She pinched a nipple in retaliation, and he chuckled. "You're really something else though."

"What's that supposed to mean?"

"It took all this to make me realize how little getting ahead at work had gotten me. You, on the other hand, never cared about titles or politics. You cared about people."

"I cared about saving my own skin."

"You cared about your dad."

"Did I really? I haven't given him much time since I started working."

"You did it for him. Probably more for him than he deserved."

It didn't matter what Linus deserved. But that was probably what Eric was getting at. "Okay, fine. But you." She felt warmth rise in her chest. "You cared about me. Even when my head was up my own ass."

"I'd say stop beating yourself up, but you were pretty absorbed in your own problems. Enough that everyone noticed that you'd vanished."

"I'll talk to Jenna and Imei." She had a lot of explanations she owed her friends.

Eric met her eyes with a soft gaze. "You're going to talk about this with your psych too, right?"

"Don't see how I can avoid it. But there's the whole my-mother-is-a-terrorist issue. Gah. If I really want to go into things, I need someone outside of Harbor. But that won't be cheap."

"You want we should ask the Makos for a referral?"

She couldn't tell whether he was joking. "Are you serious?"

"It's worth considering. I know you don't want to be any

more indebted to them, but like I said, I think Dorgo likes you. He may be able to point you in the right direction."

Thinking about him made her think about Santorini's capture. "Maybe. I'll talk to my friends first."

"Fair enough." He smoothed her overshirt over her shoulder.

"I know I have to start somewhere." She owed Eric that. Hell, she owed herself that, he'd say. And she knew he was right. "But what about you?"

"Huh?"

"You've got emotional shit to shovel too. Why don't you talk to Vail? They'll understand what you've just gone through."

He drew a heart on her forehead with his fingertips. "That's not ideal."

"They're the person who knows you best. Besides me and your family."

"Vail and I . . . things might be rough for a while, working with them. Like I said, I'm sympathetic to their situation, but there's a lot to sort out between us. We'll have to work through it." He didn't sound confident, but at least it sounded like he had a plan. "I'm a little leery of trusting them now, but I don't want to lose that friendship."

It wasn't like she could throw stones, not with her testy unresolved relationship with her ma. They had time now to give their lives real attention. "Anyone else you can talk to?"

"I could confide in Staplehead." Eric yawned.

This must be a bigger joke. "You want to get life advice from the Makos?"

"There's also Esperes."

While hilarious, she wasn't sure if that was a better idea. "I should dare you to do that."

"Mmmm, dares," he said. He rubbed his nose in her neck. "She does offer some good insight, you just have to turn it inside out."

"She has a unique perspective, I'll give her that."

"Sounds like you want to explore that perspective."

"I think so. It's a chance to start fresh. But I should sleep on it first. Tomorrow I'll be thinking more clearly."

They had as many tomorrows together as they wanted for the foreseeable future. It may be a long time until she felt steady and whole, but they had each other's backs until she got there.

He smiled and closed his eyes. "I'll see you first thing tomorrow then."

They held each other until they drifted asleep.

ON SACRES

Before the Quiet Revolution in the 1960s, the Roman Catholic Church was the dominant institution in Quebec. This led to residents swearing by invoking words from Catholic liturgy. These became known as sacres.

There is an art to using sacres, but the ones in *Razor Strike* are relatively simple. The words are used interchangeably and often chained together with the word "de." "Ostie de ciboire de calice de tabarnak" is much like "fuckity fuck fuck motherfucker" in English.

Here are the profanities Eric uses, along with their meanings:

câlice. chalice
ciboire. ciborium, a container that carries the host
criss. Christ
ostie. the host, the bread consecrated during the Eucharist
sacrament. sacrament
tabarnak. tabernacle, a locked box where the host is stored

It is likely that this mode of swearing will fall out of use in the future. I included it anyway, because I find it delightful.

ACKNOWLEDGMENTS

Thank you to my family, immediate and in-law. Especially Mike and John for beta reading.

Neal, for beta reading and guiding me through the process from first draft to publication.

Marcella Burnard, Vivien Jackson, and Nathalie Gray for showing me what could be done.

My writing teachers, especially Nils Osmar, Rebecca Agiewich, and Stephanie Brownell.

My typo hunters Alex and Vesper.

And again John, for giving me better support than I knew to ask for.

ABOUT THE AUTHOR

Lee Sarpel is a music composer turned software developer with a love of gritty science fiction, absurd humor, and hugging. Born in New York City and raised in New Jersey, she bounced around both of America's coasts before settling near Boston with her spouse and many robots.

Lee enjoys reading, stuffed animals, video games, chocolate, electronic music, and urban exploration.

Made in United States
North Haven, CT
01 June 2022

19720259R00190